Enthusiastic reviews for Lior Samson's novels —

Bashert (The Homeland Connection)

"Perfect! . . . a page turner that spins a good story."

— Peter Gordon, publisher

"Samson writes with a crisp elegance, like John Le Carré, and weaves his plot magically, sustaining suspense throughout the novel. The ending is a satisfying and surprising climax."

— James A. Anderson, author

"An ambitious novel, . . . moving with the speed of light between interconnected events, three continents, and a group of unique and memorable characters. I recommend it."

- Avraham Azrieli, author

The Dome (The Homeland Connection)

"Suspenseful and timely, . . . I cannot say enough good things about this novel." — Alan Caruba, critic, BookViews

"Crisp, sardonic, sometimes amusing, and highly entertaining. [Samson is] a real story teller." — James A. Anderson, author

"An excellent read, and very highly recommended."

— Midwest Book Review

Web Games (The Homeland Connection)

"An outstanding tech thriller—better than Tom Clancy. . . . This ranks up there as one of the best [thrillers] I've read in 2011."

— James A. Anderson, author

"This extraordinary author has the ability to anticipate events in ways that enhance his novels, and Web Games, his latest, is no exception. . . . You will not put it down."

— Alan Caruba, critic, BookViews

Chipset (The Homeland Connection)

"[A] multi-dimensional thriller that will satisfy discriminating readers who crave realistic stories populated by flesh-and-blood characters."

- Avraham Azrieli, author

"Lior Samson hits another one out of the park. . . . Few thriller writers can match Samson's ability to deliver a gripping story."

—James A. Anderson, author

Gasline (The Homeland Connection)

"Samson turns up the heat with a high-energy plot and . . . a perfect mix of techno thrill and human conflict. . . . a rip-roaring ride. Excellent!" *—Avraham Azrieli, author*

The Four-Color Puzzle

"[A]n authentic thinking person's ideal mystery; an eloquent feast of words and an excellent story. . . . [M]ay be the best [book] I have read this year." *—Jeanie B. Clemmons, author*

"[A] fast-paced crime story that had me rooting for the hero while also feeling conflicted by his choices. The story challenges the reader." *—Patricia O'Sullivan, author*

The Rosen Singularity

The Rosen Singularity

a novel by Lior Samson

GESHER PRESS

Gesher Press is an imprint of Ampersand Press
Rowley, MA 01969

Gesher Press | Ampersand Press
58 Kathleen Circle
Rowley, MA 01969
Author site: www.liorsamson.com

Gesher Press and the bridge logo are trademarks of Ampersand Press.

Printed in the United States of America.
5 4 3 2

ISBN 978-0-9843772-4-4

Cover and book design: Larry Constantine.
Text set in Gentium and Gentium Book, title in Blue Highway Condensed, chapters and running heads in Vera Sans.

To Sami—my Rabbi, my friend

In memoriam, Steven Paul Jobs, 1955-2011

Acknowledgements

My previous novels have all been long-haul treks. The writing would start with small steps and skips of inspiration and would build slowly, the final form emerging over a journey of years on a trail marked with numerous detours and stopovers. This time around, writing seemed more like base jumping off a cliff in a wing suit, ideas and words rushing up at me in a whirlwind of intense creation over a span of mere months. Then the work began.

It was Lucy, my bashert, my wife and best friend, who provided me with the gem of an idea that sent me diving into the uprush of air. It was Lucy who prompted me to set aside another project to write with a sense of urgency and who pushed me to fix the problems in my early drafts. Expressions of gratitude to the wives and husbands and partners of authors have become almost mandated cliché, but, in my case, the depths of my debt to Lucy cannot be measured. This book is a completely different and far better work because Lucy goaded me into starting over and doing it right.

I am also indebted to my readers and reviewers who suffered through earlier versions and gave me the benefit of their intelligence and insight. Old friends and erstwhile debate partners were, once again, pressed into service. Jim Hawkins, sailor and counselor extraordinaire, was helpfully supportive, and David Tutelman, friend and critic, told me straight out that my first draft simply failed. David told me enough about why and how I had missed the mark for me to correct my aim and zero in on the target.

This novel, my first foray into a subgenre of thrillers tied to the medical field, takes me well outside my usual technological comfort zone. Mark Raizin, M.D., an amazing internist who actually spends time listening to his patients, did his best to keep me from making boneheaded mistakes regarding modern medicine and medical practice. My friend and good university colleague, Jos van Leeuwen, a careful reader and my consultant on matters Dutch, suggested small but important changes.

To my hard-working, underpaid, but not under-appreciated copy editor, Janet Lemnah, go my closing thanks. If the commas are in the right place and the spelling is correct, if the names are consistent and the scenes connect, you, also, can thank Janet. Her sharp eyes and sharp pencil have made the difference.

I must also credit one person I have never met: the late Steve Jobs. His tenacity and untempered honesty, his blunt words while staring into the very face of Death itself, were another inspiration for this story. His words and his works live on.

Singularity: the state or quality of being singular, unique, particular; a discontinuity in space or time; a point, such as a black hole, where the normal laws of nature cease to operate; an event of such complete and abrupt alteration that history is changed qualitatively and fundamentally.

Prologue

The keys slipped from Janella's shaking hand. She did a perfect grand-plié to retrieve them, then struggled to guide the front-door key into the lock.

She was chilled to the core of her small frame. The forty-minute hike down Mass Avenue from Bram's apartment near the West Somerville line to the icy porch of the white Victorian in Cambridge had left her sobered but shivering. She opened the front door, sending a swirl of powdery snow onto the mat inside. She stepped cautiously, but the old wide-board flooring creaked as she entered the darkened house. She paused, listening, trying to control her shaking as she removed her wool tam and placed it with her keys and purse on the stand by the door. The house was silent.

She jumped suddenly.

"Oh, shit!" she whispered. She had forgotten the manila envelope with the research paper at Bram's apartment. "Douglas will kill me if he finds out."

Douglas was even more possessive of the paper and the work it represented than he was of her. He did not approve of her involvement with Bram Dekker but had said nothing. He had, however, said clearly that their work was strictly confidential and no longer to be discussed with anyone. Not only had she shown the paper to Bram, but Bram had been the one to confirm her sense of its singular importance. They had spent the first part of the evening at the kitchen table, washing down pepperoni pizza with cheap Chianti and talking their way through the highly technical research results. They had spent the rest of the evening in bed with Dutch beer from Bram's stock, arguing about the grim developments in the war in Vietnam, about the proper care and feeding of laboratory rats, and about the correct way to write DO loops in FORTRAN programs. Between debating the implications of Gödel's Theorem and disagreeing about Chomsky's notions of deep-structure grammar in natural language, they had managed to squeeze in two rounds of lovemaking.

Janella, realizing she would have to retrieve the paper, replaced her tam over her dark hair, grabbed her keys from the table, and slipped back out. A dusting of new snow was already beginning to obscure her tracks on the sidewalk. She crossed her arms and set off at a jog in hopes of warming herself. Like a member of the corps de ballet crossing a darkened stage, she ran through the night with sure-footed steps, her long plaid scarf a pink-and-purple banner streaming behind her.

It was long after midnight on a winter weekday, and she ran alone, unnoticed on the deserted streets. Gradually, her pace warmed her, the heat starting in her thighs, then rising and spreading until she had to loosen her fur-trimmed jacket to keep from overheating.

She was almost within sight of Bram's basement apartment when she finally slowed to catch her breath. As her breathing quieted, the winter stillness deepened. Through the muting curtain of falling snow, she could hear the sound of hurried steps behind her.

With a dancer's heightened sense of place and position, she waited until the unseen follower was nearly upon her before planting her left foot, kicking off with her right, and spinning around with determined precision.

1

The world tilted sharply as the Gulfstream 650 banked and angled down toward pebbly cloud cover that revealed a teasing mosaic of the bronze and blue-green African landscape below. Veteran traveler though he was, Ferguson felt his stomach lurch as the plane started its sudden steep descent. The co-pilot, who had left the flight deck to chat with the two minders seated at the front of the near-empty plane, stumbled and ended up in the lap of one of them. He struggled to pull himself erect and up through the open doorway to the flight deck while the pilot shouted to him in rapid-fire Portuguese. Ferguson caught only one word of it. *Merde!* Shit.

The plane suddenly rolled left and into a precipitous dive, followed immediately by a sharp right turn again and a gut-wrenching climb that pressed Ferguson deep into the glove-soft leather of his seat. The plane continued to climb so steeply that Ferguson wondered if they were on the verge of stalling out. For a moment, they seemed to hang suspended before the plane rolled again into a plunge nearly straight toward the center of the earth, the twin engines screaming as the fuselage shuddered in protest.

Not this way, Ferguson thought, not like this. The obvious question sprang into his always analytical mind: what way, then? What way, good doctor, what way and when? Sooner or later, someway, somehow it had to come. Even he had to die—a painful reality that he preferred to postpone as long as possible.

The plane shook violently as the pilot struggled to pull it out of the steep dive. A bright flash, like a stab of sunlight, filled the window beside Ferguson, and the plane seemed to hop to one side. The thud of an explosion and thump of a compression wave left his ears ringing. Slowly the plane settled back into what seemed to be a normal flight, and his hearing returned. The pilots and the two men up front were laughing, shouting something about Matata and his people.

"Can somebody tell me what that was all about?" Ferguson called up toward the front of the plane.

"Matata, the troublemaker," the pilot said. "He lives up to his name. Matata Sabri and the EUN." His accented English mixed Portuguese overtones with the rhythm of the Lusanyu dialect, the language of the Busanyu majority. "They must have gotten their hands on a surface-to-air missile, but these Gulfstreams are pretty maneuverable if you know how to handle them, and we can out-fly that outdated Russian crap. That's all they can afford, those poor peasant bastards. Now the army will hunt them down and cut out their hearts." He snorted as if enjoying the prospect. "If we can't catch the traitors, our soldiers will go to the villages of their families and kill everyone with machetes. Matata will not try this again."

Ferguson was not reassured. The *Exército de Unidade Nacional*, the Army of National Unity, which government forces referred to as the Army of National Disunity, was only the most visible evidence of many hidden enemies. That President Mbutsu had enemies was not unexpected, given his totalitarian regime and long history of human rights violations. It was always a risk coming to Busanyu, but there was no choice. They needed Edgar Jabari Mbutsu as an underwriter. And, of course, he needed them. He could not come to the clinic outside Moscow any more than he could drive through the streets of downtown Mbutsu City unless in an armored vehicle with heavily armed escorts. Indeed, Ferguson knew the truth, that Mbutsu rarely stepped foot outside the grounds of the Presidential Palace. There were even rumors that he had actually died back in 2010, and that his third son, Edgar Abimbola Mbutsu, was secretly running the country. Ferguson knew the rumors were just that—without substance but nevertheless convenient. It could be a comfortable fiction for a country that hated and feared its leader in equal measure.

Ferguson wondered whether the insurgents would have fired a missile had he arrived on one of the regular commercial flights. Now that Busanyu had finally gained U.N. recognition, there were two flights a week from Lisbon and one from the Canary Islands. No, the insurgents knew nothing of Ferguson's travels. The attack was targeted for Mbutsu; it was his private plane, his ostentatious display of wealth and power, like a sleek, subsonic peacock, the orange and blue livery of its tail proudly defiant—and inviting. Ferguson much preferred the anonymity of commercial travel to the luxury—and uncertainty—of private accommodations. But this was not one of Ferguson's regular visits to Africa; it was a command performance at the request of Mbutsu to jump the queue of Ferguson's short list of patients. The charter flight from London in his own jet had been Mbutsu's idea, a gesture of hospitality, he claimed, one that he knew could not be turned down.

The whole trip was also a power play, a claim to equal standing in the long stalemate between the underwriters and the organization. Ferguson, for one, regretted they had ever entered into the devil's deal with the underwriters, although there had seemed little choice at the time, a time when there was so much research still ahead and so little in capital behind them. Now—or soon—there might be alternatives, but a transition would not be straightforward.

Ferguson stretched, hitched himself fully upright in the spacious leather seat, and massaged his aching neck. The scare from the rebel forces had abruptly brought him out of the semi-conscious trance in which he had passed the last hours of the nine-hour flight from London. He was slipping his unused e-book reader back into the medical bag beneath his feet when he looked up to find the co-pilot standing next to his seat.

"We're coming into Mbutsu International, Dr. Ferguson," the man said. "We'll be starting our final approach in a few minutes." Though he wore the insignia of a lieutenant colonel in the Busanyu Air Force, he spoke with quiet deference that evidenced how keenly he was aware of the high status and importance of his only passenger. Although the cabin of the Gulfstream could be configured to carry as many as eighteen, in this one, luxuriously finished in soft beige and camel tones offset by the bright blue-and-orange signature of its owner, the plane had been appointed to carry only eight in spacious comfort. The other two men, seated at the front of the near-empty plane, did not count as passengers. Though they were out of uniform, Ferguson knew they were military police, minders charged with keeping an eye on himself and the pilots. He had been entrusted to top officers in the Air Force, but the current regime in Busanyu was not one built on trust, and Ferguson imagined that the minders, too, were somehow being monitored in turn.

Dr. Charles Ferguson was a real doctor of medicine, but his medical credentials, like his passport, his name, and his entire personal history, were fictitious. The transformation had become necessary more than two decades earlier when colleagues had begun voicing suspicions and resentment—all in good humor, of course—about his excessively long tenure as head of the Cancer Biology and Genetics program that he had created at the Dana-Farber Institute outside Boston. The program was largely a cover for the real work that he directed elsewhere, but the handwriting was on the wall and clearly writ. When glossing over the good-natured graffiti of his detractors with humorous brush-offs no longer quelled their suspicions or quieted their envy, one leading Welsh oncologist based in Boston "disappeared" while on holidays in South America, and the unassuming Dr. Ferguson was born, created by the magic of money and resources that knew few limits.

Ferguson stared out the window past his own reflection. He was Hollywood handsome in the classic mold of generic good looks and appealing but forgettable faces. The translucent image that interposed itself atop the shifting scenery softened the lines in his face, lines that spoke less of mere years than of years of responsibility. His medical practice, and the peripatetic life it demanded, both aged him and kept him young. It was not the life he would have imagined when he graduated from medical school and began his research career. It was not the life he had imagined when he married Ruth Pincus in Newton. He missed Ruth. He missed having someone to come back to other than his housekeeper in London. But housekeepers kept their places and stayed in role and could be replaced every few years—not so wives.

There were compensations, of course, in the life he had chosen, and not merely the obvious one. He had learned that companionship comes in many costumes, and impermanence has its intrinsic charms. He smiled as he thought ahead to his next visit to Russia and to Sveta, the bright young lab technician who found talk of telomeres and oncogenes and nucleotide polymorphisms to be such a turn-on. She was as talented in bed as she was in the lab, and she had dark Russian eyes and thick Slavic thighs that reminded him of Ruth as a young woman. But, where Ruth had regarded sex as a wifely duty, Sveta was a screamer who approached bedroom antics with the same enthusiasm with which she attacked the ski slopes or maneuvered her Mercedes along the narrow country roads that led to the unnamed and all-but-invisible artificial village where she worked on projects for Ferguson and The General. The differences between Sveta and Ruth, including the half-century difference in birthdates, were not enough to completely erase the small reminders that sometimes brought back sweet and painful memories. Ferguson had come to believe that we live with our first loves for all our lives; the later ones all come with an expiration date. He was not sure whether Sveta qualified as a love or merely as a current love interest, but he knew that it would not last, could not last. The organization would never approve extending her expiration date—she was too unstable, too unimportant, too ordinary, too obvious. Too bad.

Ferguson would not have counted himself as either jaded or a cynic, but he went about the complex business of maintaining his life and those of his few patients with a well-modulated sense of resignation. As a doctor, he had lived too long not to have distanced himself somewhat from the melodrama of life and death that played out on the human stage. He had finally become, somewhat unexpectedly, more a part of the audience and less and less a participant in the on-stage story.

The final fifteen minutes of the approach into Mbutsu International Airport kept Ferguson's attention focused on the immediate present. Even in the nimble Gulfstream and with no more missiles to dodge, it was a white-knuckle landing, with a steep, banking descent to avoid Kinyetu, the next peak in the chain of mountains, followed by hard braking to avoid going off the edge of the flattened top of Mount Durban. Sir Anthony Durban, nineteenth-century explorer and raconteur, would have been appalled had he lived to the twenty-first century to see what had become of the dramatic summit of his namesake. Ferguson supposed it could be called progress of a fickle but effective sort, since the mountain had first been beheaded by strip mining to recover its mineral wealth only a few years before the overburden had been recycled as backfill to transform it into an airfield.

Ferguson remembered the early days of his involvement with Edgar Mbutsu, when his transportation into Busanyu was a chartered C-130 and the runway was hard-packed red clay. Now, at the edge of the modern airport, surrounded by a moat seething with the pulse of submerged fountains, a white-winged terminal building sailed like a graceful giant of a water bird taking flight from a wind-roiled African lake. The stunning design, one of the first commissions by Paolo Pereira de Canha, student of the Brazilian architect Oscar Niemeyer, was typical of the extravagance with which the Mbutsu government displayed its public face.

Niemeyer, never one to have obsessed over human proportion or efficient use of space in his monumental architecture, had trained his protégé well. Pereira de Canha had created a terminal building as impressive inside as out. One wall of windows, sprinkled with rhomboid panels of yellow and magenta glass and thin stripes of the Busanyu blue and orange, looked back at the tarmac; another of clear glass faced out over a precipice, across the verdant jungle that carpeted the region, and through a cleft in the mountains offering a glimpse into a patch of sun-browned savannah beyond.

Inside the cavernous building, security guards with Kalashnikovs outnumbered the few scattered passengers. When the afternoon flights for other African cities departed, only the footsteps of the guards would echo in the terminal.

Ferguson was efficiently ushered through the terminal by his minders, speeded without ceremony past security guards and passengers and customs officers and into a waiting limousine where there was a long delay while all his baggage caught up with him and was loaded into a panel truck, unloaded again, rearranged, then reloaded amidst much arguing and gesturing. Ferguson was used to such mixes of speed and inefficiency, so he was not surprised when he was told by the driver that there would be another delay while the road ahead was patrolled and cleared.

Finally, it seemed they were ready to move when they were joined by two armored personnel carriers, fore and aft. But the gathering convoy remained idling outside the terminal for another twenty minutes until a motorcycle escort arrived to lead the procession. Through darkened windows, Ferguson watched the bare beauty of the airport surrounds gradually give way to tin and cardboard shanties erected on the slopes just beyond a deep roadside ditch that carried raw sewage.

It took nearly an hour of trailing red dust clouds down the switchback road from the sheared-off mountain and on through the crowded outskirts of Mbutsu City before they reached the far side and an isolated stretch of paved highway with no other traffic and only one destination: the Presidential Palace.

The Palace, a sprawling complex of mismatched buildings, was no

Niemeyer-inspired creation. More military than monumental, it was a small city unto itself. The main gate, a massive sliding panel of gray-painted armor plate with red-brick guard towers on either side and walls topped with razor wire, would have done justice to a maximum-security prison. To the right of the heavily guarded entrance were the military barracks, complete with their own helipad; to the left was a school for those children of the President who lived with him as well as the children of permanently stationed military families and others in a small inner circle who lived at the site. Beyond was the stark steel-and-tinted-glass façade of the fully equipped hospital, and behind the hospital, an unseen electric power station grumbled quietly. Atop an incongruous rise in the otherwise flat landscape stood a small stucco cube with a heavy, vault-like door, the above-ground entrance to an underground communication center, a complex of satellite-linked computers that might have been the envy of some of the smaller of the European intelligence services. Straight ahead, down a broad avenue lined with exotic and stately eucalypts, loomed the polished Italian marble columns of the palace proper, home to the President, three of his four wives, and some twenty-odd of his unnumbered children. Several of his closest advisors also lived with their families in the palace proper, along with an unknown number of relatives and other hangers-on.

The convoy pulled up beside the massive concrete security bollards lining the circular driveway that fronted the palace. The ugly cylinders were an architectural addendum installed in response to an earlier assassination attempt when a bomb-loaded delivery van had been driven all the way up the palace steps. The driver died in a hailstorm of automatic weapons fire, and the bomb had failed to detonate, adding yet another chapter in the myth of a President who some claimed was indestructible, who seemed to lead a charmed life protected by potent magic.

Now, as Ferguson stepped out of the limousine, stopped a safe distance from the palace entrance, a cheer went up. "Not for me, I would hope," he said, with a concerned look on his face.

"Oh, no, good Doctor," the chauffer holding the door said. "It is for the pilots who so skillfully evaded the missile and who also spotted the dust of a fleeing vehicle on the road through Samputu. An army patrol in the area immediately intercepted and captured them. I am afraid that you already missed the trial, but you are still in time for the execution, if you make for the courtyard with some haste."

"Well, no one can say that Busanyu justice is slow," Ferguson said, shaking his head. "But I think not. I am tired and still have much to do to be ready for the President's appointments this week."

"Are you sure? I could escort you there."

"I am sure. I will go inspect my suite at the hospital and make sure everything arrived in good order. I can find my way. Please have my bags taken to my usual room."

Ferguson took a few steps toward the hospital, then cringed involuntarily as the crackle of nearby gunfire interrupted the afternoon quiet.

"Not to worry, Doctor," the driver called out. "It is just the firing squad." Another ragged burst split the air. "Special justice," the driver said, retreating and leaving Ferguson standing there with a puzzled look. There was another round of gunfire.

2

The stark skeletons of winter were now peppered with the pale green and deep pink buds of spring along tree-lined Argilla Road. The trees cast pulsing shadows as Rosen sped past. He was eager this morning, eager to get back to the intriguing lead he was following. He slowed, but not enough to prevent his tires from letting out a brief squeal as he made the switch-back corner and headed up the undistinguished long driveway leading to the Ipswich Labs. A sea-blue sign, less than a foot high and located halfway up the curving drive, was the only indication that the former mansion was now the North Shore Laboratories of Biontolics Research, LLC.

Rosen's lime-green Honda Prius was the first car in the lot, yet, despite his hurry, he parked farthest from the building. He extracted his tall and well-muscled frame from the small car, grabbed his thermos and briefcase, and started to jog across the parking lot. Rosen considered everything in life as amenable to optimization. His preferred parking spot would be shaded from the afternoon sun by the adjacent trees, and the modest trot from the far corner of the lot, around the house, and up the broad steps into the front entrance of the building counted in his mental ledgers as exercise. Others might simply use their keycards to enter by the convenient parking-lot entrance, but Rosen's everyday life operated on the accumulation of small tweaks that he believed added up to noticeable effects, even as in his work, where minute patterns were magnified into visibility by his arcane arithmetic arts.

The Labs' many-gabled house and its outbuildings had once been a rich industrialist's North Shore retreat, replete with a gentleman's farm and a widow's-walk balcony that overlooked the salt marshes stretching toward the sea. In recent years, the marsh lands had become dotted by little black boxes, traps for the biting flies that had long plagued the residents of the area. Biontolics Research had quietly acquired the neglected property—and radically expanded the number of little black boxes—not long after the arrival in Ipswich of New England Biolabs, their much larger and better known neighbors just to the south. Both labs had begun tapping into the deepening pool of science and engineering talent migrating northward from the universities and older high-tech institutions inside and along Route 128, Boston's fabled Technology Highway. Biontolics had refurbished the interior of the main house to create office suites, turned a barn into a world-class microbiology research laboratory, and made a guest house into a computer center. With its long driveway and the buildings painted to match the dark New England slate on the footpaths, the compound was all but invisible from the road.

At the front desk in what had once been a sitting room, the white-haired guard greeted Rosen with a sleepy smile. "Good morning, Dr. Rosen," he said, as he ticked off an entry in an on-screen log. Rosen had long ago given up correcting the man. He was Dr. Rosen David, no middle name, because Michael David, his father, emotionally traumatized by a childhood filled with teasing for having two first names, had flipped the bird at the world by giving his first-born son a surname for a first name. Of course, Michael David insisted on telling everyone that Rosen was a perfectly fine given name, that it was of Hebrew origin, with the correct accent on the final syllable, although no one pronounced it that way, and that it meant that his son was an honored person. After growing up taunted by new variations on old schoolyard themes, the college-bound Rosen David had finally embraced fate and learned to turn the memorable distinctiveness of his offbeat name to his advantage. As David Rosen, he would have been one of hundreds on Facebook, thousands on Google, but as Rosen David, he was singular, unique.

Rosen took the stairs two-at-a-time up to his second-floor office. He hip-checked his posture chair, sending it skidding across the room from where he had left it next to the small circular conference table, then booted up his computer while still standing. He was impatient to get back to the work that his promise to meet Millie for dinner the night before had interrupted. His wife, knowing that it was one of the few ways to guarantee that Rosen would return from work at a reasonable hour, insisted on a dinner date every Thursday. Other nights, he was apt to find her already in bed when he arrived home, usually curled up with a book—usually about nature—but sometimes already asleep, her cheek creased by the edge of the book she had been reading. And tonight he would have to leave work early again because it was Shabbat, the beginning of the Jewish Sabbath, and, although neither he nor Millie were observant and both were scientists and devout non-believers, they never failed to mark Friday evening with candles and with blessings over the bread and wine.

Rosen sat down at his desk and ran a hand through his curly hair as he made a perfunctory scan of the subject lines of his email before closing the in-box without reading any of it. He was notorious for missing important memos and not responding to urgent inquiries from management, but it was not so much by any rebellion against authority or an uncooperative nature as by the tendency for his attention to be always elsewhere. Elsewhere was usually the analysis of the last batch of numbers to arrive at his desk.

He unzipped his jacket without taking it off and, at the same time, finished logging in to retrieve results from an overnight computation he had run on the supercomputer at Biontolics Southland, the company headquarters and computing center in Research Triangle Park, North Carolina. An array of unintelligible numbers swept over his screen. While the numbers continued streaming in, he pipelined the array over to his newly devised data visualization program that would turn digits into colorful graphics, abstract paintings that could more easily be eyeballed for elusive patterns. At the same time, he started another program on his local work-station that took the results of the overnight computation as input and generated yet another set of numbers.

This was how he did biology. His work was all about looking for patterns, identifying results in experiments that even the experi-menters had missed, the subtle and unintended consequences of science scaled up. His specialty was known as meta-analysis, a di-scipline that looked at dozens or hundreds, sometimes even thou-sands of old studies, and mixed them all together into one statistical stew to see if any newer or clearer results bubbled to the surface.

He was correcting a formula in an internal memo about a previ-ous project, when his computer chimed and the big 26-inch LCD monitor to his right started painting the tinted shapes generated by his visualization program. He stared in eager anticipation as the high-resolution display filled in successively refined levels of detail, sharpening the boundaries between contrasting colors in the patchwork. To the uninitiated, it might have resembled a nightmare painted by Chagall or the false-color x-ray images generated by air-port security scanners, another form of visualization that used sharp contrasts in color to highlight tiny differences.

Rosen's heart started pounding as a small but distinctive, red-hued patch began taking shape amidst a field of blues and greens and yellows. His reaction was not unlike what a TSA agent staring at a screen in an airport might feel, an agent who had suddenly spotted a pistol-shaped shadow in the x-ray of someone's carry-on bag. The patch of red was a signal amidst the noise of irrelevant blue and green, a sign of success, an indication that some small numbers among many thousands of measurements had been ever so slightly different than expected.

Rosen lived for such moments. Most of his work, most days,

meant telling researchers and funding sources the bad news that the drugs they were trying didn't work or the traces of chemicals they sought simply were not there or that the theory they were espousing didn't prove out. Some days, like this particular Friday, he caught the scent of significance, the glimpse of real results, and he was like a bloodhound on the trail.

The patch in the picture was only a flag, drawing attention to buried possibilities. The real work would be teasing out exactly what the connections were in a collection of spurious results from diverse publications, and more importantly, deciphering what they meant. Behind the numbers were words, and behind the words were poetry, the poetry of new science and undiscovered truths for which Rosen rose in the morning and which still spun in his head as he drifted into sleep late at night.

Rosen became so absorbed in scanning summaries of studies and setting up another analysis on a subset of the data that he did not even notice when his officemate, Jeannine Carsten, arrived for work or when she left for lunch. He finally looked up from his keyboard and screens when he realized his thermos of tea was cold and his bladder was uncomfortably full. The clock told him it was nearly one-thirty.

When he returned from the bathroom, Jeannine was back at her desk, chin resting on one hand as she entered data on her numeric keypad with the other. "Oh, hi," she said, her husky voice filled with good-humored sarcasm. "Nice to see you, too."

He gave her a lopsided grin. "Sorry," he said, "I was really into it, I guess. I think I am onto something. A lot of checks and counter-checks to run, still, plus some new tests, but this is looking good. Something subtle is going on in this mess of research that my new program has flagged. I'm not sure what exactly it is yet, but I'm going to pull in all that old work on telomeres from Bischoff and Muybridge, you know, the studies of rat longevity, plus, well, a bunch of stuff." He had to remind himself that Jeannine was a statistician—simply that, a pure mathematician, competent in her work but largely uninterested in the science behind the numbers she manipulated. Despite his frequent disclaimers, Rosen actually was a real biologist in that he understood the meaning of the numbers on his screen and the significance of the experiments he analyzed. In a string of papers published while he was still a student at Tufts University, he had broken new ground by combining deep scientific insights, particularly in genetics, with original and powerful mathematical techniques.

Jeannine smiled at him and twirled a finger in the air. "Well, ride 'em cowboy. Corral all them stray numbers and line them up in neat rows." She turned back to her screen and started tapping out strings of numbers again.

"No, really, this could be something big," he said. "I am going to have to go back and re-read all the papers from this collection." He waved a finger at the reddish patch still displayed on his screen. Jeannine swiveled in her chair and nodded but immediately turned back to her own work and otherwise ignored him for the rest of the day. They were two number-crunching introverts who had long since worked out their quiet pas-de-deux for sharing the small office. If Rosen were to be asked how tall Jeannine was or the color of her hair, he might make something up that he believed was an acceptable approximation, but, in truth, he hardly noticed her, certainly not the way she watched him when he was not looking.

She was still tapping away behind him when, late in the afternoon, his cell phone rang. It was Millie. "Do you know what time it is, Rosen? Do you even know what day it is?" she asked, the casual lilt of her voice salted with irritation.

"I know I'm in trouble. Does that help?"

"Not unless you get your distractible self home real darn fast. The sun is setting, my love, and I should be lighting the candles."

"My *eshet chayil*, my woman of valor, thank you for reminding your clueless love that the world keeps turning even when his computer slows to a crawl. I'll leave right now. I just have one more text clustering to do, then I'll shut down for the weekend."

"No."

"No? No what?"

"No, you do not have one more analysis or one more test or one more anything to do. I know you, Rosen. One becomes two and two become a dozen, and I won't see you before midnight."

"Okay. I'm really quitting. I'm logging off and shutting down," he said, even as he typed a new command to run another long job at the Research Triangle computing center. "Hear that? I'm on my way." He grabbed his jacket off the back of the chair as he continued to reassure Millie that he really was leaving work. Jeannine watched as he scowled at the long error message that popped up on his screen. Her IM to him popped up beside it. "I can correct that. You go home," it read.

Rosen nodded to Jeannine, told Millie once more that he really was leaving, and headed out the door.

Jeannine sat down at his desk and corrected the error in his remote job command before resubmitting it. Unlike Rosen, she had no one waiting for her; like Rosen, the work was an addiction. It was more than an hour until she reluctantly returned to her own desk where she finished the data entry job before logging onto a remote facility in Europe to post her weekly report.

= =

It was well past seven o'clock that night when Rosen got home to the small, white, black-trimmed Cape Cod colonial on the far edge of Essex, a modest little house on a small lot that had been bargain-basement priced when they bought it but was more than enough for the two of them. Millie welcomed Rosen warmly but let him know her displeasure with his late arrival by heading for bed immediately after dinner. Rosen did his usual perfunctory job of cleaning up before heading down the short hall to join her.

Their so-called master bedroom was tiny by modern standards, having been carved up by the previous owner to create an equally tiny *en suite* bathroom. Millie sat propped up in the queen-size bed that nearly filled the room. The current issue of *Edutopia* was in her hand, and an assortment of Audubon field guides were spread around her. Rosen belly-flopped down beside her, bouncing the field guides a few inches into the air and sending one handbook onto the floor.

"Thanks a heap," she said, as she stretched to retrieve it.

"Anytime," he answered. "So, tell me Millie, how would you like to be married to a Nobel Laureate?"

"Depends which Laureate you mean. I always thought Krugman was kind of ruggedly handsome in a classic Ashkenazic mold. And Kornberg, in chemistry—balding, yes, but still kind of cute."

"Krugman? Paul Krugman, the economist? You think he's handsome? Brilliant, yes, but... Anyway, I meant me. How would you like that?"

"Being married to you? Hmmm?" She paused for a three-beat. "Could take some getting used to." She was teasing, of course, but there was also a tautness to the tease that Rosen in his excitement missed completely.

"I'm serious. I am that good!" he said, gesturing with his highly controlled version of a fist pump. "I think I am onto something at the Lab that is big, really big."

"It's all really big to you, Rosen, always has been. The first day we met you were already telling me that you were going places. A plumped up ego can be charming in an undergraduate, but it can wear with time." She spread her magazine in her lap, turned the page, and frowned in concentration as she bent toward it.

"Millie, listen. I mean it. This might be the most important work I've ever done. I wish I could tell you all about it, but you know, it's, like, top secret and all. If I'm right, though, this really is potential Nobel material. As soon as I can confirm it, I'm going to see if I can negotiate a release and get a paper accepted by *PLoS Medicine* to get it out before somebody scoops me." PLoS, the Public Library of Science, was an open-access, online collection of publications that made it possible to disseminate scientific findings much faster and more widely than in traditional bound journals. "You don't seem all that happy at the thought of being married to a world famous mathematical biologist," Rosen added, his voice filled with unspoken hurt.

Millie forced a smile and gave him a wet kiss on the cheek. "I'm happy for you, sweetheart." She was not happy for him, though. The very thought of their settled life being disrupted by fame terrified her. Rosen, straight-tacking Rosen, had been the safe, easy choice for her, her Mr. Spock, relentlessly rational, his cool logic protecting her from facing inner fears. "Send me an email when the Nobel Committee announces," she said.

She gathered her books and stacked them on the nightstand before turning out the lamp on her side of the bed. As she closed her eyes, she was thinking about being married to Rosen and about being married; as he watched her feign sleep, he was thinking about signal-to-noise ratio in research results and about the optimal place to publish his blockbuster journal article. He drifted into sleep while mentally composing the draft of his Nobel acceptance speech.

= =

The weekend, having started late, ended early for Rosen and Millie. By Sunday afternoon they were facing each other across their laptops on the kitchen table, logged into different systems and working in different worlds.

Millicent Geller David was a biologist, like Rosen. But unlike Rosen, she was what he referred to as a real biologist, one who picked up insects and could name trees by their leaves. Rosen had long ago given up trying to explain his obscure profession of mathematical biology to dinner guests or to new acquaintances at school functions. Millie, on the other hand, taught middle school, which was easy to explain and meant that she was up before the sun to be in her classroom by seven and spent weekends planning lessons that would challenge her students, the easily bored teenage and pre-teen children of the iPod generation.

Rosen and Millie were, by every measure, an odd couple. She was short and slight, with wispy honey-blond hair; he was six-two and somewhat beefy, with a head of thick, kinky hair the color of fresh asphalt. Despite her waifish physique and a long list of allergies, Millie loved the outdoors, hikes in the woods, swimming at Crane Beach, and kayaking on the Ipswich River. Hers was a passionate, visceral, and immediate involvement with Nature, which she had always spelled and spoken with a capital N, even as a small child. Rosen, who never liked to sweat without purpose, had a mechanically mediated approach to the natural world. His version of staying in shape involved mowing the lawn or ferrying groceries from the neighborhood store on his bicycle or, on rare occasion, weather permitting, cycling to work. His three bicycles, work stand, and tools took up most of their small garage, relegating his Prius and Millie's bright yellow VW to their short driveway. Millie had tried for years to get him to go backpacking with her, but his idea of camping out was a half-opened bedroom window in the dog days of August.

They had met in college, accidental lab partners in an organic chemistry class, and were instantly connected by their shared love of science—and of sex. "I'm someone who is going someplace," he had told her, as they walked across campus after class. "How would you like to come along for the ride?" She was drawn to his soft-spoken arrogance and said, "Sure. Where are we headed?" That afternoon, someplace turned out to be his dorm room. By the end of the semester, they had moved in together, and they were married in the summer before starting graduate school. But Millie had her heart set on a career as a biologist doing field research, and Rosen was beginning to discover that the real fun for him lay not in preparing specimens for electron microscopy or in discovering new species of soil bacteria but in crunching numbers.

Rosen had slalomed from specialty to specialty, taking courses in biochemistry, genetics, and even bioengineering before settling down to pursue a doctorate in mathematical biology, a field of applied statistics that was more math than bio. That suited Rosen, who had come to dislike chemicals and animals and plants in equal measure. He took his time on an ambitiously original doctoral dissertation while Millie doggedly searched for field research jobs before giving up and going back to college for her master's in education. She was already settled into teaching at the Nock Middle School in Newburyport before he finally finished his dissertation. That work, on the application of an obscure branch of information theory to the analysis of experiments, had attracted the attention of Biontolics, which had pursued him aggressively and put him under contract the week before he defended his dissertation. He had been working at the same desk in Ipswich ever since, doing an interesting job that, until now, had seemed to be an end in itself, a journey without a destination other than the completion of one project and the launching of the next.

Sitting at his own kitchen table, Rosen called up another research paper from the remote server, read the abstract, and saved it off in one of a dozen folders he had created. He was a biologist again, following a trail, sorting species unearthed along the way, immersing himself in the experience of discovery. As he waited for the next paper to download over the sluggish connection, he looked up from the screen to find that Millie was no longer across from him and her laptop was closed.

3

Orange and blue bunting draped the semicircular dining hall of the Presidential Palace in honor of what the government spin-doctors were describing as a major victory over opposition forces of the EUN. Ferguson, among the last few to enter the hall, spotted Raul Gomes, Minister of the Interior and former Angolan smuggler of blood diamonds, motioning toward an empty chair to his left. "I hear you had some fun coming into the airport yesterday," Gomes said to him, as Ferguson seated himself. "You must fill me in. I want to hear all the details."

Ferguson was about to answer when a slim giant of a man, his nearly blue-black skin set off by a bright yellow traditional tribal wrap, entered from the doorway to the far left and ceremoniously thumped his carved wooden staff on the floor twice. He held his staff aloft and called out in rhythmic Portuguese a phrase that Ferguson knew by heart: "His Excellency, the Doctor Edgar Jabari Mbutsu o Basanya, President for Life and Supreme Commander of the Armed Liberation Forces of the Sovereign State of Busanyu." The herald repeated the announcement in Lusanyu, the language of the Basanya people, the dominant tribal group of the region for whom the country had been named. The hundred or so guests in the hall rose in unison as the President for Life took a step into the room and the opening bars of the national anthem sounded. "*Basanya kyahm ngala*," they sang—Basanya people now unite.

Edgar Mbutsu did not look like a man born in 1922, although he did look like one who had fought in wars and insurrections in half the countries of sub-Saharan Africa. His knobbled face, red-brown and mottled like the earth of the land around, bore the irregular pink line of a poorly stitched gash from a machete that had nearly severed his left ear, and his chin sported an off-center dimple from a bullet wound. He was proud of his scars and even of the slight limp that spoiled his gait when he hurried, so he had a tendency to stroll when he wanted to appear dignified, stride when he wanted to draw attention to his long service and humbler origins.

He was a military man turned politician in the old style of twentieth-century Africa. He had been leader of a successful secessionist movement and survivor of more coup attempts than anyone had counted. He was a man of unmeasured personal wealth, fueled by his country's oil, diamonds, and newly discovered minerals, as well as by his percentage off the top of an extensive trade in contraband that went largely unreported. He was ruthless and fearless in defending what was his, but relentless in his pursuit of stability in the region, which made him a friend to Western governments and the latest in a long history of brutal dictators tolerated or supported because they were good for business. Except to encourage trade and honor treaties, Mbutsu was without personal or political ambitions beyond Busanyu's borders. He had everything he wanted and more, and the time to enjoy it. He would proudly declare his simple foreign and domestic policy positions in a single statement, that Busanyu was enough for Mbutsu—and Mbutsu was enough for Busanyu.

As the anthem ended, Mbutsu, tall and imposing, unbent by age, strolled with dignity toward the focus of the semicircle, where his immediate family waited for him at the head table. Just short of the table, he turned his head and looked straight at Ferguson, then picked up his pace to walk past his family and approach Ferguson instead. Grasping Ferguson's hand in both of his, the President for Life of Busanyu nodded gravely, then grinned and administered a crushing bear-hug and a thumping back-pounding.

"You are looking better than ever, old friend, my doctor," he said, stepping back. "The medicine man's medicine keeps you well."

Ferguson frowned at Mbutsu, then covered by smiling and looking around the room at the many faces turned their way. "We are both well," he told Mbutsu. "That is what counts."

"I do have much to thank you for, Doctor, particularly yesterday. If you had not accepted my invitation and drawn the fire of the criminal scum that follow Matata, who knows what might have happened. Why, I might have been killed." He said the last without irony or humor. "I must apologize, though, for the humble transportation that was not of the class that you deserve and have earned. You know, I am sure, that the Gulfstream 750 is still in such regrettably short supply and orders can take years before they are filled. So, in the meantime, while I await delivery, my guests must all resign themselves to transport in my humble G6." Mbutsu was bragging rather than apologizing, as Ferguson knew. The false modesty of a man who personally owned a G6 and had a G7 on order fooled no one.

Mbutsu continued. "The skill and bravery of our pilots and troops were not quite enough, alas, because that bastard coward Matata got away, leaving behind eight of his men, including two of his top aides and one of his grown sons, all for us to capture. Convenient. We gave them a speedy trial and special justice. This is a country of laws and of swift application."

"Emphasis on the swift."

"Thank you," Mbutsu said, acknowledging the remark as if it were a compliment. "I have been at this business of building and running a country for a very long time, Doctor, as you know. One gets good at something when one does it long enough. But in this case it was not all that difficult. The criminals were caught red-handed. They had the launcher still in the back of the Land Rover, the one that was spotted from the air by your most able pilot. You really should have come into the courtyard to see how effectively special justice is carried out here in Busanyu." He patted Ferguson on the shoulder before leaving to join his family at the head table. There he raised his glass in a traditional toast that Ferguson already knew: *Franda bmeli ontani!* May we outlive our enemies.

= =

As the thick after-dinner coffee was being served, Ferguson turned to the Minister seated next to him. "What is meant by this term, 'special justice,' Raul?" he asked. "I am not sure whether I have heard it used before."

"Special justice is the term we now use when the crime is very bad, like this one, since theirs was really, in effect, an attempt on the life of the President. It was the President's personal plane they tried to shoot down, thus it was an attack not only on the State but on the Head of State as well. In such cases, the entire village of the criminals is brought to watch, or as many as can be rounded up in time, so the lesson can be learned by the neighbors and relatives as well. Because the evil that is in these men is in their blood, we must be sure also that the evil is not carried on, so first we take care of the children of the criminals. His Excellency, our President, graciously gave the rebels a choice: they could kill their children themselves or the Presidential Guard could do it for them."

"You ask the accused to shoot their own children?"

"Oh, no! For children, a firing squad is unnecessary. A machete works just fine."

"But why? Why would anyone ever choose to kill their own children?"

"Because they can do it quickly, perhaps with a single blow. When the Presidential Guard does it...well, they are trained as soldiers not marauders or field workers. In the hands of one who does not wield the machete that often, it can be somewhat clumsy and slow, taking sometimes many blows, especially if the child runs or tries to fend off the blows." The Minister demonstrated by raising his arm as if to shield his face. "You can see the problem, of course."

Ferguson lowered his head and covered his eyes. He told himself that he had always known who he was dealing with, although it made the present circumstances no easier. He wondered what it said of him that the man known to the world as The Butcher of Busanyu was his patient. Aloud, he said, "And then the firing squad for the rebels themselves."

"Yes, of course, but first we bind them to posts and gag them so they cannot scream."

"Scream?" he asked, but quickly wished he had said nothing.

"Well, yes, because the first volley is for their feet, the second for the kneecaps, the third for the navel. We wait between. For effect. And then for the heart. That usually is enough."

"Yes, I would imagine," Ferguson said, rising from his chair and steadying himself on the edge of the table. "You will have to excuse me. It was a long flight, and I still have much to do in the morning."

Minister Gomes rose with him, determined to finish the story. "We also take care of the women," he said. "The firing squad get the first chance for the wives and daughters. Then the others. But that is more a matter of tradition than of law. At least this way they do not go to waste, the women and girls, before they are gone. But all that comes first, so the criminals can watch their women raped by their enemies. I do not know exactly what the legal status of that is, but it is custom sanctioned by the President. It is not only good for morale in the forces, but it discourages rebellion. That is the theory, at least."

Ferguson nodded slowly and left without saying any more. In his room, he reminded himself that Mbutsu had, in his unprecedented long reign, brought stability to the region, that African nations like his were, relatively speaking, enjoying prosperity and strong growth, lifting their citizens out of poverty—or at least helping those who survived, the ones who kept their heads down and their mouths shut. He reminded himself of the ongoing mutual dependence between them, that both their very lives depended on maintaining that relationship.

Still, he slept fitfully, awakened several times by gunfire and screams that were only in his dreams.

= =

In the morning, he was a doctor again, carrying his battered black bag across the compound to the hospital where he had an appointment with the Butcher of Busanyu. Mbutsu casually entered the special suite of the clinic forty minutes late, flanked by his personal bodyguards and accompanied by an old man. "This is Fallu," Mbutsu told him. "He is to be my tester today."

"I don't understand," Ferguson said. "What do you mean, tester?"

"It is a new procedure that we have thought of, a security measure. We trust you, of course, but we do not know who else might have had access to your drugs, your equipment. Everything you do to me, you will first do to him; everything you give to me, you will first give to him. That way, we will know it is safe, just as when my tasters try my food before I do."

"That is crazy, Mbutsu, madness. You have become paranoid."

"I have enemies. They stalk me and fire missiles at my plane. That is not paranoid."

"In any case, Mbutsu, the organization will not allow this plan of yours. What if it works? You know what that would mean. We cannot risk a..." He stopped without finishing.

"There is no risk, my shortsighted doctor. He will not live long at any rate; we will see to that. He is old and has served his purpose already. Now he is to become a defensive weapon, a single-use weapon. Do not concern yourself for him. Just give him the injections before you give them to me."

"Mbutsu, you know full well that the effects can take hours, days, months in some cases. Are you going to watch this man for ill effects while you become ill yourself, waiting for the medication you depend on? Besides, I have no extra with me, none to spare. You know how difficult the treatments are to produce. This is...this is simply stupid!"

Mbutsu slammed his palm on the examining table, causing his guards to jump and to reach reflexively toward their weapons. "You! You do not call me stupid!" he shouted. "No one ever. Not even you. You will die here, today, and the organization will send someone else in your place."

Ferguson, his heart pounding, struggled to control his voice. "They will send no one. You know that. You may not be stupid, but that does not save you from stupid ideas. What you want of this man will not work. Send him back to his village."

Mbutsu glared at Ferguson for long moments before nodding. One of his bodyguards opened the door, said something in Lusanyu, and shoved the old man in the back.

Mbutsu laughed loudly and signaled to his bodyguards, who followed the man out the door. Mbutsu placed his hands on Ferguson's shoulders. "It is not wise for men such as you to live dangerously. I have a lifetime of practice at it, and you are still just a novice.

"But, you are correct; it would not have worked. It was a stupid idea, and my head of security, the one who first suggested it to me, will find himself working the yam fields again. Now, let us begin this uncomfortable ritual that will take us days to complete and leave us both tired. Yes, tired but rejuvenated, is it not so?"

Ferguson shrugged but said nothing.

"Not to worry. We will, my doctor friend, outlive our enemies. All of them. And most of our friends as well." He started to undo the buttons of the midnight-blue military dress uniform that was his everyday attire. "Remember this, that stability requires continuity. The revolutions that swept the Arab world north of us reminded everyone of that lesson. Mubarak and Gadhafi were growing old and were no longer able to hold on, to provide that continuity for themselves or their countries. The outcome might have been different had they the arrangement we have. Is that not so, Dr. Cass? Oh, forgive me, Dr. Ferguson, I must have been thinking of someone else, someone from the past."

Ferguson ignored him while he busied himself smearing the EKG leads with electrode jelly. There were no assistants when he treated one of the underwriters. Fortunately, there were only a handful, which meant he had time—time for research, time for reflection, time to figure it all out.

4

Monday mornings tended to mean a late start for Rosen, but finding Jeannine already in the office when he arrived was unexpected. He was also surprised to see that his system was on and the big monitor was displaying the work that had now obsessed him for several weeks. Jeannine turned quickly from where she was standing by his desk and crossed over to the conference table, where she casually picked up a copy of a Biontolics internal publication and carried it to her own desk as if it were an important document and not a piece of company puffery.

"Are you interested in my work? Or are you trying to cut in on my territory, now?" Rosen said, his sarcasm sprinkled with seriousness. "Would you like a demo? I didn't think data visualization was exactly your thing, but maybe some of the information theory behind these new techniques I've been working on might be of interest."

"Maybe, later," she said. "I've got a presentation to deliver to the Foundation that I need to polish before heading downtown." The Foundation was the Boston-based Gerard and Hannah Berkowitz Charitable Foundation, one of the major funding sources supporting the Ipswich lab. Catering to representatives of the Foundation was a necessary, but largely resented, part of their jobs. Biontolics carried out the sort of obscure basic research, long-haul programs or long-shot gambles, that was difficult to fund from ordinary sources.

Occasional contract work for drug companies was the exception, but most of their research was supported by a handful of American and European private foundations. Rosen had never figured out precisely why the Berkowitz Foundation or any other private group would fund their sort of research nor what was in it for their contributors, but the money and the requests kept coming, and that meant that Rosen had a job he loved at a time when the economy was still on the long, slow slope up from what had been a prolonged recession, even though most economists had been reluctant to use the term and had declared its end on multiple occasions.

Rosen sat down at his desk and did his ritual scan of the email in his in-box. One message, leapt out at him. The subject line read:

FW: RE: IP release request.

The body was mostly boilerplate reminding him that all his research was proprietary work-for-hire and all Intellectual Property belonged to Biontolics Research, LLC, and/or the sponsors of its research projects. The final paragraphs delivered the real message.

> Your request to publish a paper with the working title of "Role of selected oncogenes in regulation of telomere activity in genetic chimeras: a multi-factor meta-analysis," has been denied by the funding source. It was felt that the work does not merit publication at this time. It does not represent original research and is of limited scientific significance. In any case, further work would be required to develop and refine the research sufficiently.

> We appreciate your excellent contributions to the research agenda of Biontolics and its partners and look forward to more in the future.

"Can you believe this?" he said, waggling his finger at the screen. Jeannine gave him a quizzical look. "They turned down my request to publish. They have never turned down any of my requests before. The first time I do something really good, and they reject it. 'Does not represent original research.' Quote-unquote. It's a meta-analysis, for God's sake. Of course, it doesn't represent original research. Who are these clowns? 'Limited scientific significance.' Didn't they even read the abstract. The conclusions are a game changer. Then this: 'Further work would be required.' It's a meta-analysis of completed research, you idiots. What further work do they have in mind?"

Jeannine shrugged. "It's just one paper, Rosen. You already have dozens in print. You're one of the most productive people in our section."

"But this is the one that matters!" he snapped, surprised at his own rising anger.

"Don't bite my head off. I didn't reject your request. Blame Widmark in the Intellectual Property group. IP can be bull-headed at times."

Rosen scrolled down to the signature block on the email: J. Thomas Widmark.

"How did you know it was Widmark?"

"Er, I guessed. I suppose he's always the one to deliver the bad news. Well, anyway, he turned down my paper last month."

"I didn't know you were working on a paper."

"Yeah, well, one of many things you didn't know." She tilted her head to one side letting her short brown hair fall across her face. "Like, for one thing, I think you are good, but also too serious for your own good. Let this one pass and propose another project. There are a lot of good ideas waiting to be studied.

"Oh, yes, and another thing. I like sushi but not wasabi," she added with a quick laugh.

Rosen wondered whether she was flirting with him but decided against commenting. He did not want to prolong the conversation at a time when what he really wanted to do was fire off a long email to Mr. J. Thomas Widmark. That, however, was not Rosen's style. His style was to line up all his ducks in a row, polish his arguments, and methodically build his case, then deliver the whole thing in one surprise attack that left the opposition dumbstruck. He turned back to his desk and started building his intellectual roadside bomb.

It turned out to be a dud. They turned down his second request. And his third.

= =

Two weeks later, he was working on a fourth submission when the email arrived. WE NEED TO TALK, its subject line shouted all in caps, as if some junk email had snuck past the corporate spam filters. It was the return address, however, that really grabbed his attention. It was internal, from Atchison Dougherty, CEO of Biontolics, a man whom neither he nor anyone else at the Ipswich offices had ever seen, but who was a legend. A summons from the man known to his far-flung troops as "The General" was unprecedented. Rosen opened the message. The body was an Outlook appointment: Monday, 15:30-16:00, Suite 1100, Berkowitz Building, Boston.

"I have until Monday to figure this out," he said aloud. "I have to puzzle out what is going on before I go in there." He reached for the phone, called Millie's school, and left a message for her at the school office. It was only the second time he had ever canceled a date with her. The first time was when they were still in college, after which she had broken up with him and refused to see him for a month. He wondered what the consequences would be this time around.

= =

Suite 1100 in the Berkowitz Building consisted of a mahogany-paneled reception area, a large corner office with views out over Boston's financial district, and a small conference room furnished with a walnut table that barely left space for the chairs around it. The suite was hardly more than a drop-box, a luxurious but little-used serviced facility that supplied an address and a place for meetings. When Rosen introduced himself to the receptionist, a plump woman in her fifties with an Eastern European accent, she ushered him into the conference room, told him to have a seat, then left and closed the door behind her. Rosen flipped open the port-folio that he carried and tried to concentrate on rereading the syn-opses of the two reports he had prepared. He cringed when he spotted a misspelled word in the second paragraph. So much for trying to impress the big boss, he told himself.

Atchison Dougherty kept him waiting, but not for long. A few minutes after the hour, he opened the conference room door several inches and announced that it would be a few minutes more before they could meet.

"Not a problem," Rosen said to a door that was already closing again. Dougherty returned twenty minutes later and motioned Rosen to follow. He wordlessly waved Rosen toward the large office on the far side of the reception area, paused and accepted a stack of papers from the receptionist, then entered the office himself and closed the door behind him.

"Well!" he announced. "You are a determined young man, Dr. David. Determination is a meritorious quality so long as it is not one's only quality. Please, take a seat." The General remained standing, his legs slightly apart as if at parade rest. He had slate blue eyes topped by untamed eyebrows. His mouth was a thin-lipped stroke across his square face. He looked like a man who had earned every letter of his nickname, one who might have launched a military career pacifying villages in Viet Nam.

"To get right to the point, your excellent work on a number of projects has not gone unnoticed. We want to put you in charge of an important line of investigation funded by a rather sizable new grant. I have already spoken with your supervisor, and you are to be reassigned to the Nutrition Sciences Group. This is a promotion. You will have three junior staff working for you, your own office, and a not inconsequential increase in salary. Oh, yes, and we have upped your allocation on the North Carolina facilities. We expect you to make good use of our supercomputer down there."

"What about the research that I have been trying to publish? I'd like to see that through to some resolution."

"I don't think you understand, Dr. David. Your paper is not going to be published. It has already been decided not to pursue further research and not to publish. I brought you here to tell you about your promotion but also to impress something on you. To put it bluntly, no matter how many times you submit a request and no matter how many pages of appendices you attach to your application, the answer will always be the same: a plain and simple no. So, you can cease wasting your own good time and that of our overworked Mr. Widmark in the IP Group. It is a dead end, and we will be doing no further research in that area. None whatsoever.

"So, if there are no questions, please accept my congratulations. And don't forget to have the receptionist validate your parking ticket." He reached out for a handshake but Rosen remained seated, with his hands in his lap. The General's expression darkened with a mixture of annoyance and puzzlement.

"I do have a question," Rosen said.

"Certainly. Anything."

"Why are you here, Dr. Dougherty? I mean here in Boston. Corporate headquarters is in Research Triangle, and you live in London, at least according to the company magazine piece about you. When I rang our London office, they said you had flown over for a meeting in Boston. Why am I so important?"

"Well, I would not want to deflate your ego too much, but perhaps you are not that important. I just happened to have had business here with the Berkowitz Foundation and thought I would take the opportunity to deliver the good news to you in person."

"I am yet to be convinced that it is good news you are delivering."

Dougherty turned away for a moment, then sat casually on the edge of the desk. "Trust me, it is definitely good. We think you have a bright future with us and that it will be brighter if we focus your considerable talents in an area of more value to us and our underwriters."

"That is difficult for me to believe. Just let me try to explain my paper and its significance."

"I read your paper, son. I did molecular biology at university," he said, with rising impatience. "I am telling you that we are not going to publish it. Period."

"Why?"

Dougherty's face took on an expression that suggested he was not accustomed to being asked to supply reasons for his actions. He grunted. "Let us just say that our underwriters do not think it serves their interests. They pay the piper, hence they call the tune. In this case, that tune is a dirge for your research. Finis. I would not want it to turn into a tragic grand-opera finale for you. You are too valuable. And I would remind you that, should you leave, you would still be bound by non-disclosure and non-compete agreements."

Rosen raised his eyebrows. "Perhaps, then, you could answer a different question. Why were all my other earlier publication requests approved?"

"Because they were better, I suppose, more appropriate. I don't involve myself in that level of detail. I can't afford to indulge in micromanagement or in second-guessing my people."

"Might I suggest a possible explanation?" Rosen said. "Perhaps they were less important. Over the weekend, I completed a small-scale study of my own, an impact analysis. Did you know, sir, that out of a random sample of 1000 papers published by Biontolics people over the last decade, only two appeared in so-called first-tier journals? Two-thirds appeared in journals ranking in the bottom quartile on Impact Factor, the accepted measure of influence in scientific publications. And the vast majority of our papers were cited once or not at all."

Dougherty shook his head slowly from side to side. "I've always believed that Biontolics has an enviable publication record. I am told that, for our size, we are one of the most productive research enterprises in the world."

"With all due respect, sir, we are purveyors of mass mediocrity.

My analysis shows we are publishing material that nobody cares about. With few exceptions, it's mediocre and irrelevant."

"Now wait one minute, I don't have to listen to this sort of talk."

"Bear with me, please. As you probably already know, my specialty is meta-analysis, the art and science of sifting through other people's work, mining the discarded detritus of research to reveal trends or patterns, the forest overlooked by others too busy examining all the trees. The science is statistics, but the art is spotting patterns. When I finished the analysis for my last paper, the one I can't publish, I went back and read through all 54 papers in the core cluster of studies. You know what I noticed that wasn't in the tables or the statistics? Not one of those papers was written or co-authored by anyone from Biontolics, not one. That is amazing, sir, because those papers, those important papers, are all in areas that fall within our primary mission: oncology, genetics, epigenetics, gene expression, apoptosis, and cellular growth and longevity. These are our bread and butter, yet not one of our people were represented by a paper in that group."

Dougherty shrugged and spread his hands. "Do you have a point?"

"That was my point. But I also have another question. It struck me as strange that no one from Biontolics was publishing in that area, so I went back into our own archives, reran my earlier analysis, and found more than thirty internal, unpublished papers that would have fallen into the same cluster and lent even greater strength to my conclusions, yet none of these studies had ever been published. Why do you think that is?"

"Because they were not good enough to be accepted by the journals, perhaps?"

"No!" Rosen said, lightly tapping his clenched fist on his thigh for emphasis. "They were unpublished because Biontolics would not allow them to be published. I cross-referenced with the IP Group's database and found that Biontolics had turned down every publication release request for every one of those papers. What do you make of that, sir?"

Dougherty clenched his teeth as he mulled it over, trying to decide what tack to take with a conversation that was lurching out of control. "I don't know, exactly. I think it is a matter that someone will have to look into, but I am certain we will find an explanation, one that will satisfy you. At least I hope we can, since I would hate to have us lose someone as resourceful as you seem to be." He tried to modulate the level of threat in his voice. "So," he pronounced as he stood, signaling that the meeting was at an end.

Rosen ignored the hint. "If you are going to have someone look into the matter, sir, perhaps they will find this useful. Several of the earliest unpublished papers in our own archives cited this one as an unpublished research report, but it was not in our database, so I tracked it down on the internet. It was never published, that much I confirmed. From the references it cites, it would seem to date from the 1970s. Apparently, someone had once scanned it into a .PDF document and left it forgotten on a server at their university. It took some real digging, but I have learned that if you are clever and persistent enough, you can track down almost anything on the Web."

He slipped a stapled document from his portfolio. The cover sheet was darkened toward the edges and peppered with a telltale accumulation of speckles from too many generations of successive photocopying. It was a typewritten manuscript with the word "CONFIDENTIAL" repeated across the top and bottom of the page. The title, "Cancer expression, cell longevity, and mosaicism in Rattus norvegicus," was succinct testimony to close parallels with the research integrated in Rosen's own meta-analysis, except this paper reported experimental results from decades earlier. The authors were listed on the cover sheet as Atchison D. Dougherty, Ph.D., Llewellyn A. Cass, M.D., Emile Aubuchon, Ph.D., and Janella Kai.

When Dougherty didn't take the paper from his hand, Rosen stood up to leave and laid it on the desk. "I guess you were barely more than a grad student then, and now you are the last man standing, it would seem."

Dougherty's face remained placid save for a double crease that subtly deepened between his eyebrows. "Meaning?"

"Well, all the other authors are either dead or disappeared."

"All? How do you...," he stopped himself and locked eyes with Rosen.

After an uncomfortable few seconds, Rosen broke the silence. "You have someone look into that. And I trust you will let me know what this is all about." He walked out and strode past the receptionist without remembering to get his parking ticket validated.

The General sat down again on the edge of his desk, rocking back and forth ever so slightly as he thought through the scenarios. He picked up the phone on the desk, punched a long series of digits, and waited. After a half-dozen warbling rings, the voice on the other end said, "What?"

"Andras, it's Dougherty."

"I know who it is, but do you know what time it is?"

"Sorry. Where are you?"

"Moscow, the clinic."

"We have a problem. We have to meet."

"Do I know about this problem?"

"Not yet. I'll see you at the Center tomorrow night."

"No, you come here. I just got in from Africa. Are you certain this can't wait? At least give me a hint over the phone."

"No, it can't wait, but, on second thought, I can take care of it, or at least engineer a short-term solution. So, until we next meet in Zurich. The chemist. I have to go. I have to make some arrangements here." He set down the phone and picked up the mottled paper from his desk. He had not known that a copy still existed outside the safe in his London townhouse. Who had made it? They had shown the draft to almost no one once they had decided what to do about it. But someone among the handful they had trusted had given a copy to someone else who had passed on another copy. This version looked like it might have been scanned from a sixth or seventh generation copy. It wasn't possible to go much further than that in those early days of photocopying.

Dougherty made another phone call. "Holzinger, it's Dougherty here. I want you to track down something on the internet and make it disappear, completely, even on the Internet Wayback Machine. Every copy, every reference, every link. I don't want a trace left behind. Can you do that?"

"I know the team that can do it, but it will not be instantaneous if the distribution is wide. And if there is anyone on the other end trying to preserve it, we can get into a put-and-take game that can drag on and on."

"We'll head that one off by starting with every system inside Biontolics. Begin with the Ipswich Lab and work outward from there. I'll send you particulars by secure email. Start scrambling the moment you get it. And put a tail on a Dr. Rosen David in the Ipswich Lab, infect his workstation, and get into his home system if he has one. You report back to me directly. Understand?

"*Ich verstehe!* I understand. *Tchüss.*" The line went dead.

5

Rosen knew he should have gone straight home after the meeting in Boston, but he had been driving on automatic pilot and had continued on directly to the Lab instead. Once there, he had gotten caught up in tracking down new references cited in a fresh batch of unpublished papers that he had retrieved from the internal archives. Millie would not be happy. In the weeks since his discoveries began, a murky shadow had descended on their relationship, and the distance between them had been growing. It would have worried Rosen had he been given to worry, but in their division of roles and responsibilities, worry was Millie's department, just as taking out the garbage and mowing the lawn were his.

The house was dark when he arrived, but he could see that a light was on in the bedroom. When Rosen rattled his fingers on the half-closed door there was no response. He pushed it open enough to see Millie lying with her back to him and her arm cantilevered straight out over the side of the bed. The coverlet was heaped like a tent over her, leaving only the top of her head exposed. A pocket guide to edible weeds lay on the pillow beside her.

He whispered, "Sorry," in hopes that he hadn't awakened her but in fear that he had. He tiptoed out again, gently pulled the door to, and quietly walked back down the hall to pour himself a drink and watch something from the TiVo. The tension of the meeting was still with him, though, and he found it impossible to concentrate, so eventually he poured himself a second single-malt scotch and headed back to the bedroom.

Millie hadn't moved.

Rosen froze, a wooden totem pole standing watch over the fragile figure of his wife lying still on the bed. A breeze from the open window stirred her hair where it peeked from beneath the covers, but there was no other movement. His heart hammered in his chest as he forced himself to edge around to her side of the bed. His knees cracked as he slowly lowered himself until he was eye-level with her motionless face. He did not have a label for the feeling that gripped him as he reached out to touch her shoulder.

"Millie," he whispered. There was no response. He gently shook her. "Millie, I am sorry. Please."

Her eyes fluttered half open and she looked into his. "Are you all right, Rosen?"

"Yes. No. I thought,...for a moment I thought maybe...You didn't move."

"I'm exhausted, Rosen. These nights when you have been working so late, I try to stay up to see you, to talk, but then I have to leave so early in the morning. It...I...I just can't do it. It's not working."

"I'm sorry, Millie." He lifted her gently and pulled her to him. "I was," he searched for a word, a synonym for the fear he had felt. "I thought," he said, choosing a safe and neutral verb, "I thought that maybe, maybe I had lost you. That's crazy, I know, but..." Her head lay deliciously against his chest and a wisp of her hair tickled his lip. "I love you, Millie."

"I love you, too. Come to bed my future Nobelist, my noblest of biologists. And please come home earlier more often." His tenderness and concern had touched her. She started kissing him with the little popping kisses that were her way of inviting him in.

He drifted in and out of their lovemaking as Millie's sudden passion and his dark thoughts of conspiracies warred for his attention. Millie, on the other hand, mounted and rode him with undivided concentration. She climaxed astride him, then bent to whisper in his ear. "We have to talk. I'm taking a sick day tomorrow and so are you. We have to talk."

It was a litany that he had heard before, and his discomfort rose as he lay beside her. Whether in whispers in bed or shouted in capital letters in an email, the message did not usually mean that what followed would be easy for Rosen to manage.

Rosen's wide-ranging intelligence did not extend to insight into the subtleties of human emotion. He interpreted the feelings of those around him by formula and only with some difficulty. His own emotional experience was largely one-dimensional, ranging from moderately good to moderately bad. Good could be anything from simple satiety to his own carefully modulated version of elation; bad could mean anxious or angry, discouraged or disappointed. Feelings, he had once written in a note to a friend, were like numbers: they could be positive or negative, real, or imaginary, but mostly complex. It was a mathematician's play on words that brought a groan and a grin from his friend, an excitable electrical engineer who wore his feelings up front, next to his pocket protector. To Rosen, though, numbers, including the so-called complex numbers, made simple sense in a direct way that feelings never did.

Ask Rosen how he felt, and he might say "I don't know." Press him on it, and he might elaborate. "Good, I guess," he would add, or, "Not good, but okay." Millie accepted his handicap as she accepted the tin ear that rendered him incapable of carrying a tune. His muted emotions often served as a convenient counterbalance to her many anxieties, but acceptance did nothing for her need for engagement and intensity, which periodically rose to the point of crisis between them.

= =

The day spent playing hooky with Millie had proven to be a good idea and not nearly as taxing for Rosen as he had anticipated. She told him she was unhappy and becoming unsure whether they should stay married. She missed him and wanted more time with him. She wanted more independence and more togetherness. She felt the pulls of their very different careers and wondered if they might just slowly drift apart. She was proud of him but also felt diminished by his glamorous job in cutting-edge research that contrasted so critically with her own position teaching biology and health science to adolescents.

They had been holding hands as they walked in silence along the harbor front in Gloucester with freshets of the fishy Atlantic breeze tossing Millie's silk-fine hair. Then her small hand tightened on his, and the core of her perennial pain poured out. They had just reached the Morgan Faulds Pike sculpture of a young woman and her two children gazing out over the sea.

"I wish we made love more often," Millie said.

Rosen nodded, but it was a nod of agreement not of understanding. They stood silently for several minutes, each appreciating in their own very different ways the beauty of the three figures in bronze. Rosen, having completed his visual survey, spoke first. "Isn't it extraordinary, such lifelike detail," he said. "Look at the drape of the dress seeming to blow in the wind as if it were thin cotton rather than solid metal. I read somewhere that the artist had her models pose nude for the initial sculpture. That way she could build up the clothes more realistically in the original from which the bronze was cast."

Millie looked at him with sad eyes then turned her gaze to the young child in the woman's arms as the tears began to flow. "I wish we made love more often," she repeated, "even though..."

Even Rosen understood this for the trope it was. She regretted that they couldn't have children. The regret, which was deep, real, and recurring, surfaced someway in every such talk. It was most painful to both of them—painful to Millie because she saw it as her failing, painful to Rosen because he knew how much it meant to her. He liked the idea of children but had always found the reality less interesting than the idea. He was willing to adopt—emphasis on the willing—but the issue to her was as much about bearing the children as raising them. As she saw it, her career gave her abundant opportunities to mother-hen a young brood. What she couldn't do was conceive and give birth.

She had all but convinced herself that it was a blessing not to be having children. The biologist in her said that it was Nature's way of keeping reproductive handicaps from being passed on to another generation. She worried about the growing number of couples who bore children only with the help of expensive and elaborate medical technology. Their investment would only ensure that future generations would be even more dependent on intervention. She took secret comfort in the fact that she had persuaded Rosen when they were in graduate school to donate to a sperm bank. At least one of them might continue to contribute to the human gene pool, but she said nothing of any of this in their day-long talk.

Later, he had stood, stroking Millie's hair as she sat on a rock, knees tucked under her chin, hugging herself as she cried and the incoming tide washed the gravel beach. Back home, they had made love in the afternoon with the late sun streaming in the bedroom window.

It had been a day filled with conversation and without conclusion, a day that Rosen could replay in his head but without insight. He knew these times transformed, that even without resolution, even without change, they made life better between them, but he had no idea how. He only knew that it felt good to have Millie's head on his shoulder and the scent of her hair in his nostrils and her breath warm against his neck.

6

Mbutsu glanced quickly around the long ebony table, its highly polished surface dancing with reflections from the chandelier above, and realized that it was good to be dining alone again. Alone was only a relative concept for the President for Life of Busanyu. Both of his newest wives were across the table from him, but the children had already dined separately and been paraded before the table, then herded off to studies and to bed. Tabansi Faruq, Busanyu Minister of Defense and the youngest son of one of Mbutsu's old school chums, was on one side with his wife, Daib. On the other side was the mayor of Mbutsu City who had arrived with a petition at the palace and managed to invite himself to dinner, along with his pudgy teenage daughter. An aide had quietly informed the President that the Mayor was shopping his daughter to high-placed officials and might even have in mind her becoming number five in the President's household. Mbutsu, who had seen the daughter before, had laughed.

Mbutsu pushed his plate away and leaned back in his chair. The plate was immediately swept up by one of the servers, a young girl who shyly stole a glance at Mbutsu as she retrieved his cutlery.

Mbutsu raised a finger, bringing the butler to his side. "That one," Mbutsu said, nodding toward the rapidly retreating serving girl. "Who is that one? I do not recognize her."

"She just returned from Angola where she was studying. One of the drivers recommended her. She is a hard worker and a quick learner."

"And very pretty."

"And very young." The almost inaudible remark came from across the table, but it was not clear who had spoken. Mbutsu shot a glance at his wives, who both stared straight ahead, grim faced.

"I like them young," he said. "You should both be glad of that, or you would not be here, now, eating like the queen of Egypt."

Boipelo, the older of the two sisters and mother of three of his children, sniffed in reproach before wiping her mouth slowly and deliberately with her brocaded napkin. "And the older you get, Edgar, the younger you like them. Is it not so, husband?" She drew out the last word for emphasis.

"It is not so, wife number three," he said, putting her firmly in her place. "I simply never lost the tastes of my youth." The tastes of his youth were legend. As a soldier, he had encouraged the men under his command to rape the women of the villages they overran, and he was said to have saved for himself the prettiest among those who were barely more than girls.

While locking eyes with Boipelo, Mbutsu signaled again to his butler.

"Excellency," the butler said, leaning slightly forward in anticipation of the request to come.

"Have her brought to my room in an hour," Mbutsu said, speaking quietly but loud enough to be heard by those across the table. He did not shift his gaze from Boipelo.

"The serving girl," the butler said in confirmation, but with a subtle hint of question. Mbutsu nodded and dismissed the man. Boipelo held her husband's eyes as she rose from the table, made a show of straightening her chair, and backed away without turning, as if she were leaving the presence of royalty. Her mouth remained fixed and unexpressive, but her eyes flashed anger.

"Wives," Mbutsu said, leaning forward and speaking to the Defense Minister who was seated just past his own wife. "It is probably that time again, when they get moody and jealous. At least eventually that monthly inconvenience stops, although then they are not that desirable, either, as you know."

The Minister squirmed with visible discomfort, but neither he nor his wife spoke, and the rest of the dinner proceeded in silence until Mbutsu suddenly rose. Everyone still at the table stood.

"I think I shall be off to bed. I have meetings early in the morning," he announced, before walking slowly from the room.

= =

Mbutsu ignored the soldier from his personal guard who stood at attention outside the door to his bedroom suite. He entered the room and found the girl already waiting for him, standing beside the bed, barefoot, wearing the simple, light-blue shirtwaist dress of a schoolgirl.

"You are early," he said.

She kept her head bowed slightly in respect. "I asked them to bring me here so that I would be ready."

He looked surprised and pleased. "You are eager, then?"

"You are Mbutsu. I am only one who serves. That is why I am here: because you are Mbutsu."

"Does the one who serves have a name?"

"Afya." She didn't offer a family name.

"And how old is Afya?"

"Nineteen."

"You do not look even fifteen."

"Is that a good thing or not," she asked, "to look younger than you are?"

"In a woman, it is a good thing, and in your case a very good thing. In a man, it is another matter, and in a President, it can be a definite problem."

"It is said that our President is more than ninety years old. My grandfather told me that he saw you on the television when he was a boy in school, and you were already a grown man, a soldier fighting against the government. But that is impossible. You do not look to be ninety."

"No, I do not," he said, dismissing the subject.

He crossed over to her and started undoing the buttons of her shirtwaist. Her breathing deepened and picked up in pace as he proceeded. He placed a finger on either side of her neck and traced the lines of her collarbone, slowly spreading his hands, pushing the top of her dress apart until it slipped from her shoulders. She was wearing nothing underneath. Mbutsu trembled slightly as he slowly lowered both hands until his fingers rested lightly on her large nipples, as dark as espresso against the light cocoa of her skin.

He pushed her gently but eagerly down on the bed and started to undress himself. She lay there, atop the covers, legs slightly spread in invitation, arms raised and hands beneath the pillow behind her head. She opened her mouth as if to speak.

Mbutsu climbed onto the bed, spreading her legs still farther as he lowered himself.

He screamed.

The pain, at first a mere stitch in his side, shot through him, ripping him apart like lightening through an old tree in a storm. Her arm had come around suddenly, catching him low in his left side. He grabbed the arm and twisted it with such desperate violence that he heard a snap as a bone in her wrist gave way. She screamed as the guard, already at the bedside with his gun drawn, jerked her erect.

The knife had done real damage, but Mbutsu knew he would heal. He was an old soldier who had survived worse. He calmly grabbed a pillow from the bed and jammed it against his side to staunch the rush of blood. A pistol lay there on the bed where it had been hidden under the pillow.

"Pity she decided to use the knife instead of finishing me off with a single shot," he said, laughing with grim humor.

"You deserve more than a single shot!" she spat. "Special justice, like you gave my father. I will cut off your balls and feed them to you."

Mbutsu laughed and winced in pain. "I think you will do no such thing. I think it is you who will get special justice."

Three soldiers suddenly entered the room. "Get the doctor. Now!" he barked at the last of them. "And take her away," he said to the other two, as his personal guard helped steady him. There was a traffic jam at the door as the three soldiers all took the same moment to try to exit.

"Wait, leave her." The soldiers hesitated a second but then threw the girl to the floor and stood over her with their side arms drawn. She lay there, her hand wrapped around her broken wrist, and glared up at Mbutsu.

"Who is your father, Afya? What is your family."

"My father was Ntansi, Matata's half-brother. And you are nothing beside either of them. Matata will eat your eyes after he is through with you. You will beg for him to be through. They will butcher the Butcher of Busanyu. The people will win in the end. Bastard! Pig!" She spat again.

Mbutsu looked down at her and grew thoughtful. The sound of running feet reached them from the hall. Mbutsu scanned the soldiers in the room and reached for the pistol on the bed.

His personal guard flinched and took a step back. Mbutsu calmly shot him in the head and the man fell to the floor beside the girl. The Captain of the Presidential Guard, rushing into the room, shouted, "What happened? Are you all right, Excellency?

Mbutsu gestured with the pistol. "Take these men away. This girl had help. There was a gun and knife in here with her. I want you to find out how they got here, who all was involved."

"Look out!" the Captain shouted. Before anyone else could react, Mbutsu kicked at the girl's good arm, sending the gun she had retrieved from the dead guard skittering across the polished wood floor.

Mbutsu, his face turning scarlet, lowered the pistol he held, turned it sideways, and pressed the barrel to the bridge of her nose.

He waited until she raised her eyes to meet his in defiance, then pulled the trigger.

"Get this mess cleaned up, Captain. And I mean more than just the mess in this room. And where the fuck is my doctor?"

"Your doctor left this morning, on your jet, Excellency. You said your goodbyes."

"Yes, of course. Then the other one, the clumsy butcher from South America. Just get him." Mbutsu staggered and pressed harder on the blood-soaked pillow at his side. "And I said to get this mess cleaned up—before I slip on someone's brains and take a fall. Unless you want it to be your blood that I next wash my feet in."

He stood there, naked, badly wounded, but still very much the feared Butcher of Busanyu.

7

Rosen had spent the entire week trying to be a good boy, trying to behave himself while getting used to a new position in which he was quickly learning that his main responsibility was keeping three junior analysts busy believing they were doing real science when they were actually pursuing make-work assignments handed down to Rosen from unknown sources in Research Triangle Park. He was not succeeding very well in his new job and was finding that more and more of his time was spent sending emails of protest to North Carolina or London or trying to persuade the local Lab Director to take yet another meeting with him.

Millie actually liked the new regime at first. Rosen's lack of real responsibility and the absence of any engaging challenge that might keep him at the lab meant that he was coming home at seven or even six most evenings. But his sullen disposition and growing unease, muted though it might be, was beginning to worry her.

Rosen, however, remained worry free but impatient as he glanced at the clock gadget on his monitor screen and wondered how much longer it might take him to wrap up the last of the many routine electronic forms for which he was now responsible. He was watching the animated second hand slowly circle for the third time when he had a flash of inspiration to take another look at the author names on some of the unpublished papers. He realized that he could define a query and pull them off the server again, but there was a folder and a database with everything he needed already sitting on his old machine. He typed in its address on the network, but instead of getting a login dialog got an error message. He double-checked his spelling, tried again, but got another message that the address was invalid. He did a search for the computer by name and this time got a response that no computer named SULTANA1 could be found. Rosen, figuring it must be a network or local search glitch, switched to a global search and tried again to connect to his old computer. No luck.

It seemed unlikely, but it was possible that the machine was turned off, since no one had moved into his old office yet. Rosen took the back stairway to the second floor and rapped on the closed door. There was no answer. He pushed the door open. The room had been cleaned out except for the desks, chairs, and conference table.

Jeannine, who seemed perpetually present wherever Rosen was, poked her head around the corner from the hallway. "Looking for something?" she asked.

"Yeah, my old system. I wanted to pull some files from it."

"Oh, I guess when they moved my stuff over to Nutrition Sciences they must have grabbed it, too. Must be around someplace."

"Well it doesn't show up on the network, so if it's around it's not connected. And you've been sent to join Nut Science, too?"

"Please, I prefer to use the official name, even though 'Nut Science' might be the favored terminology in the hallways."

"No, I tell you, it really is Nut Science. Haven't you heard the latest findings from my group that 500 grams of walnut meats a day cuts your risk of cardiovascular disease and colon cancer in half?" He paused, waiting for a laugh or a rabbit punch that didn't come. "Which team have you been assigned to?"

"Yours. You're my new boss." She grinned at him and mimed a curtsy. "I want to keep an eye on you, see how you do it, so I can become a rising star, too."

"Rising, falling, who can tell the difference? Right now I'm headed down—to check with the IITS people to see what happened to my computer."

Information and Infrastructure Technologies and Services was located in the converted guest house, which was itself larger than most single-family homes in the area. One had to go outside to get there from the labs or the offices. There had been talk of building a tunnel or covered walkway, but IITS had always vetoed the idea. They liked the separation. Those in Technical Services, the "help desk," particularly preferred to be able to put people on hold or stack them in a message queue rather than have to face them across a counter.

Rosen now leaned on the Technical Services counter and looked down at the chunky nebbish in a flowered dress standing on the other side. "You are saying that the computer—my computer—was scrubbed and rebuilt?"

"That's what it says here on my Equipment Disposition Log," she answered, with more than a hint of impatience. "The hard drive was reformatted and the OS was reinstalled on Tuesday."

"Why?"

"Security policy. We sent you an email last week, but you didn't respond."

Rosen fluttered the fingers of his left hand against his jeans, his version of getting steamed. "You wiped the hard drive."

"Yes, Dr. David, multi-pass random overwrite to DoD standards. Even the Pentagon would approve of our procedures."

The pace of Rosen's fluttering fingers picked up. "Right, I guess that's it, then. Thanks. Carry on."

Rosen left and shifted gears into his determined problem-solving mode. Back in his new office, he accessed the backup share for SULTANA1. The Lab automatically maintained a backup copy of everything from its many scattered computers. More than once Rosen had been saved from redoing work after accidentally overwriting the wrong file.

He let out a sigh of relief and a quiet "Yes!" The backup share was still there. He opened it to scan through folders. It was empty.

Rosen stared at the screen, thinking of his next move. The report and project archives might have a copy of his data if he had a-ttached them at the time of filing. It was worth a try. He accessed the archival database and once again sighed in relief. Everything was there. He scanned down the list until he came to Project Zoetrope, his last assignment, and opened the folder. It, too, was empty.

Rosen could feel his heart speed up, but he calmly switched to a corporate directory, located the listing for Chief Librarian of Librar-ies and Archival Storage, and sent off a message to Enid Amundsen. The reply came within minutes.

> The files you were attempting to access have been removed from the Libraries and Archival Storage databases.
>   –Enid Amundsen, Chief Librarian, LAS

He typed a reply and got another quick response.

> I am not in a position to say the reason except that the removal was made at the direction of Corporate Security. And, yes, removal means expunged completely. We have no backup copy or any other means to restore the information removed.
>   –Enid Amundsen, Chief Librarian, LAS

= =

It was over take-out pizza for a late dinner that Millie brought up the matter of his mood. "Tell me what's going on with you, Rosen," she said. "Something is really eating you."

"No, I'm okay. Anyway, I really shouldn't talk about this stuff," he said, which Millie recognized as his coded declaration that he could and would talk about it in his own good time.

"You have to trust me," she said, reaching across the table to take his hand. "I can keep a secret, you know."

"I know, it's not that. I trust you, but it's complicated. I'm under contract; they could go after me for talking out of school."

Millie said nothing but waited patiently for him to decide to talk.

"You know what happened today?" he began at last. "I went to suck over some files from my old system, and the computer didn't show up on the network. I went over to the other building, and they told me the system had been scrubbed and rebuilt. I asked why. Actually, I insisted. They said it was a security issue, that they had nothing to do with it. Corporate Security had told them to retrieve my machine and all my media and scrub them clean. I stormed out of there. Back at my office, my nice, new, antiseptic office—it's on the back corner with a view out over the picnic tables—I figured I would just pull what I was looking for out of the archives. Nothing. Gone. I searched the backup servers and found zip. I called the head of IT and asked her what had happened, and she gave me the same song and dance about security. Corporate had directed that everything be deleted. Everything.

"It's as if the last months never happened. My old reports and my published and internal papers are still in the reference database except for my last project, Zoetrope, which has vanished completely."

"What do you think is going on?"

"It doesn't make sense, but I'm becoming convinced that the company might be actually suppressing research. From what I can tell, they are giving away dreck and censoring the good stuff."

"That could make perfect sense. Don't corporations usually keep the best ideas to themselves?"

"Sure, if they are building cars or developing drugs or manufacturing computers, but Biontolics doesn't make anything real. Their only product is research; they manufacture and distribute knowledge."

"What about your clients? You do research for clients, right? Keeping important stuff proprietary would make sense for them."

"Yes, for the drug companies that we do stuff for, but that's less than maybe ten percent of our business. Most of what we do is for foundations funding pure research. There is nothing to be gained by not publishing and everything by publishing, particularly in this area that I've been working on. It's really important research that needs to be put out there so that others can followed up on it."

"What's it all about? Just tell me in general terms if you can't be specific."

Rosen took a deep breath and another bite of pizza before answering. "It's about what causes cells to age and die and the genetic and other factors that regulate that. On the one hand, you have ordinary cells that only live so long and can only go through so many cell divisions before they give up the ghost."

"Apoptosis, cellular suicide," she offered.

"Right, and without that you end up with cells that go on living and multiplying forever. Cancer. Like the immortal HeLa cancer-cell culture so widely used in research. There doesn't seem to be anything in between, not in nature, but researchers have been trying to figure out an end run around nature, to regulate cell aging and longevity and, ultimately, to extend the lifespan of the organism."

"You mean like calorie restriction, anti-oxidants, that stuff?"

"Not exactly. Some of that more superficial stuff may eventually be proved out to be useful, but most of what passes for life extension is just snake oil and pseudoscience. Besides, who wants to live to a hundred and twenty if the price is to spend your life being cold and hungry or eating nothing but wheat grass? No, what I am talking about are more fundamental mechanisms, like telomeres."

"The little strings at the ends of DNA that protect the DNA but gradually wear away with each cell division. At least that's how I explain it to my students."

"Right, except that it turns out there are a bunch of studies with small samples and inconclusive or incomplete results that happened to have included chimeras."

"You mean animals with a mosaic of genetically distinct cells from more than one set of parents. And?"

"And, I can't yet tease out all the details, but the presence of certain oncogenes, genes that would normally lead to or increase the likelihood of cancer, have a modulated effect on normal cell aging and longevity when they are part of a genetic mosaic in a chimeric organism."

"You're saying a chimera, like a rat that has cells with the genetics of different sets of parents, one with mosaicism, could live longer?"

"Maybe. The problem is that most of the experiments were investigating cancer and cancer treatment, so the animals were 'sacrificed' at a certain stage in the experiment. Somebody would have to do a whole new series of studies solely with chimeras in which they were allowed to reach natural death."

"And?"

"And this is an extremely promising line of research toward a possible mechanism for life extension."

"If you're a chimeric lab rat."

"It's not limited to rats, remember. Chimerism turns out to be fairly widespread in nature and not all that rare in humans. Nonidentical twins have been found to have swapped genetic material in the womb. And most women who have had children end up incorporating cells from their offspring in their bloodstream."

"Are you suggesting that if I could have children, I could live longer?"

"Well, you can reduce your chances of breast cancer. That's been shown." He stopped and looked at his hands before reaching out to her. "Sorry. I didn't mean anything by it, just...well, it's true.

"Anyway, the point is, there has been a lot of good research that adds pieces to the puzzle, some of the best within Biontolics, and all the Biontolics work has been censored. They put a lid on good science and smothered my work." He told her about the direct orders not to pursue his previous line of inquiry.

"The kicker is that Dougherty himself was lead author on a paper that anticipated my findings on a small scale by maybe thirty or forty years; there's no date on the paper, so I'm guessing about when it was written. Something is not right with this picture." He stood up suddenly. "I think I'll go log into my account at the Lab and try another tack. The company contracts with an off-site firm out in Colorado to keep ultimate backups in some underground bunker or something. I think I may be able to find a way to retrieve my stuff from there.

"Here, you can finish the pizza," he said, crumpling his paper napkin into a small ball and snapping it across the room into the sink.

"Don't do that. Put it in the trash, dummy." She walked over and retrieved a soggy wad from the sink and gingerly transferred it to the upright bin in the corner.

"I could have done that," he said.

"Yeah, I know. But you're you, and I'm me, and this is how I do it. Go analyze your whatever, my messy mathematician."

"Biologist," he corrected, as he blew her a kiss. "Mathematical biologist. Soon to be famous mathematical biologist. Either that or unemployed."

= =

Millie, deciding to check in with him before she headed for bed, found him still working in the den. He was uncharacteristically agitated, shaking his head and muttering under his breath as he alternated between short bursts of typing and almost savage clicking on his mouse. "Well it seems to be gone from the data archiving company, too. It took a while, but I finally managed to tunnel in through the lab and back out again using my new credentials to get read-access privileges in Colorado, but my paper, the raw data, even the .PDF that I pulled off the internet, are all gone. I don't know how they did it." He pulled up a browser. "One more shot; I'll try going back to the Web. Let's see, what the fudge was that URL where I found the old paper in the first place? It was something like trollhouse dot some university dot some country. The Netherlands, I think." He tried several guesses before switching to Google, where he entered the first five words of the title in quotes. Google dutifully reported back in 0.13 seconds: No results found.

"It's gone," he said.

"Are you sure about that? Things don't just disappear from the Web. Quite the opposite. They hang around forever, even when you want them to go away—like those pictures of us skinny dipping at the lake that your dear little cousin posted. I am sure they are out there, someplace, still, if not on the Web itself, then on some pervert's hard drive."

"Shush, Millie. I have to think. Where could there be another copy of any of my stuff."

"I thought companies had to keep copies of everything."

"Millie, I told you," he said, with growing impatience. "I already checked the share server. My backup files have also been purged. This is so crude. Somebody must be real scared—or real stupid."

"What about your laptop? Don't you sometimes work on this at the kitchen table? Could there still be copies there?"

He was already heading for the closet to retrieve his laptop bag.

= =

Millie awoke at 5:30, as usual, to find no one in the bed beside her. Rosen was at the kitchen table where she had left him at 10:30 the night before. "Don't tell me you pulled an all-nighter."

"I did. Call me in sick again. I'm going to see Steven," he said, pushing back his chair and closing the laptop.

She knew immediately who Rosen meant. Steven King was one of his few heroes, a man of broad interests and deep intellect who had taken the young Rosen David under his wing and coached and coaxed and cajoled him through his disillusionment and his dissertation. Professor Steven King held an endowed chair at Tufts and had appointments in three departments. He would start every semester by writing his name on the whiteboard, underlining the V in his first name and announcing, "I'm the Steven with a V; I write journal articles. The Stephen with a PH writes novels. One of us is rich, the other is not. I'll leave it to you to hypothesize which is which." It was lame, college-lecture humor, but it always got a laugh, and none of his students ever misspelled his name.

8

Rosen finally located his former advisor in Halligan Hall, a brick building removed from the heart of the Tufts campus. It housed an odd mix of disciplines and activities, and the office Rosen had been directed to was sandwiched between a supply room for the athletics department and the locked double doors of the Intelligent Robotics Project, its title spelled out in Legos cemented to the door. A standard-issue plastic plaque below declared it to be for Authorized Personnel Only.

Rosen walked past the closed robotics lab and peeked through the open door of a tiny, windowless office. It was not what one might expect, not the typical academic abode lined with bookshelves, littered with boxes, and festooned with piles of papers. The walls displayed a few framed posters, the largest for a Marc Chagall exhibition from a generation earlier, and the modest desk held a single neat stack of student essays alongside a keyboard and a small computer display screen. Professor King believed that books and bound journals were of little value in his profession, particularly in an era when nearly everything of consequence could be accessed online.

"You're a hard one to find these days," Rosen announced, as he tapped on the doorjamb and entered. "Is this how the University now treats the Shmuel Pfeffer Distinguished Professor of Mathematics and Medicine?"

Steven King looked up from the stack of papers he had been

grading and smiled broadly. "I'm Emeritus now, just plain old Professor King. They put me wherever they can find an empty closet. But look at you, Rosen David! What an unexpected pleasure." He stood and took Rosen's hand, pumping it enthusiastically. "Please make yourself comfortable in my little den."

"You will never be plain old anything to me, you know," Rosen said. He remembered Dr. Steven King as a giant, a man who went nowhere on campus without at least one attentive student in attendance, a man whose most casual comment could trigger a flurry of note-taking among his graduate students. It was hard to reconcile the memories with the man in front of him, a smallish gentleman in a gray Van Dyke beard who now squeezed himself back into a squeaky secretary's chair behind a battered metal desk in an office the size of a large janitorial closet. "What's up? What are you doing," Rosen said, gesturing, then adding, "here?"

"I'm retired. I still teach pro bono, one course a term, usually alternating Experimental and Quasi-Experimental Design with Non-Parametric Statistics, which let's me meet the new students and mess with their minds before the younger faculty completely corrupts them. Besides, nobody wants to teach that stuff anymore, certainly not to students who come from a half-dozen different departments and might have to be told how to pronounce 'chi-square.' I'm yesterday. 'Let the old guys teach the old stuff.' That's what they say when I am not at the meetings, which is almost always, because I never liked meetings or departmental politics, and now I am simply too old to waste time on that crap."

"You don't seem old to me. I didn't even think you had reached retirement age."

"I took early retirement a few years ago when the University was desperately trying to cut expenses while clearing out the deadwood to make room for new growth. The payoff they offered was modest compared to the parachute my older brother got when he left Burroughs-Welcome, but Miriam and I are comfortable. Both kids are grown, off on their own, happily married—or at least married—

so it doesn't take a lot for us. Did you know that we're going to be grandparents? Elspeth is pregnant. You remember Elspeth? She had a crush on you, you know, when she was in middle school. She married a WASP, a musician, and moved to San Francisco. Somehow Keith manages to make a living in this so-called indie music scene—even has his own label and a studio in their attic. It's amazing what these kids can do these days with a Mac, a few mikes, and some software.

"Speaking of kids, what about you?"

"No, not in the cards. But back to your retirement," he said, quickly changing the subject. "That blows my mind. I had no idea. I mean, you're still publishing and all. I read your last paper in the *Journal of Neuroscience and Cognitive Studies*. It was good."

"That was all Jacobson's work. I just helped fix his statistical analysis."

"You're too modest. That was a clever technique you applied to test for the significance of volumetric differences in functional MRI scans."

"Clever, maybe, but hardly groundbreaking. Jacobson and his neuroscience whiz kids are the ones exploring new territory. I'm just tilling old soil, replanting the same old crops in Latin Square plots."

Rosen smiled at the play on words that only someone who knew experimental design would get. It was a coded message in the private language between them, an acknowledgement of their connectedness. Like Rosen, Steven King was not given to much in the way of open emotional expression, but both of them knew that their affection was mutual and deep.

"Frankly," Steven continued, "I think the neuroscience people are straying too far afield, getting too full of themselves. Take Jacobson's work. It's interesting, incremental science, but I am not sure it proves anything, certainly not that consciousness is an epiphenomenon, a side-effect of complexity, as he claims. If consciousness is merely an illusion, then the question I ask is who or what is experiencing the illusion? Jacobson and his cronies are convinced that's all it is. They speak as if the debate were concluded. Awareness is illusory, they write in uppercase, which may well be true for them, I grant. Frankly, I think the whole lot of them exhibit certain deficits in self-awareness, particularly at conferences when they are dealing with those whom they regards as lesser beings, meaning anyone who does not share their views.

"As for me, my own consciousness is self-evidently no illusion, therefore, with a single counterexample their thesis is disproven." He snorted disdainfully, then leaned forward and dropped his voice into a conspiratorial tone. "Besides, that magnetic imaging stuff is over-rated, a research fad that became popular in large part because of the pretty pictures you get to publish—that and the fact that the equipment is massive and expensive and makes for good demonstrations when taking prospective benefactors on laboratory tours. This," he tapped the side of his head, "and this," he added, patting the top of his computer monitor, "are less dramatic, but that's where the real stuff happens.

"So, tell me what brings you here, Rosen? You didn't drive into Medford and search all over campus just to pass the time listening to me pontificate. You've certainly heard all my sermons before."

Rosen laid two papers on the desk and turned them to face the right way. Steven bent toward them and tilted his head back to study them through his reading glasses.

"So, I see you are forcing me to wear both my hats in order to understand these. Oh, my poor head. It's been such a long time." He was referring to his double degrees in medicine and mathematics. Like Rosen, who had gradually moved from straight biology to applied math, Steven had found out during his early work as an internist on the cancer ward at Dana-Farber that he was more interested in the experiments in treatment than in treating the patients. He had completed a Ph.D. in statistics in record time and was immediately snapped up by Tufts to fill a joint appointment created especially for him in the Medical School and in the

Department of Mathematics. His Biology appointment was a later addition.

Steven swiveled in his noisy chair as he read the abstract of Rosen's meta-analysis, then flipped through the pages of the blotchy older paper. "So, what do you make of it?" he asked.

"That's what I'm asking you. But let me fill you in on the background, first." He outlined what had been happening at Biontolics up to and including the point where his files had disappeared. "Do you think I'm paranoid? Paranoia is so,...so illogical."

"I was an oncologist not a psychiatrist, Rosen—cancer not gray matter—and I never put much stock in nosology, anyway. Just because you can classify and label something doesn't mean you understand it. Modern psychiatry, when it isn't all about drugging patients into submission, is preoccupied with putting them in a box with a name on it. Back in the 1960s, the radicals used to say that what the establishment called paranoia was merely a heightened sense of reality. Of course, the APA, the Ancient Psychological Association, as I like to call it, keeps changing the definitions of the boxes and renaming them with each release of their *Diagnostic and Statistical Manual*. But I would say that the reality is pretty much the same as it always was. Just because something sounds paranoid doesn't mean it might not be real. End of today's second sermon.

"So, Rosen, stop beating around the bush trying to get me to say something. What's your best guess? Do you think there is some kind of cabal controlling research in this area?"

Rosen took a long time to answer. "Look, Biontolics has research programs in many different areas—in geriatrics, pharmaceuticals and biochemistry, genetics, nutrition, oncology, cell biology, neuroscience—but there is a single subtext running through all of them. Everything we do is tied somehow into the issue of longevity. And it is becoming clear to me that the best of what we have been creating is being buried. I want you to help me make sense of it, to get to the bottom of it, to figure out why."

"I can think of several possible reasons, most of them having to do with money. A real life-extension technology, one that actually worked, that could be packaged and sold, would be worth billions. No, I take that back. As it is, the long-life industry with their pills and supplements, their diets and treatments, must be worth many billions—and that's all big bucks for little or no difference. The real deal would be worth trillions and would change the game."

Rosen shook his head. "Doesn't quite ring true, because they are making it harder for even their own people to see the whole picture. It's like they want us to keep working on little pieces but not know how the pieces fit together."

"That might be exactly what they want, like the Soviets and the Americans during the Cold War, each with their secret chemical and biological weapons research and no one but a handful at the top knowing what was really going on. Maybe what your people are working on now is just improving techniques, streamlining a process that is already worked out but perhaps is still too crude, complicated, and expensive. Have you considered that, Rosen?"

"You mean, they may have already succeeded but don't want the world to know, at least not until they are ready."

Steven looked over the top of his reading glasses and stared into Rosen's eyes. "It just might be possible, you know. I would have to study these papers more carefully, of course. Still, from my own, somewhat casual, reading in the area of life extension, I'd say we are a very long way from figuring this one out. There are a lot of very bright people going full tilt at the problem, and a lot of big money is being poured into it, not only by the usual bunch of foundations but also by super-rich individuals who want to use money to cheat death. So far, though, all we have is hints and hopes and hype. Maybe in a few decades we will be able to add another ten years or so to the average lifespan, but I simply do not see the Ray Kurzweils or the Craig Venters of the world getting their wishes granted and living forever. Like everyone else, whether they admit it or not, the life-extension lobbyists are afraid of death."

Rosen gave him a look that said he wasn't buying it.

Steven continued. "Hey, some people make up stories of an eternity in heaven, others fantasize about reincarnation, and still others invent scenarios in which science rescues them from the abyss of a personal end. But it all comes down to one thing: death, coming to terms with it. Do these people think it will be any easier to face the void after living another twenty or even two hundred years? The end is the end."

He shuffled the two articles on his desk before continuing. "I'm no expert in this area, but I just do not see us as being on the verge of a singularity where medical science will suddenly enable people to live for hundreds of years—much less indefinitely.

"It is wishful thinking by a few rich men with enormous egos who would like to believe that their wealth will enable them to survive, even thrive, until this singularity is upon us. It is the wishful thinking of people of lesser means but equally exaggerated senses of self-importance who hope that, if only they are disciplined enough, if only they work out every day and eat enough buckwheat bran or drink enough carrot and banana-peel smoothies, they, too, will be able to reach the ripe age of 150, to live until the singularity when they can join the immortals. It is the fantasy of other poor deluded souls who grasp onto isolated and widely misinterpreted experiments and then choose to go through life perpetually hungry, shivering in the July sun, because they think by eating little they will live long. Modern science and pseudoscience aside, that is symbolically and physically straight out of the thirteenth century: the denial of the flesh in pursuit of immortality.

"But there I go, mounting my soapbox again, while you sit there, polite but pained. Let's see." He looked down again at the papers on his desk. "This one," he said, tapping the mottled front of the older paper. "I know some of these authors. Well, everyone knew Llewellyn Cass, or Andras, as he preferred to be called. He was a force on the Boston cancer scene for decades before he disappeared on some kind of expedition in South America. Soft-spoken but with boundless energy. He gave a series of lectures here at Tufts that were later published as a monograph, something about slow-growing cancers, varieties like certain prostate cancers that are best left untreated because they never become life-threatening during the patient's life."

Steven became suddenly thoughtful, staring at the Chagall poster on his wall for several seconds. "I was going to say that Cass must have been in his mid-to-late seventies when he went on that ill-fated eco-tour to Patagonia, although he looked and acted more like a man in his fifties. Funny, that, wouldn't you say?"

There was a long silence between them. Rosen started to say something, but Steven interrupted him. "I remember this Janella Kai, too. A biochemistry major, I think, very bright, wanted to start her own drug company and retire rich, if I remember right. Petite, athletic, very pretty, too. Mixed race, from Mexico or something. More than one of the Assistant Professors in her department would have loved to become her mentor in more than one manner of speaking. She came to me a few times for consultations on experimental design." He noticed Rosen smiling at him. "Just consultation," he added. "I don't know what happened to her. Probably married a CEO in big pharma, with a ranch in California and two beautiful teenagers away at private school in Europe."

"Isn't that a bit sexist?"

"Sexist? Me? Talk to Miriam about that. I'm a devout realist. Had I been born female—and observant Jewish men thank God every day that they were not—with Janella Kai's brains and good looks, I could imagine the appeal of such a career path. But, like I said, I don't know what path she took."

"Neither do I, which is interesting, because it is so easy to track down people on the Internet. Everyone leaves footprints on the Web, but Janella Kai is the only one of those four authors who doesn't exist, except in Tufts alumni records and on Reunion.com, where her high-school classmates at Cambridge Rindge and Latin have her on a 'does anyone know what happened to' list. I even checked marriage records through two genealogy sites but couldn't find anything. Who knows.

"The interesting thing is that two of the authors are dead, according to the records, Kai is missing-in-action, and only the lead author is still around. I've met him and I've done the math. He's in his nineties, if it's the same Atchison Dougherty, but he doesn't look a day over fifty. Interesting, I'd say."

"Yes, interesting. Maybe it's his son. Or maybe the father has joined the gods. Maybe this line of research does lead—or already has led—to life eternal. That doesn't make it a good idea."

Rosen cocked his head in question as Steven continued. "Cells die to enable the individual to live on. Individuals die to enable the human enterprise to survive and thrive. Death is a curse to the person but a gift to the race. I once read a science fiction story called 'Death's Children.' I remember the title and the story vividly, although I've forgotten the author. It's about a race that had solved the mystery of life and death, that had found a way to live for many hundreds of years, but they threw it away, took a pass on immortality—or its approximation."

"Why?"

"It's in the title of the story. At one point, one of these aliens is speaking with a visitor from earth and draws attention to the sound of children laughing in a courtyard below. Such music, he tells his guest, the sound of youthful joy, of renewal and unending rediscovery, that is Death's greatest gift. If everyone lives forever, that's all gone. Children are the gift made possible by Death."

"Not everyone has children," Rosen said, with an edge in his voice.

"Not their own, perhaps, but ours, humanity's. Remember when you were my teaching assistant? Remember the incoming freshmen, their naïve energy, their unbounded belief in themselves and what they could and would do in life?"

Rosen shook his head vigorously. "I remember them sleeping through lectures and saying 'Yeah, duh!' and 'So?' I remember lame stories to justify missing assignments."

"That, too. But you and I were no different in our own times and ways. We could sleep through classes and skip assignments because we already knew it, already knew everything, knew that what we were being taught was bullshit that we could ignore and transcend. The future *does* belong to the young, and with good reason. They do things the old would never do, because we already know it couldn't be done. They don't know what's impossible, so they just go ahead and do it. They are ignorant, so they see with fresh eyes. One can only see something for the first time once.

"Caution and conservatism are the coin of advancing years, and the cost is creativity. That applies to me as much as to anyone else." Rosen started to protest but Steven held up his index finger and continued. "Do you think it's some kind of a fluke that the important developments in our field, in mathematics, have always been the work of younger people? It's been said that a mathematician who hasn't done something important by the age of 35 will never contribute anything of significance."

"Now you've gone from sexism to ageism," Rosen chided.

"Realism, my son, simple realism. I'm not saying geezers are worthless. As long as you can move and speak, you can contribute. Why do you think I'm here? I can still teach introductory classes in statistics. I've done it enough times that I could probably do it in my sleep, and some of my students would probably say that I sometimes do. I don't believe in retirement in any form, Rosen. I don't care how much you worked or how much wealth you've amassed, my view is that as long as you are consuming you ought to be producing—at least doing something useful.

"My Miriam once told me about her family stopping at a farm stand selling nuts. Her parents bought a small bag of walnut meats from a girl of twelve or so, who proudly told them that her grandfather had cracked all the nuts on the table. She nodded toward an old man with gnarled hands and a weather-ravaged face hunched over one of those big old long-handled affairs, cracking walnuts one at a time, very, very slowly. Miriam said he looked like he was a hundred to her girlish eyes, but there he was, doing his part to keep the family orchards going. Maybe he read to his young grandchildren in the evening when he was too tired to crack any more nuts. Maybe he entertained the family with stories from the old days, polished and embellished by years of retelling and by flagging memory. Who knows? But that man was not off playing golf or mahjongg in some retirement community or taking up bed space in a nursing home while waiting to die."

"That's a bit harsh. Not everyone gets the gift of vigorous golden years. Don't we eventually earn the right to take some time to ourselves, to do what we please, or at least not to have to get up every morning and drag ourselves off to some stupid job?"

Steven jabbed his finger at Rosen. "I'd say no. Everyone contributes, everyone adds something, whatever they can. It's what Miriam and I call TANSTAAFL economics: There Aint No Such Thing As A Free Lunch. Everybody pays part of the bill, each according to their means."

"I never would have taken you for such a communist at heart, Steven."

"Communist, hell, that's chapter and verse from an icon of right-wing libertarianism, Robert Anson Heinlein."

"I always thought he was an icon of the flakey free-love left."

"That, too. And he started out as an active socialist. He was an icon of more things than the ubiquitous Apple logo. And, like the others of his strange species, *homo sapiens*, he was a messy mix, an inconsistent collage."

"Wait, didn't Heinlein continue to write well into his seventies?" Rosen said, smiling in smug triumph.

"Yeah, but the later novels just kept getting longer and more discursive," Steven countered. "The best of his oeuvre were all in his earlier works."

"Look, Steven, we have gotten off into literary criticism, which I remind you that I dropped in college even though you insisted it would be good for me, that it would help to sharpen my critical thinking skills. Plus, frankly, I never did care for science fiction."

"You darned well better care for it, since you may soon be living it, if the crew at Biontolics are on the trajectory we are extrapolating. And you need to figure out what you're going to do next."

Rosen looked lost in thought, his eyes focused on some point a meter beyond the top of Steven's head. "I'm going to do what any good academic would do, Steven," he said at last, pushing his chair back and standing to leave. "Thanks for the inspiration."

Steven broke into a broad smile. "You're welcome, Rosen," he said, nodding slowly and repeatedly. "Anytime. And thanks for the papers. Keep me posted."

Steven listened to the sound of Rosen's retreating footsteps, then spent the next several minutes in thoughtful concentration before waking up his computer and launching a browser. He was suddenly excited at the thought of beginning a fresh line of investigation. He whistled to himself, a soft and breathy tune, as he started digging into the University's archives.

9

Fuck!"

Ferguson jumped. "What is it, Douglas?" he asked, closing his laptop with a soft click. The only other sounds in the third-floor conference room were the soft buzz of the overhead fluorescents and the almost inaudible thud of Atchison Douglas Dougherty knocking his fists together as he made faces at the screen of his computer. It was past midnight, and they were alone in the building, except for the security guard down in the lobby who had recognized them but still insisted on seeing their ID cards and passports before letting them in. Revic AG was a tiny Swiss pharmaceutical firm with offices on the picturesque but business-like Talstrasse in Zurich and its plant in its own building in an industrial park nearer the airport. Revic carried out small production runs on rare and hard-to-manufacture drugs for selected customers. Only one of their customers mattered: the owners. The owners used the company for many purposes, including quiet meetings on important matters.

After filling in Ferguson about events at Biontolics and the meeting with Rosen David, Dougherty had logged into Revic's wi-fi to collect his email only to find that an RSS feed had delivered bad news unbidden to his desktop.

"Our boy has published," announced Dougherty. "He didn't even wait to go through an accelerated peer review on *PLoS Genetics* or

Medicine. He obviously just wanted to get it out there, post it as fast as possible. It's an e-print in, of all places, arXiv Quantitative Biology." ArXiv, pronounced 'archive' as if the X were the Greek letter chi, was a pre-publication repository maintained by Cornell University. Dougherty fussed with the touchpad on his laptop and clicked on something. "It's a .PDF file, and judging by the size, the little bastard has expanded his paper. I'm downloading a copy now."

"Do you really think anybody is going to find it there? I mean, arXiv is basically just a database, a listing."

"All it takes is one, one reader who recognizes what they are reading. This is not like all the other little near-miss studies we've let go by in the past. This is a meta-analysis. Rosen references our paper. Our paper, Andras. Besides this is an important database. The arXiv q-bio listing is closely watched by anyone who has an interest in computational biology, genomics, cell behavior. Needless to say, we follow it closely ourselves. It's where precedent is set and early claims are made. The people who read in these areas are not ignoramuses. Our boy's piece won't be hard to spot among the 25 or so papers a month that are usually posted. We may already be too late. If it popped up on my feed, you can bet that others are probably having a look-see right now."

"Then let's take it down," Ferguson said, looking at his watch. "The IP Group in North Carolina might still be on the job if we act quickly. Or we can get our crew in San Diego to get on it."

"All either group can do would be to lodge an objection requesting that the paper be taken off the site. The thing is administered at Cornell where it is also the end of the day. Best case scenario, with extraordinary luck, is that it will take hours; more likely, it could be late tomorrow before any action is taken. We need to act fast."

Ferguson smiled triumphantly. "Ah, but the original poster can withdraw the paper at any time."

"You think Rosen can be persuaded to kill his own work? He's already gone renegade on us."

"No, of course not. I was thinking of Holzinger. You told me he has access to Rosen's computer and files; how long can it take him to hack into Cornell under Rosen's login credentials?"

Dougherty picked up the cell phone from beside his computer and placed a call. It took a dozen rings before he got an answer. "Holzinger. Get on your computer and Skype me. Now!" He thumbed the phone off and fiddled with his computer again. Skype was their preferred mode of communication for sensitive subjects and to keep the phone records relatively sparse and clean. With its built-in encryption and fragmentation of conversations into small packets that caromed around the Internet along varied paths before rejoining at the other end, it was the closest thing to truly secure communication available to the ordinary citizen. The organization had looked into getting its own encrypting telephones, but when they learned that even the clandestine services of a number of countries used Skype, they stuck with the cheaper alternative.

A German-accented voice, gravelly from sleep and distorted by the tiny speaker on the laptop, announced, "Okay, I'm here. *Was ist los?*"

"What is the matter? What is the matter is that I need you to do something immediately. I want you to retrieve Rosen David's login credentials for arXiv Quantitative Biology hosted at Cornell, then use them to withdraw his recently posted paper. After you've confirmed the paper is gone, change the password to keep him off the system for a while. Can you do that?"

"It's as easy as cooking bratwurst," he said. "I'm already working on it." The connection dropped.

"How long do you think it will take him?"

"I don't know. Ten minutes maybe?" he glanced at the time on his cell phone. "We'll see. Holzinger is the best." Gus Holzinger had been one of Germany's leading security consultants before Biontolics had hired him. He was now part of an inner circle that knew at least some of the scope of interlocking companies and foundations and captive professional societies that made up the organization. He was not a true insider, so he did not know exactly what they did, but he was aware that the annual reports and the scattered websites did not tell the story. He was paid very well not to ask questions. Ferguson, who had met with him in Germany on several occasions, sometimes wondered just what Holzinger thought the organization did. The man was the quintessential security type, someone who did whatever he was asked and never talked of anything but the technical elements of his work, even after several rounds of good German beer.

It was an hour before Dougherty's laptop trilled with an in-coming Skype call.

"He's not using our system, and he's not using his home computer," Holzinger began without introduction. "So, I was not able to recover his user name and password from our logs."

"What are we going to do, then."

"It's already done. Go look at the site."

Dougherty and Ferguson both switched to browsers and accessed the page at the same time. The paper was gone.

"How did you do it?"

"I hacked into Cornell and disappeared the paper plus a couple of others to throw people off the scent. Then I changed the email address on the system so that we get any notices from the arXiv that would otherwise go to Dr. David's Gmail account. It will likely be a while before he even learns that the paper is gone."

"Excellent work."

"That's what you pay me for. But the fix is only a temporary. Once he finds out, he can always post someplace else. You are going to have to deal directly with this Dr. David." He disconnected without saying more.

Dougherty picked up his phone, thumbed it off, and carefully set it down beside his computer, squaring it up perfectly with the laptop. Ferguson had seen this before in Dougherty, whose compulsive rigidity grew with increasing agitation. Dougherty realigned his phone once more. "Holzinger is right. It's not enough to kill the paper," he said quietly. "We have to take care of Rosen, too. I just don't see him as the sort who will keep quiet."

Ferguson was reluctant to follow the implications of Dougherty's announcement, but he knew better than to argue, particularly when Dougherty dug in his heels. Still, he did not want an impulsive move to jeopardize what they had managed so well for so many years. "Douglas, this guy is not some unknown little research assistant, like Janella was." Dougherty bristled at the mention of Janella but said nothing. Ferguson continued, "This one has an established career, a reputation, his own bio in the Wikipedia. It is going to be tricky."

"That's why we are going to have to go outside the organization. Maybe we should have given more consideration at the outset to using mafia money. At least that way we might now have a trail we could follow to some talent. Aside from Mbutsu, maybe we have depended too much on altar boys."

"I would hardly call Xander Quarry an altar boy."

"True, but different sins than what I had in mind. Actually, that might be the germ of an idea. I think you should pay a call on Xander and Bernice. They might have some ideas of their own or some useful names from their days of wheeling and dealing in Las Vegas real estate. After all, they also have a stake in the outcome of our current crisis."

"Why me?"

"Because you have better excuses ready at hand. You're the doctor—an early checkup, perhaps? You can pump them for information without tipping the entire hand. If I showed up at Quarry Ranch, their radar would be sounding alarms like it was a raid from the DEA. They've only ever met me once, whereas you're a regular at their little retreat."

"Retreat, maybe, little, no." Ferguson sighed forcefully. "Okay, I'll do it. California, here I come! You know, you think I live in London, like you do, but that shows how much you know about your oldest friend—and I do mean oldest. I do not live in London, I live in planes: Boeing 787s, Airbus 340s and 380s, and the occasional Gulfstream G650. That's my residential address: goddamned airplanes."

"First class, though, Andras. You always go first class."

"True. But you know, you shouldn't call me Andras. Makes for habits that might lead to a slip up in public sometime. Llewellyn Andras Cass has been dead for decades. You know, it's funny, but I'm not even sure I remember him anymore."

Dougherty gave him a concerned look. Ferguson reacted with a reassuring shake of his head. "No, don't fret. I retested just last month and the cognitive, new trace, and recall scores are all fine. I'm not starting to go senile on you. I just find that Dr. Cass seems so distant, as if he were somebody else instead of me. It's hard to explain. You didn't have to go through that; I did."

"Sooner or later I will, too. And you will do it again, when it becomes necessary. It's a small price, wouldn't you say?"

10

It had been years since Steven King had last made the trek into downtown Boston to attend one of the brown-bag lunch-time seminars on the Med School campus. He had little interest in the topic of the day, a presentation on a new class of immuno-suppressant drugs for organ transplant patients, but he was confident that he would intercept Dr. Edwards there. The ride on the T and the short walk from Charles Station had taken longer than he expected, so he arrived just as the session was letting out. His old friend's bald head was easily spotted bobbing above a knot of shorter colleagues exiting the auditorium. "Marcus, wait up," he called out, as he hurried down the hall. He caught up just as Edwards was entering an elevator.

"Steven King! It has been a while. How are you doing?"

"As well as can be expected at my age. And you?"

"Bored. But what can you expect after yet another big pharma pitch disguised as continuing ed. What brings you downtown? I thought you retired."

"You know how it is, you can't stop an old professor from lecturing—not even at a cocktail party. So, I still teach a couple of courses and consult for some of the young turks who are too busy to learn how to analyze their own bloody brilliant, ever-so-important experiments. I—"

Marcus interrupted him. "This is my floor," he said, stepping out of the elevator and blocking the door open with his arm while Steven followed him out. "My office is just down the hall."

"Are you still active in immunology?" Steven asked, hurrying to keep up with the taller man's long strides.

"I suppose you could call it active," Marcus said. "I have three doctoral students doing their own thing. It's not like the old days where you could shape a long-term agenda. These kids have minds of their own, and it's really hard to steer them." He unlocked the door to his office and ushered Steven in.

"You know who still drives research the old-fashioned way?" he said, gesturing toward the only extra chair in the small office. "The genetics people just up the river, that's who. They have things under control with old Gabriel Costa still at the helm, hanging on forever and dominating his department as if he had invented biology. The man is pushing 80, and they can't seem to be able to get rid of him. He's the Energizer Bunny of biology. Brings in grants, honchos conferences, serves on the editorial board of more journals than you can count. He is the ultimate gatekeeper. No one enters the kingdom—or the phylum—save by him. Stubborn as ever and convinced that the new paradigm, epigenetics, is garbage. Nothing will persuade him. He calls it the return of the rancid residue of Lamarckism—his exact words. He says it's the last gasp of long discredited Soviet science invading America. The younger faculty are just waiting for the day when they can dance on his grave." He paused and pulled a battered paperback book from the shelf beside his desk. "You've read Kuhn, haven't you? *The Structure of Scientific Revolution*?" he said, sliding the book across the desk.

"Of course."

"I mean actually read it through. Everybody but everybody cites it, and it's probably almost as common as *Gray's Anatomy* in offices around campus, but I'll lay odds that not one in ten of our colleagues has actually read it, and fewer still remember what Kuhn really had to say about scientific paradigms."

"I think I know where you are going with this, Marcus."

"Maybe. My point, the point Thomas Kuhn made and that so many conveniently forget, is that the old paradigm is ultimately overthrown and replaced by a new one not because of better experiments or the accumulation of superior evidence or the perfection of persuasive arguments but because the adherents and advocates of the old paradigm eventually die.

"That's us, too," he said, tapping the book for emphasis. "So, what do you want to talk about, Steven. You obviously came here to ask me for something. I hope it's not another one of those damned committees for the preservation of whoop-dee-something. The only thing I give a flying fig about preserving anymore is the equity in my retirement accounts." He knuckled the desk top. "Knock on wood that I last long enough to see retirement. You remember Jamison, Hanny Jamison, the molecular biologist? Retired last year and croaked on the plane on the way to his retirement digs in Miami. Sixty-six. Young guy.

"So, are you looking to sign me up for something?"

"No, I have a puzzle for you, Marcus. I'm interested in the immunology of chimeric organisms, and I wanted to get the opinion of a real expert."

"It doesn't take an expert. In a chimera, two or more distinct tissue types are combined, but, being present from before birth, often from the blastula, their surface proteins are recognized by the organism as self rather than other. There's no rejection, no problematic response from the immune system. The immunology is really straightforward."

"What about chimerism in adults, I mean where the genetic mosaic was not present from birth but originated later."

"Sure. Microchimerism. It happens all the time in multiparous women. They incorporate small populations of fetal cells during each pregnancy. We had long known that the fetus can get DNA directly from the mother through the placenta, but then in the late 1970s it was discovered that it can work the other way. A woman was found to have cells with Y chromosomes in her bloodstream.

They obviously had to have come from her son *in utero*.

"You know, Steven, maternal microchimerism is an interesting case for a couple of reasons. One could say that the relationship between mother and fetus is immunologically privileged, otherwise you'd see graft-versus-host and host-versus-graft disease all the time in pregnancy; the mother's immune system would reject the fetus or the fetus would kill the mother. Obviously, evolution selected against those outcomes. The other interesting thing here is that the incorporated cells in maternal microchimerism are very often stem cells. They even have been found to take on a tissue repair role in mothers with certain maladies: thyroid or liver damage, things of that sort. The cells and the effects can linger for decades. The incorporated fetal cells can reproduce indefinitely and remain pluripotent if not totipotent; they can become almost any tissue.

"Does that answer your question?"

"Yeah. That's more or less what I figured. But one more question. If you wanted to generate chimerism in an adult organism, how might you go about it?"

"Not sure why I would want to in the first place, but let's say I did, for some reason, such as to create some really exotic version of a lab rat. Okay, embryonic stem cells would be one promising line, if it weren't that research in that arena is so tightly restricted by the residue of a religious-right agenda. Of course, all along, pregnant women have already been benefitting from natural fetal stem cell transplants. Ironic, wouldn't you say?"

He gave the paperback on his desk a spin. "Okay, back to your question," he said, picking up the book and gesturing with it. "Maybe you could find a way to engineer retroviruses that could be used as a vector to introduce new DNA. Or one might directly manipulate the nuclei of cells. It would be damned tedious and expensive, but might be worth a try. That's off the top of my head. I would imagine that if you wanted to badly enough and were backed by generous enough research grants, you could probably find a way to pull it off eventually. Why do you ask?"

"Acute curiosity, an intellectual puzzle, that's all."

"You know, the issue of chimerism takes on a whole new twist in light of the new paradigm in genetics. Epigenetics has really brought to the fore the influence of environment and the experience of the organism on gene expression. Not so long ago our colleagues in genetics were convinced that genes were genes, that genetically controlled traits were inherited and fixed. Now they are learning that the environment and experience of the individual can influence gene expression through methylation, maybe other mechanisms, and the effects can be passed on to succeeding generations. So, what and how you ate as a child can end up affecting whether your children and grandchildren are prone to obesity or vulnerable to diabetes. Old Gabriel Costa is right in his labels but wrong in his conclusions. I really do not understand why he is always trying to quash any interest in this area among his students."

Marcus was obviously on a roll and Steven just let him continue. "With a chimera, when you factor in epigenetics and gene expression, the whole picture becomes enormously more complicated. Cells from one genotype could influence gene expression in another. The history of one cell population could regulate the expression of some genes in cells from another genotype. Intriguing. I wonder if anyone has done any work on that."

"Probably," Steven said. "Look, I must go back to the more boring work of preparing my next statistics lecture. Cheers." He stood to leave.

"Well, I will say this, Steven. You've gotten me to thinking. There are some promising lines of research in this discussion. Thanks."

"Anytime. Give my regards to Phoebe and the boys," Steven said.

"Oh, Phoebe and I are history. We split years ago."

"Oh, I'm sorry."

"I'm not. I remarried. Janet is fifteen years my junior and really good for me. Keeps me young. Are you still married? I mean, to the same woman?"

"No," Steven said, smiling. "Miriam has never been the same woman. Not for more than a few months in a row. Keeps me young."

11

Ferguson gunned his rented yellow-and-black Mustang up the zigzags of the unpaved road leading to Quarry Ranch Retreat, a 47-acre estate perched in the hills roughly an hour-and-a-half's drive south from the San Francisco airport. It had become notorious for its free-wheeling, week-long parties in the 1970s but in recent years had managed to stay mostly out of the spotlight. None of the underwriters were without original sin, although compared to Edgar Mbutsu, Alexander and Bernice Quarry would seem almost angelic. They had made their money, first in insurance and then in Las Vegas real estate, with only intermittent suggestions of impropriety that never blossomed into full-flowered investigations. Ferguson knew that the improprieties were real but well buried. Bernice, always the cannier of the two, accounted for the bulk of the couple's assets, which was a constant irritant to Xander, who would have to turn to his wife whenever he needed real money for some of the more grandiose of his idiosyncratic improvements at the Ranch. The Quarrys had well-earned reputations as sybarites. Aside from their involvement with the organization in its earliest days, the Ranch and its self-indulgent, laidback lifestyle were their life.

Xander may have been envious of his wife's wealth or her gift for financial manipulation, both above and below the table, but he was not jealous of the younger men who lounged naked by the Olympic-sized pool and fetched drinks for her. He had no need to be jealous, having his own clutch of forest nymphs happy to consort with him at poolside or to cavort in the sun playing nude volleyball on a man-made beach while beside them, high in the hills and miles from the ocean, his custom-engineered wave machine generated artificial surf. Ten years earlier, a *Sacremento Bee* exposé had dubbed them the last of the swingers, painting Bernice as an anorexic, sex-crazed septuagenarian and Xander as a dirty old man whose wealth and reputation kept a rotating retinue of well-endowed young hopefuls eager to show him what they had learned in school.

Ferguson was only glad that the private parties with under-age participants seemed to have stopped—or at least gone so deeply underground that there had been no fresh scandals for years. The organization had worked long and hard on a quiet campaign to place sympathetic or indifferent officials in positions of authority throughout the county. The DEA was still a problem, but in recent years they seemed to have turned their drug-enforcement attention farther north to the medical-marijuana outlaws of the Bay area and to raids on cannabis plantations in the hinterlands. The sophisti-cated psychotropics and designer drugs that were *au courant* with the Quarrys and the rest of the retreat's residents and visitors were probably not yet even on any government list.

Ferguson pulled into the circular drive and left his car parked in front of the glass-paneled building that housed the Ranch's second Olympic-sized swimming pool, an indoor pool kept at body heat for the experiments in sensory deprivation that had first made the Ranch famous. With nothing left to learn about or from sensory deprivation, the pool was now just an extravagant curiosity that held the attention of newcomers only briefly before they discovered that mindlessly floating in tepid water was not as interesting an aquatic activity as screwing in a hot tub or doing laps in the sun-warmed outdoor pool.

Bernie Quarry waved to Ferguson from the 24-foot redwood hot tub that had once been cited in the *Guinness Book of World Records.*

"Chas, come on in and join us!" she called. Bernie, who had always had a thing for Ferguson, insisted on using the nickname that he preferred to reserve for a tiny circle of real friends. He had always cultivated her erotic interest without ever allowing it to blossom beyond flirtation. It was useful in sustaining the complex relationship between the Quarrys and the organization. They had been the first underwriters, and though there had been other bigger donors since, their initial investment had made the whole operation possible. They had been the angel investors, and Ferguson had always found that term more than a tad ironic.

Ferguson blew Bernie a kiss. "Thanks," he called out, "but I'll sit this one out. Later maybe?" He tried to keep a small residue of promise in his voice, but there would not be any 'later.' Meeting in the hot tub was about neither hygiene nor good clean fun; at Quarry Ranch it was tantamount to an invitation to group sex. Ferguson had tried that once—not at the Ranch but long before, in his college days—and found it not to his liking.

Xander Quarry, wearing only a Hawaiian shirt that hung like a tent over his ample form, came out of the Conference Center, the main spread of buildings facing onto the tennis courts, the pool, and the surf machine. Xander Quarry had silver hair that hung to his shoulders when it wasn't tied back in a pony tail as it was now. He was shaped like a wine barrel, and the joke was that it was obvious what he had consumed to acquire his figure. In truth, it was Bernie who was the lush. Xander was rarely far from a glass of expensive California white, sauvignon blanc preferred, that he would nurse until it was too warm to drink, but Bernie was the one who could start drinking heavily before noon and not let up until she passed out after midnight.

It was a lifestyle whose rhythm was not lost on the young sycophants who surrounded her. The more observant among them—particularly the ones who found her dyed hair, sun-leathered skin, and silicone breasts less than a turn-on—would aim their erotic attentions toward her at the end of the day, accompanying her to bed knowing full well that unconsciousness was not far off. In the morning, they would score points for still being in bed with her and would flatter her with tales of how wonderful she had been the night before. Then they would rush off to their own daytime dalliances in other of the many suites in the sprawling ranch.

Xander grinned as he emerged from the building. He had one hand holding his ubiquitous glass of wine and the other around the waist of a girl in a hot-pink bikini. She looked to be not a day over twelve, and Ferguson gritted his teeth as they approached. Xander removed his hand from her waist and extended it to Ferguson. "Welcome, Doc. Again. Seems like it was only a month or so since you were last here."

"Seems like it because it was. I have some extra tests I want to run."

The girl steadied herself on Xander's arm while she stood on one foot and extracted something from her flip-flop. Ferguson made sure that Xander was looking his way as he raised one eyebrow, an unspoken inquiry with a subtext of silent criticism. Xander laughed. "This is Nadia, my daughter. Her mother dumped her here with us for the summer."

"I didn't know you had a daughter."

"Neither did I. All these years I thought I was shooting blanks. Low sperm count and very low motility, so they say, right? Anyway, I have the DNA profiles that prove that Nadia is mine, so I guess it's all just probabilities, right? Fuck enough women enough times and sooner or later..."

Nadia screwed up her face and turned it toward Xander. "Dad!" she said between clenched teeth.

"She doesn't like me saying fuck."

"Dad!" she growled, drawing out the single vowel into two syllables.

"I think she is trying to civilize me, which my friends all tell me is about time, and which she just might succeed at. It's been days since I've been drunk, weeks since I've done any drugs, and I can't remember the last cluster-fu..."

Nadia gave him another fierce look.

"The last orgy, I was going to say. Anyway, her mother is not the most reliable and together person on the planet, so this is probably a righteous thing that she got dumped here. I think the Ranch is good for her."

Ferguson shot him a skeptical look. "I'm not sure this is exactly a child-friendly environment, Xander."

"Oh, there are those who would say it can be a mighty child-friendly place. No, no!" He ducked and feinted in mock defense. "Just kidding. Actually everybody knows that if they even think any thoughts about Nadia, I'll shoot off their..." He paused and glanced down at her. "Their *cojones*."

"I know what that means, Dad." She elbowed him in his blubbery stomach, and he doubled over in faked pain.

"See what I mean, Doc?" he said.

"I do see. I don't know about how good the Ranch is for her, but I do suspect that Nadia is going to be a positive influence on you."

"So, Doc, what really brings you here?" He noticed Ferguson's eyes shift to Nadia, who was once again standing like a stork while she worried at something between her toes. "Nadia, sweetie, why don't you go have a swim. Your tutor will be here this afternoon and then it's your sax lesson with Jeremy, so there won't be time later."

"I understand, Dad. You want to talk without me. I'll get lost." She did a high kick, sending her remaining flip-flop soaring into the air, and took off at a run for the pool.

"Cute," Ferguson said. "And savvy, too, I can see. She really is your daughter?"

"Yeah. Mind blowing, isn't it? Do you know how old I am? Yes, of course you do. This is so wild. I don't think I've found it so interesting to get up in the morning in a very long time. Years. Decades. Every day it's something new. Last month she was listening to an old Coltrane cut and announced that she wanted to do that. I found someone from town who could give her lessons, and she is really starting to sound like something. Amazing. The tenor sax is almost as big as she is. She is more fun to talk with than," he waved his hand, "than any of these fuckers—excuse my French—who hang out here to entertain Bernie or to be entertained."

"No French, no excuses," Ferguson teased. "You're the father of a preteen girl now, and you are going to have to watch your words." There was a girlish screech from the pool. Ferguson glanced over and grinned.

"What?" Xander asked.

"Just thinking, how odd. She's the only one in the pool wearing a suit."

"Yeah, well, that's new. When she first came here, she was just like everyone else at the Ranch. I mean, you know that these hills are caught in some kind of time warp, that it never stopped being the 1960s here. At the Ranch, we wear clothes when we eat, because hot soup in the lap can be a pain. The rest of the time, unless it's too cold, we are pretty casual about what's covered and what's not. And I have always argued that swimming suits are the stupidest invention in the history of civilization. But, well, Nadia, she's skinny but cute, and there was one of Bernie's Boys, as we refer to them, who found her little titties quite appealing. He's long gone, and she now wears clothes, including in the pool. We have this deal. I don't get falling down drunk, and she doesn't run around naked.

"Last week she asked me if I would make an exception for her when her boyfriend shows up. I freaked, I tell you. So I started asking about this boyfriend. They start so goddamned young these days. She's not going to be thirteen until December. But she was kidding. Her quote boyfriend lives in Switzerland. They met once, and he kissed her. It was a big deal to her. She told me about what she likes in men—boys—what she thinks makes for a good relationship. She thinks a lot about that, owing in part to the fine example her mother set with a long string of good-time lovers and fair-weather friends.

"But look, Doc, Nadia is off swimming, Bernie is about to climax noisily in the hot tub, and you still haven't started telling me what this is really about." Ferguson shrugged and looked around. "Okay, Doc, I get the message, a private conversation. Let me grab a pair of trousers and then let's go for a hike. There are too many people around today. Today? Hell, there are always too many people around here, period."

= =

An ambitious and lonely young man who had frequented the Ranch in its heyday had carved out a meandering trail through the brush that led to several notable vistas before looping back to the main facilities. As they walked along the narrow and neglected path, Ferguson gave Xander a condensed-book version of recent events. Xander was puffing from exertion by the time they rounded the corner of the pool house on the return leg. Ferguson had been on his case for years advising him to lose weight, but Xander Quarry was a giver of advice and not one to listen to others.

"Take my advice, Doc," he said. "Don't dick around on this one. We need to take care of this guy. I know some people who know some people, Doc, from Vegas. I think this thing can be fixed." He stopped in the middle of the driveway, frowning. "Where's Bernie?" He scanned the compound and noticed that her MG was no longer parked in its usual spot. "Hey, where's Bernie?" he yelled,.

One of her Boys, a dark-skinned Schwarzenegger-type wearing a torn tee-shirt declaring, 'I'm Tad and I'm Bad,' called out from the pool. "She and Annie drove into town to get something or other. I don't remember."

"She and Annie? Annie doesn't drive. Was Bernie..." he didn't have to finish the sentence.

"No more than usual," Tad answered. "I mean, how can you tell with Bernie. I don't know if I've ever seen her sober. With the way she takes it in you'd think she would have succumbed years ago to...what's that stuff called, sir something?"

"Cirrhosis," Ferguson said.

"Yeah, that stuff. Anyway, they left fifteen or twenty minutes ago—I don't know—in kind of a hurry. Got some kind of bee up her ass to get something at the farmer's market, I think she said. Annie, did. Bernie said she'd take her, so they hopped in that little car of hers and off they go, down the road." He made a flying gesture with his hand.

Ferguson and Xander looked at each other. Ferguson put his hand on Xander's sweaty shoulder. "She'll be fine. She could probably fly a triple-seven drunk. Inebriated has become the norm for her neurons. Her brain wouldn't know how to function without ethanol for fuel."

Xander did not look convinced, but he spread his hands in a gesture of helplessness and said, "Sure, Doc."

They were headed inside for some ice water when they heard the sound of a car traveling fast on the gravel switchback not far below the ranch.

"That's probably them," Ferguson said, reassuring Xander with a pat on the back just as the car rounded the last curve and shot into the driveway. It was the County Sheriff in his black-and-white.

"Xander," the sheriff shouted, leaning out of the door. "It's Bernice. A motorist spotted her and her friend at the bottom of Fitts Canyon and called it in. We got a rescue team and an ambulance on the way. My deputy, who arrived first, said she's alive but looks like she's lost a lot of blood. He doesn't think her friend made it. She ended up under the car. Hop in, I'll drive you down to County General; that's where they'll take her."

Ferguson grabbed Xander's arm. "We can't let them take her there," he said, turning his head so that the others gathering around the sheriff's car couldn't hear.

"Why? I don't understand."

"Because they'll type her and check her blood, and then it gets complicated, real complicated."

Xander stood open-mouthed for a second.

"You coming, Xander?" the sheriff called out.

"A minute, give me a minute," he answered. He gave Ferguson a pleading look.

"Has the ambulance arrived from County General yet, Sheriff?" Ferguson asked.

"Don't know. Let me check with the dispatcher." He ducked back into the car, then popped back out a minute later. "No, not there yet, but the driver says they'll be there in ten minutes, twelve tops."

Ferguson walked over to the Sheriff and pulled him aside. "I'm Mrs. Quarry's doctor. She has an extremely rare blood type and an even rarer blood disease that can make a transfusion fatal. We have to get her up to University Hospital where they are equipped to deal with this kind of thing."

"We'll have to get a helicopter down here."

Ferguson looked at his watch. "Can you patch me through to the EMT in the ambulance?"

"Sure thing."

Ferguson said who he was to the woman who answered from the ambulance and tried to explain the situation without telling her any more than necessary. She told him there was nothing that she could do without orders from her supervising doctor at the hospital. "And who's that?" Ferguson asked?

"Dr. Morrison is on duty now."

Ferguson coughed. He had met Abel Morrison once, and the two had taken an instant dislike to each other. He had to figure out another way. He clicked off the radio mike and leaned to within inches of the Sheriff's face. It was a gamble, but he had to chance it. "I think you can guess who I am with, Sheriff. And I think you know that we have done an awful lot to help this County, to help you." He paused for effect. "I need you to do something for me, now. I'm going to get a medical chopper to fly directly to Fitts Canyon and to take Mrs. Quarry from there to University Hospital."

"You can do that?"

"I can do that. What I need you to do is tell your deputy that he is not to let the ambulance leave with Mrs. Quarry. The EMTs can stabilize her and ready her for the life-flight, but they are to wait for the chopper. Your deputy can tell them to call in for instructions if need be, but his orders are to wait for the helicopter. Can you do that?"

The Sheriff looked grim but nodded. "Let me get on the radio before the ambulance arrives."

Ferguson pulled back, scanned the compound, and turned to Xander again. "Do you still keep up your license?" he said, nodding in the direction of the tennis courts. Just beyond, a little Robinson Raven four-seater was tied down on the helipad but looked serviced and ready.

"Yeah. I usually let Frank fly, though. What's your plan?"

"My plan is to get us up to University Hospital about the same time as the other chopper, so I can talk face-to-face with the people I know there and can take charge of Bernie's treatment. If we are not there before she arrives or within scant minutes after, all this will have been for nothing."

"Okay, but it will take me a few minutes to ready the Raven, and we'll have to overfly the SFO air space, and..."

"Go take care of it. I'll talk with the Sheriff and use his contacts. We'll set things up with the hospital en route."

With the sheriff's help, Ferguson arranged the medical evacuation, then put the organization to work on getting him set up with University Hospital. Xander quickly got clearance for their own emergency routing up to Berkeley, but he was out of practice, and it took him much longer than he had expected to go through the preflight check on the R44. The Sheriff's Department rescue team had retrieved Bernice from the canyon by the time the ambulance arrived, and the deputy spent the next fifteen minutes arguing with the EMTs before the helicopter coming down from San Francisco was spotted. The medical helicopter was already airborne again from Fitts Canyon before Xander had finished warming up the engine of the Raven and lifted off from the Ranch.

Fitts Canyon was to their southeast, a longer run up to Berkeley, but with every passing minute, the gap between them and the much faster Bell aircraft flown by the medical service increased. They were still over ten minutes out when air traffic control told them that the medical flight had already landed at the hospital. Xander kept shaking his head and apologizing to Ferguson over the intercom in the helicopter

When they arrived, they faced another delay, as they had to wait for the other helicopter to leave the helipad before they could land. Ferguson scrambled out of the Raven and ran across the lot toward the emergency entrance of the hospital.

He was met by a surgeon in green scrubs. "You're too late, doctor," the surgeon said. "Your patient was DOA. I'm sorry. You and your foundation went through a lot for this woman. It was quite a scramble here when we got the call."

A part of Ferguson was relieved, and he had to admit that he suspected the same might be true of Xander Quarry when he found out.

"Oh," the surgeon added, "we heard from your county hospital. It seems the other passenger survived. When they lifted the car off her, she was still breathing. The ambulance hadn't left yet, so they transported her to the county hospital."

Xander, just arriving from securing the helicopter, took one look at their faces and could read the truth. "Can I have a minute with her?" he said.

The doctor nodded and pointed toward a cart, its wheels visible below the pale green privacy curtains that already discreetly surrounded it. Xander pulled one curtain aside and exclaimed, "Oh, no!" He grabbed Ferguson and started pulling him toward the exit. "It's Annie. Bernie must be at County General. We have to get down there."

Xander restarted the Raven and had them airborne again as soon as he had clearance. Ferguson tried to use his cell phone to call someone at the organization, but the noise in the cockpit made it impossible. He asked Xander if he could patch him into the hospital or the sheriff. "I can try to raise the sheriff," he said, his voice high-pitched and distorted by the headset intercom. "We'll have to land at the county airport and take a taxi. There's no helipad at the hospital, and I think it would only make matters worse if we pulled some stunt like landing in the parking lot."

"Okay, let's just do it as fast as we can."

"We're doing 110 knots, that's what this baby will do. The shit will be waiting no matter when we arrive."

"Yes, but the longer the shit sits, the more it stinks up the place."

It was getting dark when the taxi from the airport finally dropped them at the small county hospital. They were greeted by Dr. Morrison, who told them that Bernice Quarry was in intensive care.

"You have some explaining to do, doctor," he said to Ferguson, the irritation in his voice evident.

"How is that?" Ferguson answered anxiously.

"Shuffling patients between hospitals, getting the sheriff's deputy to interfere with our emergency medical personnel, raising alarms about non-existent rare blood types, sticking the county with a big fat medical evacuation fee, a wholly unnecessary one, at that. How's that for a few things to answer for?"

"Look, the foundation I work for will pick up all the charges. But what was that you said about non-existent blood types?"

"Your patient, doctor, the one you claimed to be something of a hematological freak. She tested AB positive, we cross-matched her against blood that we had rushed over from the blood bank, and no agglutination, no reaction, no problem. The patient is in serious but stable condition."

Ferguson was puzzled for a moment, then smiled as he realized what had happened. The hospital lab was just not sophisticated enough to detect the abnormalities in Bernice Quarry's blood, and the organization must have already pulled off the modest miracle of getting some of their engineered antigen-neutral supply to the area blood bank. He had years earlier proposed being ready with appropriate supplies in the vicinity of each of his patients, but had forgotten to follow up. Perhaps he actually was beginning to slip in some subtle ways. He grinned broadly at the smug Dr. Morrison and said, "I am so glad to hear it all worked out."

To Morrison's annoyance, within 48 hours Ferguson was able to move Bernice Quarry to the research ward at University Hospital where he could more closely monitor and control her treatment. It was there that she died suddenly two days later. The cause of death was listed as multiple internal injuries sustained in an automobile accident, but Ferguson knew the story was more complicated than that. He knew that the damage to her internal organs was not all from trauma.

After claiming the body, Xander took Ferguson aside and said, "That was way, way too close. Remember what I told you. We need to fix the loose strands before the whole rug unravels right under us. We need to make some calls."

That was the last Xander said on the long drive back to the ranch.

= =

Xander Quarry, whose indifference to his wife was legendary, took her death unexpectedly hard. When Ferguson returned to the ranch after a day of cleaning up loose ends, he found Xander slumped in a deck chair beside the surf machine, watching as a young hard-body blonde with big tits tried to stand on her boogie board.

Ferguson was about to make some comment about her sense of balance when Xander looked up at him, head lolling, eyes unfocused, and raised an unsteady arm in a futile attempt to block the sun. "Who? Oh, you. Who?"

"Xander, Xander. You can't do it this way." Ferguson looked around and noted that the dark muscle-builder was still around. "Hey, what's your name again?" he called out.

"Thadeus. They call me Tad."

"Well, Tad, give me a hand here with our friend Xander."

Together they managed to drag Quarry to his feet and steer him into the house. Ferguson had Tad fetch his bag from the car and then gave Xander an injection. Xander sat up, blinked repeatedly, jerked his head and shoulders a few times, and said, "Yes, right. I think I better go take a shower. Maybe a cold one."

Ferguson grabbed him by the shoulders. "You made a deal with Nadia. Remember?"

"Nadia's gone. She left with one of Bernie's Boys when I started drinking."

"Then you better go after her, Dad. Go take your shower, take two of these pills with a caffè latte, then get Nadia back. And be warned: when you crash you are really going to crash. Okay?"

Xander nodded and padded off toward the nearest bathroom.

Tad looked amazed. "You sobered him up just like that?"

"Yup, but it'll only last for ten hours or so, then he'll be out for a day."

"That's amazing. Can I get me some of that?"

"No," Ferguson said, as he left for his car.

He was enjoying the drive down the canyon road when his iPhone beeped. There was no place to pull over, so he just stopped in the middle of the road at a spot where he hoped an approaching driver would have time to react.

It was a text message from Dougherty. "Big M trouble, u back to Africa."

"One bloody mess after another." he said to himself, as he put the car in gear. "One bloody fucking mess after another."

12

Rosen looked out over a morning sky like buttered toast spread with ripples of marmalade: warm, golden, inviting. It was the first truly warm morning of the spring, cool by the standards of summer in Massachusetts, but warm enough to stir the blood of any New Englander impatient to put mud season behind.

Rosen was inspired. Bike to work, he thought. Perfect! Millie did not like him riding his bicycle to work, a route that took him along well-traveled highways and narrow roads narrowed further by construction and repairs that never seemed to finish. But Millie was already gone, already in her classroom, and what she didn't know couldn't worry her. Rosen checked online. Both Weather Underground and AccuWeather sites promised a sunny day with high, thin clouds and no precipitation in sight.

Rosen dressed, slugged his coffee, and went out to the small detached garage where his bicycles hung from their overhead racks, tires filled, chains oiled, and ready to roll on the long awaited first outing of spring. Rosen owned three bikes, which amused Millie no end, since he spent more time tinkering on them than riding them. The most used, his metallic blue Trek MultiTrack hybrid, might be taken out a few dozen times a year, mostly schlepping groceries or to pick up new parts from the cycle shop down in Gloucester. The hybrid was the only one of the three equipped with a rack to carry his panniers or his briefcase.

Pride of the pack was his carbon-fiber Pinarello, a sleek, banana-yellow drop-handle road racer with a distinctive geometry that always drew attention at meets, allowing Rosen to brag without bragging aloud. Rosen's secret pride was that he had gotten the $6,000 bike for less than wholesale by badgering a cousin who had gotten stuck with it in inventory. Still, Millie had thrown a nutty when she heard what he had paid for it. Her bicycle was a Schwinn off-roader that she had picked up at a garage sale for $30, and she went out cycling three times as often as Rosen.

Rosen avoided anything he regarded as pointless activity or exercise for its own sake. He could allow himself to bike for groceries or to get to work, but he would only race if it was a charity event that would raise money, which meant that the Pinarello saw action only a few times a year at best. The Pan-Mass Challenge two years earlier had been his bragging-rights run, when he had finished on the toughest route. After 190 miles in two long days of hard pedaling, it had taken him nearly a week to recover.

His beloved mountain bike, another Trek, with fat knobby tires and hydraulic suspension, had been his since high-school. He still lovingly cleaned and oiled and adjusted it and had always meticulously repainted every nick and scratch, but these days he almost never rode it except on test runs after each round of routine maintenance.

Oddly, the vernal vitality of the morning drew him toward the Pinarello, but it had no rack on the back. He briefly considered dismounting the rack from the MultiTrack, but quickly recognized that it would be a messy mechanical job even if the rack would fit on the Pinarello, which it probably would not. He thought of stuffing the briefcase into his backpack, but the extra weight combined with the Pinarello's dropped handlebars meant risking throwing his back out again.

Somewhat reluctantly, he lifted down the hybrid, strapped his briefcase on the back, and rolled it out of the garage. He removed the reflective strap from where it hung from the right handlebar and wrapped it around the right leg of his jeans. Rosen owned one authentic cycling outfit, which he reserved for meets where proper attire was de rigueur and trousers would be an embarrassment, but the rest of the time he rode in street clothes. There were a couple of serious cyclists at the Lab who regularly rode to work in spandex, then showered and changed, but that degree of fashion-conscious fussiness was not for Rosen.

= =

The ride to work had been exhilarating, but the rest of his morning was spent in meetings that left him enervated and longing for the good old days of college classes where one could catch a catnap in the back of the room. By early afternoon he was ready to be anywhere but where he was, doing anything but what he was doing. Without thinking much about what he was doing, he opened a browser and Googled his own name. The first results were headed by his page on the Biontolics site followed by his Wikipedia bio and an assortment of old miscellany, but nothing new showed up. Rosen clicked on the "More search tools" link, slid his mouse pointer past the selected "Anytime" and clicked "Past month" to repeat and narrow the search. The dozen results were topped by his recent registration for the Essex County Bike-for-Bread to benefit area food pantries and by an item on his appointment to the editorial board of *Bio-Logical: Communications in Computational Biology*. Not a word about his new paper, not even a link to the arXiv q-bio page.

Rosen went to the arXiv quantitative biology home page and scanned down the current month's listing. Nothing. His paper wasn't there. He flipped to the login page, typed his handle and password, and got the little red-framed box at the top of the page saying "Incorrect username or password." He tried again using his email address instead of his screen name and got the same message. About the same time that he realized he was not being smart to be doing this research from the Lab, Jeannine poked her head into his office. "What's up?" she asked, craning her neck to look at his screen.

"Not much," he said, quickly closing the browser. "Just checking some Web resources."

"Well, if you're not busy, what about lunch?"

Rosen was surprised by the invitation but tried to act cool. "Ah, sure. I suppose. What did you have in mind? Who else is going?"

"Nobody, which is why I wanted company. How about The Clam Box to celebrate the real arrival of spring in New England, which, New England always being a bit behind the times, comes a month after the vernal equinox."

The Clam Box was an Ipswich institution, a glorified clam shack shaped like a giant take-out container and famed throughout the area for serving nothing but fried seafood, heavily breaded and dripping with oil. At peak times, the wait in line could be forty minutes or more. For fans of fried clams, The Clam Box rated the equivalent of three Michelin stars. Rosen, however, had never understood the appeal of fried clams and avoided them with the excuse that it was forbidden for Jews to eat shellfish. Lobster, of course, was another matter altogether, and Rosen was not alone among New England Jews ready to forget the laws of *kashrut* when lobster was in the offing.

Jeannine noticed his hesitation. "We could do Chinese. Or Greek?"

Rosen looked thoughtful. "Do you have a car? I biked to work today."

"Sure, where do you want to go?"

"You pick."

"Okay, how about trying that new place up in Rowley? We're less likely to run into the crowd from the Lab there." She smiled broadly. "I'll grab my jacket and keys."

The new restaurant in Rowley turned out to be an old one with a new name. It was the fourth attempt in as many years to launch a restaurant in the same storefront in a small shopping center. Locals always got excited with the announcement of each new arrival, but the eateries never thrived, and most were gone within a year. Rosen commented on the depressing trend.

"Most restaurants don't last more than a year or two," she said. "But the sushi here is pretty good, don't you think? Maybe this time it will work." She leaned forward. "Are you all right, Rosen? I mean, if it's okay for me to ask."

"Yeah, it's okay. I'm okay, just thinking."

"And when aren't you thinking? You are one of the most thinking-est people I've ever known."

"Yeah, well, I'm trying to work out a puzzle," he said, pushing bits of rice around on his plate.

"Is this that rat longevity stuff again? The business that The General told you to back off from? Or have you found an entirely new way to get the High Command coming down on you?"

Rosen carefully lined up his knife and fork and his chopsticks on his plate and slid back in his chair. He said nothing, waiting for Jeannine to fill the gap in the conversation. She didn't, so he took a deep breath and decided to chance it. "Whose side are you on, Jeannine? Are you working for them?"

"Them? Of course, I work for them. We both work for the same company, Rosen, at least last time I checked my employee badge." She lifted it up from where it still hung around her neck. "Yup, it says Biontolics Research, LLC, North Shore Laboratories. What does yours say?"

"That's not what I mean," he said impatiently.

"Then say what you do mean. What are you really asking?"

He shook his head. "Nothing, I guess. Let's get the check and head back. This will be my treat."

"No."

"What? No, I insist."

"No. It doesn't look good. You can pick up the tab when you take the whole team out, but it wouldn't be right to just take me to lunch."

They rode back to the office in silence, and Rosen passed the afternoon impatient to be home so that he could start surfing the

Web again without being watched.

= =

It was the end of the day when Millie called.

"You biked to work today, didn't you," she said, in a tone that Rosen had not heard since his mother stopped using it on him after his bar mitzvah.

"Yeah, well, it was such a perfect day."

"Was. It's starting to look threatening. You know I don't like you biking after dark."

"It won't be after dark. Besides, I have lights."

"And what are you wearing, darling Rosen? Your black leather jacket? Black jeans? Huh? I know you, Rosen. How do you expect drivers to see you?"

"I don't. I expect to see them," he teased.

"Well, you had better see them, and see them soon. I want you home before sundown. Do you hear? And you're on your own for supper. I have a budget and planning meeting tonight, and I expect it will go long. You had better be waiting for me when I get home."

"I will be. I'm about to leave the office right now."

"Be careful."

He laughed. "No, I will not be careful, darling. I expect to ride recklessly, weaving in and out of traffic, popping wheelies, and grabbing air at every opportunity. Just go to your meeting and stop worrying about me."

"No, I will not stop worrying about you. That's my job. You won't do it, so somebody has to. Love you. Later." She hung up.

Rosen, who was a serious eater but an indifferent cook, did not like the thought of cooking for himself when he got home. He tried to visualize the state of leftovers in the refrigerator and made a face. "Pizza night," he said to no one in particular as he shut down his computer. He stuffed a wad of loose papers and his iPhone into his briefcase, turned out the lights, and headed for the bike racks just outside the back door.

Once underway, instead of turning to cut directly over to Route 133 heading down toward Essex, he continued up Argilla Road and then into the center of Ipswich. At the Ipswich House of Pizza, another small but popular local institution, he picked up a small Mediterranean pizza with extra olives, strapped it on the back of his bike with a spare bungee cord, and headed back down 133. At the turnoff where the highway split from Route 1A, he upshifted and started pedaling hard through the long, lazy curves, past the Corliss Brothers Nursery where Millie was a regular customer and irregular consultant on matters horticultural, and finally into the straightaway at top speed. It felt good to be taking the road flat out. The traffic was already thinning, and, although the sun was down, the twilit sky still provided plenty of light. Rosen reached behind him and turned on his red blinker even though it was mostly blocked by the briefcase and pizza strapped on top of the rack. He switched on his headlight, then flipped it to strobe mode to make himself more visible.

The breakdown lanes in that stretch were wide, but out of habit Rosen rode as far to the right as practical and kept checking his handlebar mirror for traffic from behind. There was a long string of cars doing 50 plus in the 45-mile-an-hour zone, then a break in the traffic, and then the flash of high beams reflecting into his eyes. He shifted his gaze down and to the right in front of him as the blinding lights in his mirror grew bigger and brighter. As the vehicle closed rapidly on him, he steered to steady his front wheel on the very edge of the asphalt and slowed, waiting for it to pass. Instead of passing, it slowed as it approached, as if to make a turn. As it pulled alongside, Rosen, no longer blinded by the headlights in his eyes, could see that it was a white pickup truck, a big 4-by-4. He coasted and downshifted, but the pickup slowed, too, staying beside him and signaling for a right turn. Rosen braked to let the truck pass, but it slowed still more and paced him, all the while edging farther and farther into the breakdown lane.

Rosen crunched hard on both handbrakes, fighting to keep from pitching over the handlebars. The driver in the pickup edged over enough to bump Rosen's mirror. Rosen's front tire hit gravel, and he lost control. At the last second, he spotted the telephone pole flying at him and threw his bike into a skid in front of him. The bike slammed into the pole, wrapped around the backside, and continued, with Rosen sliding and tumbling after. The truck took off down the highway in a squeal of tires and was gone.

Rosen tried to sit up. His arm hurt and wouldn't support him. His whole left side was on fire with pain, and his face was hot and sticky. He reached up and wiped pizza sauce from his cheek.

Another set of lights was approaching. Rosen struggled to try and drag himself farther off the verge as the car slowed and stopped with its lights flooding the area. He waved weakly at the driver. His Trek was a mangled mess just beyond him and his briefcase and its contents were scattered twenty feet up the road. Rosen's vision blurred.

"Are you all right?" Two people got out of the car and stood over him, a couple in their thirties or forties.

"I think so," he said softly. He looked down at the hamburger that was his left leg where his torn slacks exposed the road rash beneath. His vision blurred again, but he gritted his teeth. "Did you see anything? Did you see the pickup?"

"Yeah, hit and run. But they'll catch him."

Rosen groaned in pain. "Better call an ambulance. I think I need to be looked at."

"Heidi already called, and the police—so they can pick up that driver. They'll get him."

"You keep saying that."

"Well, he left this behind." The man held up a passenger-side mirror. "Cut so close to that pole that he knocked it clean off. We saw it land in the field there. Shouldn't be all that hard to spot a white pickup with out-of-state plates and a missing mirror." He grinned in triumph.

Rosen struggled to stay conscious. "Have you got a cell phone on you? Can I call my wife? I seem to have lost mine." He pointed toward the briefcase still lying in the road.

"Sure thing. Just tell me the number and I'll dial it for you."

Rosen had just started to recite the digits when he heard the sirens approaching. It was the last sound he heard.

13

Ferguson looked down at the wound, an oozing, beet-red and cheddar-yellow gash. He gently pressed his gloved fingers around its margins and shook his head. In Portuguese, he told the doctor and nurses what they should have already figured out on their own, that the wound was infected, there was evidence of peritonitis, indications of possible internal bleeding, and absolute certainty of their own incompetence.

"I am from Argentina, not Brazil," the doctor responded in English. "We speak Spanish. You speak too fast, and I do not understand you."

"Well, now you understand me, then. So I will tell you in English that you can take the next plane out of here and wing it right back to Argentina, because you are unfit to call yourself a doctor. I can repeat that in Spanish, if you prefer."

"Who are you to speak to me that way? You just arrived. Do you know who I am? I am the President's personal physician. Who do you think you are?"

"I think that I am the man who is going to save your life by having you deported instead of executed. That's who I think I am." Ferguson signaled to one of the ever-present soldiers, who hustled the protesting doctor out of the room. He turned to the two nurses and spoke to them in Lusanyu. "Prep him and scrub for surgery. Show me that you know what you are doing, and I won't say anything to the President when he awakens."

He left the room to get supplies and scrub for surgery himself.

= =

The operation did not go well. Ferguson already knew that would be the case with the first incision. By the time they were ready to close, Ferguson was struggling. Anywhere else he might have let one of the nurses close, but this was not anywhere else, and there was not anyone else he trusted. By the last stitch in the four hours of emergency surgery, Ferguson was on the verge of collapse. He knew that as a young intern he had pulled much longer shifts, but he was not an intern and not young. First Zurich to San Francisco to meet with the Quarrys, then Bernie's death and Xander's collapse, then the ten-and-a-half hour non-stop back to Heathrow with the nine-hour flight to Mbutsu City waiting for him: it had proved too much. Ferguson dragged himself out of the operating theater, then collapsed on a bench. When he awoke in his room the next day, he had coffee and toast delivered before he called Dougherty.

"I operated," he told Dougherty, "but it's just a holding pattern. He needs a real surgeon. He needs Colfax."

"You know Colfax won't go to Africa."

"He has to. I can't do this. I'm an internist not a surgeon, and Colfax has done resections before. I only watched the video on YouTube."

"You're too modest. I've seen you pull off miracles. How bad is it?"

"Bad. I loaded him with antibiotics—our stuff, the latest, not the commercial crap—and pumped a new batch of cells into him, but the damage...The knife wound was bad enough, but Mbutsu apparently did most of the real damage when he wrenched the girl's arm. Then his goddamned personal physician finished the job by botching the surgery. He's out of here—on a plane home or lying by the side of a road somewhere —I don't know. I don't really care anymore. But my patient is in bad shape."

"Maybe it's time."

"Are you crazy, Dougherty? Mbutsu is still a quarter of our budget. Besides, anything happens to him now, and they will never let me out of the country. He dies and I'm a dead man. You read the news, so you already know what his army did after the attack from the girl. They razed an entire region of the country. They leveled it. You could see the fires from all the way across the border. Then the infantry went in and finished off the survivors. Red Cross sources estimate that 25,000 people were killed in a week; the army claims double that. Mbutsu was unconscious most of that week. They don't even need his leadership any more, if leadership is the word you apply to such savagery. He has been around so long that his barbarism has become institutionalized."

"Okay, I'll bring Colfax myself. He's not completely rational, you know, but he's still the best in his field, and he'll come if I go with him."

"I don't think that's a good idea—you, me, and Colfax all in Busanyu at the same time, with the country burning."

"It will be a swap. I'll hold Colfax's hand on the flight down. They'll refuel, board you, and fly right back."

"You're sure Colfax will do it?"

"Yes, I'm sure. I'll have him put under when we get into the limo, and we'll bring him around when he's in the operating room."

"So, we add international kidnapping to our dossiers."

"He's one of ours, so it doesn't count. We'll add it to the collective rap sheet when we kidnap someone outside."

Ferguson laughed despite himself. "Sooner or later, I'm sure we will."

= =

By nightfall, Dr. Abraham Colfax was at the Presidential Palace outside of Mbutsu City and scrubbing to operate. He was furious with Dougherty, who had not, in fact, flown with him to Busanyu, but had drugged him and passed him on to the capable hands of a couple of minders. Ferguson had delivered both the shot of sivilac that brought him around and the news that he had been abducted for the greater good. Colfax protested until he saw the MRIs and had examined their patient. Old memories and over-trained responses were stirred. The gifted surgeon in him took charge again over the anxious and unstable recluse he had become, a virtual hermit who could not always hold up a normal conversation. He was transformed by the challenge that was now made even more challenging owing to the population of new cells eagerly trying to repair the damage on their own. He consulted with Ferguson for an hour, then announced his plan.

Ferguson did not announce his own plan. Once he realized that his options had expanded, he abandoned Colfax and left immediately for the airport with a smile on his face. To save time, Colfax had been brought down on a flight chartered by the organization instead of on Mbutsu's G6, which would have required further delay while it was flown up from Busanyu. Instead, the chartered Gulfstream waiting for Ferguson at Mbutsu International was now his to command. He intended to command it to file a flight plan for Moscow. He would get a full night's sleep on the plane and meet Sveta for brunch.

= =

Spindly trees flickered past like pickets in a fence as Ferguson pushed his black Mercedes along the forested road in an effort to break his previous record of an hour and fifty-three minutes from the airport at *Sheremetsavo* to the *Nichevo* clinic. It was not, strictly speaking, a clinic, and the town was not named *Nichevo*. In fact, the town referred to by Ferguson and his colleagues as *Nichevo*, Russian for nothing, had once had a postal code for a name and could be found on no map. One of a number of secret cities and towns created by the Soviets during the autumn of the cold war to manufacture weapons and carry out secret and forbidden military research, this one had been spared from becoming a ghost town after *perestroika* only by way of Ferguson's inspired intervention.

The organization had bought the town outright through Russian intermediaries for several million dollars in cash, a price that was proving to have been a bargain. Its captive chemists, biologists, and engineers, who had once labored in obscurity on wholesale death, now worked on its retail defeat. Laboratories and production facilities constructed to churn out chemical and biological weapons had been repurposed to make pharmaceuticals and synthetic versions and variants of proteins, enzymes, and neurotransmitters. Some of the transition was less a leap than naïve outsiders might imagine, owing to overlaps in the basic science needed. While others of the nameless towns were now crumbling and weed-choked, *Nichevo* thrived, and its resident professionals enjoyed a good, if somewhat isolated, life. In that, for them, nothing had changed.

The setup was perfect for the new purposes: isolation and anonymity, established security, and a pool of highly educated talent eager to work on interesting challenges with no competitive employers on the tree-peppered horizon. *Nichevo* was the centerpiece of the organization's research strategy, the place where they could do precisely the experiments they wanted, even on human subjects, without having to create a cover of legitimacy. It was the gateway that gave them easy access to the supply of embryonic stem cells that were essential to their techniques and that were all but impossible to obtain through legitimate channels. The new Russian leaders, each in turn, had gladly accepted the cash compensation of regular fees, and they willingly turned a blind eye to the details of operation. Even with the surcharge of obligatory payments to the Russian mafia for protection, *Nichevo* was providing a stunning return-on-investment.

The guards at the gate in the chain-link fence, armed with Kalashnikovs and accompanied by dogs who looked as bored as their handlers, no longer wore the old soviet-style uniforms from the early days of the conversion, but they were the same guards, some now grizzled and bent, but all smiling at their benefactor, the

Brit who had let them keep their jobs and who paid them both more—and more reliably—than the Red Army ever had. Like their neighbors, their silence and loyalty were easily bought. They were the lucky ones at a time when so many of their cousins or former officers were starving on half-rations or running to stay a meter or two in front of the police or the Russian mafia.

Old Konstantinov, who by rights should outlive Ferguson but almost certainly would not, greeted him warmly in his Bulgarian-accented Russian. "We are so glad to have you back again so soon, Comrade Doctor. I will telephone ahead to the House in case they are not yet fully ready for you."

To Konstantinov, caught in a closed, time-like loop that perpetually returned him to the days of his youth, everyone was *tovarisch*, comrade, as if he were still in the same secret unit of the Soviet security machine. He raised his hand to signal his juniors to slide open the gate, which had once been powered by a motor that no one had bothered to replace. Ferguson made a mental note to bring it to the attention of Colonel Markov, who now handled security at *Nichevo*.

= =

Sveta couldn't meet him for brunch but at the end of her shift met him in the lobby with his marching orders for the evening. "You are going to a concert. Andropova is leading our chamber orchestra in two works by Gaiyden." Sveta's English was pitch-perfect in most areas, but names she had grown up with seemed resistant to correction, and in Russian, the prolific baroque composer's name was spelled with the letter *geh* and pronounced like guide-in.

Ferguson faked disappointment. "I had in mind more improve-sational music," he chided. "But, Andropova is very good," he said, switching to Russian. "Maybe she will want to go back to my suite with me to make for an encore."

Sveta shoved at his shoulders. "You are always the dreamer, my mysterious doctor, but Andropova likes her lovers with more curves than you possess. Perhaps she will come instead to my apartment after the concert."

Ferguson patted her behind as he grabbed a quick kiss. He liked Sveta's sass, but did not always know what to do with it. She was too young for him, he knew, but then, nearly every woman in the world was too young for him—or soon would be.

"A good Gaiyden concerto followed by a private duet would be wonderful," he teased.

= =

If she had been one to smoke, Sveta would be smoking, filling the empty minutes after intercourse with ritual distraction. Instead, she picked at something imagined or real on her left index finger while she coughed little chirps that signaled Ferguson to wait until she was ready to speak.

"I know what we are researching, what you are doing," she announced, fixing him with her walnut-brown eyes. "I have figured it out. On my own. I want to be one of your subjects."

Ferguson took a breath and let it out slowly. "What is it that you think we do, exactly? In what research do you want to become a subject?"

"You want me to say it because you do not think I am that smart, but I am, and I want to live to be two hundred and fifty. That is the experiment I want you to include me in—the immortality experiment. You will do this for me because you are in love with me."

"And who is it who said that I am in love with you?"

"I said it, because it is true, just like my analysis and conclusions regarding the research we are doing. We, here, at what you call the clinic when you are not here—see, I know more than you think—we are working on the next generation, aren't we. We are designing the simpler, cheaper ways to regulate the balance so there is not this perpetual race between metastasis and cellular cascade, so you do not have to monitor so closely and have treatments every few months. This is what we are doing for you. And what you will be doing for me is making me to keep young."

Ferguson shook his head slowly, again and again.

"No, I am wrong? Or no, you will not? That is not the right answer, my doctor, my love. The right answer is yes: yes I am right, and yes you will keep me young."

"It is not that easy. You are too young."

"I am 36, which for a woman, a Russian woman, is already of a certain age. That cannot be too young. I do not want to get any older."

"No, you should be in your forties, preferably in your fifties. It took a long time for us to figure that one out. I lost a friend because we didn't realize that an older, less vigilant, more complicated immune system is needed to start with. The sledgehammer approach of completely knocking out the immune system is too aggressive and brings on its own problems. Besides, I do not make these decisions."

"That is okay, because then I will make the decision for you. Otherwise, I will decide that it is time to talk to an ex-lover, a journalist in Moscow, who will be so very glad to see me again and so very glad to have a story that will see publication beyond the miserable little rag he now writes for."

"You are not a foolish woman, Sveta, and that would be a foolish move that would only guarantee you would never get anything more from us, not even another paycheck." Ferguson studied her face, the sweeping brush strokes of her eyebrows that said so little of the inferno of intelligence behind them, the thick lips that could pull him in like a vortex. He was thinking of those lips and those eyes and the woman behind them and seeing the relationship with her stretching out far into the future. It left a sweet-sour taste in his mouth, and he wondered if there would ever be anyone who could sustain his interest the way his attention was held by the film festival of women parading through his life. Even now, there was Sveta with this year's *palm d'or*, but there were also the runners-up—Brigit in London and Alicia in California—as well as the not infrequent short subjects of young women met on a Virgin Atlantic flight or in a tony London club for those who have arrived and those looking to arrive by way of some wealthy and well-toned older gentleman.

"I will talk to my employers," he said, "but I can promise nothing."

"Ah, my elusive doctor, we both know that you are the employers; there is no one else to talk with."

"And there you would be wrong again. There are many discussions to be started, and many others who must weigh in on the matter before anything could happen. And, as I said, there is time, some years' worth of it."

Her face pinched into a pout, and her thick brows lowered as she considered him. She decided to drop the matter for the time being, to enjoy the moment, confident that she could eventually wear down his resistance. She pushed him over onto his back and started the physical persuasion, running her big hands down over his belly and to his inner thighs.

Ferguson let out a groan of pleasure and surrendered—for the moment.

14

Rosen attempted a smile at Millie as she entered the hospital room, but his face didn't seem to be responding right. "I'll be ready in a few minutes," he said, pushing the words out with a tongue still thickened by sleep.

The nurse at his side turned and said to Millie, in a tone of professional impatience, "I'm just changing his dressings. Why don't you wait outside until I'm through here. This might take more than a few minutes."

Rosen gathered his strength again and said, "They're almost ready to discharge me."

"Discharge you? Wait just one minute! You're injured, Rosen. You've had a serious accident. They can't possibly be ready to send you home."

"We are not ready to send him home," announced a wide, dark-skinned Indian woman standing in the doorway. She wore an unbuttoned doctor's coat like a vest over her rose and saffron sari. "But we cannot keep him if he insists on being released." She walked over to Millie. "I'm Doctor Ramachandran. You must be his wife. I wasn't on duty last night, so I just met your husband, who is convinced that he will be better off recuperating at home."

Rosen raised his head and leaned as far as he could to talk around the nurse, who had advanced up to changing the bandages on his hip. "You know what I think of hospitals, Millie. No offence, doctor."

"Oh, none would be taken. It is not my hospital. I just work here. And my job at the moment is to try and persuade you to stay here at Beverly Hospital for at least another day."

"No luck, Doc," he said, just beginning to hit his stride. "Just shoot me full of methicillin, give me a prescription for oxycodone or your favorite morphine analog, and send me on my way."

"Oh, are you in medicine?" she said, looking down at his chart. "Mr. David? Or is it Mr. Rosen? These night admissions people can make a mess of names."

"No, it's Dr. David, but not your kind of doctor. I work in," he stopped, reminding himself of his recent reassignment. "I work in Nutrition Sciences at Biontolics up in Ipswich."

"Ah, yes, Biontolics. My sister-in-law works at New England Biolabs. Adhi Kandiyar. Do you know her? No? Well, I will give you a prescription for oxacillin, Dr. David, but ibuprofen will be the pain reliever of choice for you, I'm afraid."

"Damn. I was looking forward to feeling better—much better." Millie shot him a disapproving look. "Just kidding, of course. Working at the Labs I have access to all the opiates I need."

"Rosen, stop it. Doctor, he is just like this—doesn't know when it's not appropriate to kid around."

"Oh, it is not a problem. We consider it very appropriate. It makes it easier to fill out the police report." She looked down at her chart, made a couple of check marks, and looked back up at Millie. "Just kidding, of course."

The nurse at Rosen's side gathered her things and stood up. "I'm through here, doctor, if you don't need me."

"No, that will be fine. Are you new on this ward? I don't remember seeing you around."

"I'm part-time staff," she said over her shoulder as she wheeled her cart out into the hall.

The doctor flipped through the chart in her hand. "Nothing broken, Mrs. David. It looks a lot worse than it is," she said, trying to reassure her. "Just have him take it easy for a few days. He'll be stiff for a while. And have him see his regular doctor within the week, sooner if anything starts really hurting or he starts running a fever or shows any reaction to the antibiotic." Millie did not look convinced.

"It's just road rash, honey," Rosen said. "I'll heal. You know me. My poor bike took the real beating. Aren't you glad I wasn't riding the Pinarello?"

She gave him a withering look of disapproval. "What about your dislocated shoulder?"

"I've located it. See?" He twisted his right arm, now in a sling, toward her. "There it is, right where it's always been."

"Not funny, Rosen," she said, just as an orderly showed up with a wheelchair to escort them out. He smiled down at Millie, then helped Rosen into the chair and expertly swiveled it around the end of the bed and out into the hallway.

"I was worried sick all night," Millie said, walking alongside and continuing her monologue as Rosen was wheeled toward the entrance. Rosen kept looking up at her and nodding. "I'll bring the car around," she told the orderly. "Don't let him move!" she admonished.

Rosen looked up at the orderly, who rolled his eyes sympathetically but stood in silence as they waited several minutes for Millie to arrive with Rosen's Prius.

"I told you not to ride your bike to work," Millie started in again, as the orderly helped Rosen into the passenger seat and buckled him in. "The traffic on 133 can be something else. There are so many accidents."

Rosen waited until the door was closed and the orderly was headed back into the hospital before he spoke. "It wasn't traffic and it wasn't an accident. Someone tried to kill me, Millie. The man ran me off the road. He was signaling for a turn and there was no road there to turn onto."

Millie let out a puff of breath. "Don't talk that way. That's crazy. Who would try to kill you?"

"The same people who do not want my paper to get out."

"Biontolics? Are you losing it, Rosen? This is not like you, Rosen. I don't like you scaring me that way."

"My paper is gone. It's been removed from the quantitative biology arXiv, and I can't log in anymore."

"Rosen, stuff like that happens all the time. That's why they have those lost-password links."

"It's part of a pattern, surely you can see that, Millie. And there's something I didn't tell the officer who took my statement last night. Just before the guy steered me into a telephone pole, the pickup bumped my handlebar mirror and I looked over as I went down. I saw the guy, he was looking straight at me. It was no accident, I tell you."

Millie fought down anxiety that threatened to overwhelm her. She wanted to support Rosen but couldn't let herself accept the implications of his story. "Are you sure, Rosen? You didn't, like, imagine this? Because your head hit the pavement pretty hard. You said that your vision blurred." She was reaching for straws and Rosen was beginning to see it.

"Yeah, but I didn't pass out then, and I didn't hallucinate, Millie."

"Why didn't you tell this to the police?"

"Tell me, have the police found the truck yet? A white pickup with out-of-state plates and a missing passenger-side mirror, speeding down Route 133. So easy to miss something like that," he said, with vitriolic sarcasm.

Millie pressed her forehead to the steering wheel. "What are you saying, Rosen."

"You know perfectly well what I am saying."

"What are you going to do?"

"I'm going to go home, get on the computer, do some research, and post my paper again. That's what I'm going to do." He closed his eyes for a minute. "And I'm going to get Dr. Jervis at the Peabody Clinic to prescribe me something stronger than ibuprofen. My God, everything hurts."

= =

Rosen spent the next two days recuperating and doing research. He created new login credentials, posted his paper on three sites, and followed up on his citation studies. His leg hurt like hell, and he was beginning to think it was getting hot to the touch, but he decided to tough it out and say nothing to Millie, who was already fussing anxiously over him. On the third day, Millie came home from school to find him stretched out on the sofa in his undershorts, delirious and burning with fever. His left leg was badly inflamed and peppered with patches of discoloration.

Dr. Jervis returned Millie's call right away and told her to call an ambulance.

= =

Rosen's head rang with the dissonant warble of a siren as the ambulance wove in and out of the traffic coming down Interstate 95. He was not sure what the emergency was, but he could see that the paramedic had started a drip and had him hooked up to monitors. His leg felt like it was being scalded with steam, and he raised his head just enough to get a glimpse of it. There was a terrain map in red and purple, brown and gray painted over his left leg. He started to say something about it to whomever was holding his hand, but passed out again before he could get the words out.

He was just coming around once more about the time they wheeled him into the Beth Israel Deaconess Medical Center through the emergency entrance.

"That was my second time in a week," he said to the lights flying by overhead. "Ambulances sway a lot more than I would have expected. Not fun." He drifted off again before he could finish his thought.

On Dr. Jervis's direction, Rosen was taken directly into isolation, where the doctor's suspicions were fairly quickly confirmed: MRSA, methicillin-resistant staph. They started him immediately on vancomycin, but within a few hours, as the patches of discoloration on his leg continued to spread, they realized they were dealing with something even more dangerous. Without waiting for the rest of the lab results that could take hours, Jervis switched him to an intravenous cocktail of powerful antibiotics that included linezolid and daptomycin, relatively new drugs that had proven effective against multidrug-resistant bacterial strains. Then they waited and watched.

It was early evening when Dr. Jervis met Millie in the waiting room. She looked at him questioningly and held her breath.

"I want you to know," he said, speaking slowly, "we brought him down here to Boston because this way we have the best facilities and resources at our disposal. He is getting the very best treatment available anywhere, but I also want you to know that we are fighting a real battle now. I told you over the phone that I suspected it might be MRSA."

Millie nodded, letting her breath out in little pulses.

"Well, it is, a particularly nasty strain, one we've seen before but not often, but it's more than that. We're also dealing with necrotizing fasciitis."

"You mean the so-called flesh-eating bacteria."

"Right, in this case the lab now confirms it's a polymicrobial infection, several bacterial strains, not all of which have been identified unequivocally yet. He was not responding to intravenous vancomycin, so we switched to a more powerful cocktail of antibiotics. He's also now getting intravenous immunoglobulin. It's too early to tell, but we are hopeful. I have to ask you some questions, though, because this sort of fierce polymicrobial invasion is extremely rare, and usually would only be associated with a compromised immune system. Is there anything that might account for that."

"If you mean is he gay or bisexual or an intravenous drug user, the answer is no, no, and no. I would know."

"Well, it's very puzzling, then, because the timing would suggest he contracted these infections in the hospital, but Beverly has not had any outbreaks of MRSA, and they got a clean bill of health from the team that just got back from there."

"Can these be soil dwelling? I mean, could he have picked them up from the accident."

"Both the strep and staph bacteria are endemic. We live with them, constantly. It is theoretically possible that they were present on his skin and got access through the wounds, but I have never seen anything like this before. The onset and progression are so fast. Oops, there's my pager. Gotta go."

"Can I see him?"

"He's in isolation, but I'll see about it. I'll be back." He took off down the hall in the hurried walk of someone trying not to appear to be running.

15

In the morning, anxious despair turned to hesitant hope when Dr. Jervis told Millie that he had good news, that he had just learned about a drug research program looking for subjects between the ages of 40 and 50 with MDR-MRSA and/or necrotizing fasciitis. The research protocol seemed almost as if it had been written with Rosen in mind.

"Do you have power of attorney for Rosen?" he asked her. "Did Rosen ever give you medical authority?"

"Yes, I have the papers filed at home somewhere. Do I need to get them?"

"I'll take your word for it. I think if you bring them in tomorrow for the Human Subjects Office here, that will be okay. For now, just sign on the lines marked with an X on all these forms, and we'll get things rolling."

After Millie signed the informed-consent papers, Rosen was accepted as a subject in the study and was administered an experimental series of treatments. Over the course of the next week, he made what was being described as a miraculous recovery. The doctors were saying they had never seen such rapid healing after necrotizing fasciitis. His leg was looking dramatically better, and it was even beginning to appear that he might not need skin grafts. As suddenly as he had been admitted, Rosen found himself being discharged.

Millie drove him home in the Prius and waited until they were home before telling him what had happened. "You haven't asked about my car," she said, out of the blue as they were finishing dinner.

He twisted in his chair to look out the kitchen window. "I hadn't noticed. It's gone. Where is it? Is it in the shop?"

"I totaled it. Well, the VW is totaled, anyway."

"What happened? You didn't say anything."

"You were fighting for your life. I didn't want to add to your problems."

"Yeah, bad car karma can interfere with antibiotics."

"Rosen, be serious. I was just looking out for you. Still am."

Rosen knew it was his turn to say something meaningful, but his mind only offered up more wisecracks, so he just looked at her and kept silent.

"It was on my way home from school," she said, suddenly very solemn. "I was driving down Route 1A, giving Henry Armand a ride home—his Saab was in the shop. Just before the turnoff for his house, I noted a pickup truck at a stop sign on the right. Without warning, it shot across the road, coming right at us, broadside, tires smoking. It shoved us all the way across the road and sideways into a fieldstone wall, then backed up, looking like it might ram us again, but it took off when a minivan came around the curve."

"Oh, my God. You could have been killed."

"Yeah. But all I had was a few scratches, nothing serious—'treated and released' as they say." There was a long silence. "Henry...Henry died in the ambulance on the way to Anna Jacques. He didn't have a chance. The entire passenger side of the VW was stove in."

"What about the truck? The driver? Did they catch him?"

"No." She closed her eyes. "They didn't catch him, and they haven't found the white pickup. Rosen, when he rammed us, he was looking right at us, just like with you. It was no accident. I told that to the police. I also told them that it looked like the truck had a new mirror on the passenger side. It didn't quite match."

Rosen put a hand over his eyes for a moment. "What are we going to do?" he said, at last.

"It's like you have been sucked into a minor war, Rosen. I don't know. You realize that some people have said that Henry Armond looks a little like you. Cynthia, the secretary at the middle school, even though you two might be related."

"It's dangerous to be around me—is that what you are saying?"

"Yeah, I guess. I don't know. I don't understand what's happening, except that ever since you got into that Nobel-grade research, things have been going wrong. Maybe the universe is trying to tell us something. Maybe messing with Nature is not such a good idea. This...this whole thing is beginning to really scare me. I just want to run away. I shouldn't, but I do. Intense stuff like this is easier for you. You've always been so logical and controlled, but it gets to me. I didn't sign up for this."

"You could maybe stay with your mother for a while? Until this is sorted out."

"I thought of that. I don't want to abandon you."

"No, you should. You should go. In fact, I insist."

"My mom's place is too far, and I still have eight weeks of school in the term."

Rosen wanted to make everything all right, wanted to reassure her and reassure himself, but he could think of nothing convincing.

"The police said they would be looking into it," she added, a footnote to her frustration.

"There you go. I'm sure they'll figure it out."

"Rosen, I can't tell anymore whether you are serious or trying to be cute. This is reality, not reality TV. I'm not hopeful." She held his eyes. "I don't want to die, Rosen."

Rosen thought of many ways to answer, but just said, "Me neither. We'll think of something."

"I feel guilty for feeling this way," she continued, "but I don't think I can handle this. I'm really getting scared. You were always the unflappable Mister Cool. Nothing really penetrates, nothing rattles you. I'm not that way. I feel things. The world churns inside me."

Rosen watched as the image of his wife sitting across the table from him turned watery and blurred into visual static. He blinked and felt a warm, wet spot on his cheek. "It's not really like that, Millie. I just have trouble figuring out feelings—my own, too. But," he began, but then left the entire thought unspoken. He was already shutting down, lowering the internal pressure, sliding the safety rods into place in his mental reactor. "You do what you have to do, Millie," he said at long last. "I don't want anything to happen to you."

She reached across the table to rest her hand on his. He stared down at their hands, recording a high-contrast image of them against the bright spring colors of the table cloth, freezing the frame until he realized that Millie's hand was no longer there and she had left the room.

16

Ferguson and Dougherty faced each other across the conference table in the London office of Selian Atlantic. Ferguson had his Drambuie and Dougherty had his Irish whiskey, and both of them were tired.

"It wasn't me, Douglas."

"Nor me. So, who has been trying to do bodily harm to our boy in a very visible, very public way."

Ferguson stiffened defensively. "The only person I have talked with about Dr. David is Xander Quarry, but we made no plans and didn't initiate any action. Bernie's accident put everything on hold, and we never got back to discussing the matter. You don't think...?"

"I do. Look, somebody tried to run the guy off the road, and then we learn through a contact in the Ipswich Lab that he was taken by ambulance to the hospital where he was fighting for his life against an onslaught of infectious agents that had 'prescription cocktail' stamped all over them. Luckily, we had our informant in place and were able to concoct a cockamamie research protocol that would enable us to administer some of our private-stock antibiotics.

"It is a good thing that we had the foresight years ago to keep pushing development of a deep reserve of never-released drugs and the discipline to use them selectively and rarely enough so that nothing out there has had a chance to develop resistance. Fortunately. If our Doctor David had died and there had been an investigation, who knows how far the probe could have reached. We are talking about Boston, here, not some country clinic in rural California run by rubes. These people know what they are doing."

"Well, for the moment, Douglas, all is quiet on the eastern front, but we better quickly find out who unleashed the assault troops so we can get them to sound retreat."

"You know what I'm thinking, Andras?"

"Chas, please."

"Okay. You know what I'm thinking, Chas?"

"No, but I can guess. Whatever it is, it probably involves a plane ride."

Dougherty nodded and took another sip of whiskey. "I hate it every time it comes to this, have from the beginning."

Ferguson swirled his drink. "And it has been coming to this from the beginning."

Dougherty sucked air. "You never let it go, do you? It was so long ago, and you are still holding onto it, as if you had been the one, as if it were your story."

"It's all of our stories. And Janella's." He could picture her still, feel her energy, her determination. She had been unstoppable.

17

Janella Kai was the copper-skinned daughter of a Japanese-American businessman with a taste for Hispanic women and a Brazilian housekeeper who was determined to rise above poverty. Janella's mother saw her as a window of opportunity, and her father had added an extra L to the Portuguese word to make her name easier for Americans to know how to pronounce. Always one to look for ways to make things easier, particularly for himself, Haruto "Harry" Kai had departed when Janella was still in diapers and had never bothered to return from South America. Raised by her mother to be their two-for-one ticket up from the Cambridge projects, Janella had twice skipped a grade, then soldiered her way into Rindge and Latin High School and finally into a full scholarship at Tufts, where she had maintained a straight-A average until her mother had died suddenly. Janella, on her own at nineteen and with no promises left to keep, dropped out of school one semester short of a degree.

The pint-sized ballerina had danced into the newly opened cancer research lab at Harvard, trailing her long scarf like a young Isadora Duncan. When she spotted Emile, she snaked her way through the labyrinth of partially unpacked boxes and miscellaneous equipment disgorged on the floor to plant herself, splay-footed, right in front of him. "I'm Janella Kai," she announced, slapping a folded and marked-up copy of the *Harvard Crimson* onto the granite top of the workbench. "I'm your new lab assistant."

"Well, hi! I'm Emile Aubuchon. I didn't realize that Dr. Dougherty had hired somebody already."

"Yeah, well, here I am. Where do I start?"

Emile, a post-doc and youngest of the recently assembled research group, was not only taken aback by her entrance but was also hypnotized by her exotic looks: her skin the color of a newly minted penny, her long hair like dark-roast coffee, and her eyes, improbably bright, like polished brass. He stared, then looked around and shrugged, momentarily tongue-tied by being in the presence of a goddess.

"Well, then," she said, whipping off her scarf and coiling it atop the newspaper, "Why don't I start over there with organizing the glassware. This place is messier than a freshman dorm room during midterms."

== ==

In truth, Dougherty had not yet hired anyone, but when he checked in at the lab the next morning, Janella was already there, feeding the Norway rats and making notes on the clipboards hanging from each cage.

"This pup is off its feed," she told him. "You might not want to include her—or him, hard to tell when they're this little—in the study. It may just have a little rat-sized tummy ache, but maybe more. Why start out with an outlier? I figure, we'll get enough outliers later for reasons we'll never decipher. Right? Oh yes, you also have a whole litter of chimeric rats in cage number eight. Shouldn't make a difference, but I thought you should know.

"And I was looking over your research protocol. Emile gave me copies of everything. I think you are going about the synthesis of some of the experimental drugs all wrong. I sketched out an alternative scheme that cuts out two steps on one and three on another sequence. Of course, you'll need to use some different reagents. I can order them for you."

Dougherty scowled and tilted his head back. "And you are who?" he said, in confused annoyance.

"Janella Kai, your new lab assistant. I'd shake hands, but I've been handling the lab residents, you know. Say, you wouldn't happen to know where I might rent an apartment, like real cheap? I'm still sleeping at West Hall, but I'm not actually a Tufts student anymore." She emphasized the word *actually* as if it were ironic or ambiguous or both. "It's one of the quads and my roomies are cool about it, but it's getting sticky sneaking in and out. Pretty soon the residence police will figure out they have a spare bed and move a new student in on top of me. Personally, I prefer to pick my bunkmates myself. So, do you know somebody with an extra room?"

Dougherty, realizing the hiring was a fait accompli, offered to let her stay at his house as a temporary solution, one that turned permanent once their affair started. Emile, who remained fixated on Janella and oblivious to her relationship with Dougherty, continued to follow her around the lab like a stray cat looking for a new home. Eventually, it became evident that Janella had a boyfriend, but Aubuchon, a Canadian transplant, was too polite to inquire or even to comment. It would never have occurred to him that the object of her attachment might be the head of the project and the oldest member of the team.

Janella quickly moved from lab flunky to partner in the project, joining in on meetings, contributing design refinements, and eventually helping to write up results. The affection between her and Dougherty grew until it was obvious even to the oblivious Emile.

The real crisis in the team came not from vying for Janella's affections but from the research itself. Once the results had been analyzed and written up in draft form, their unanticipated breakthrough lay exposed. They were split two-to-one on whether to publish immediately or pursue further research privately. Emile, insisting that he could see both sides, abstained from the vote, but it was evident that he really sided with Janella, who wanted to trumpet their findings to the world.

Dougherty maintained that they could find sources—wealthy individuals or private foundations—that would quietly fund the transformation of research results into clinical technique. "The biggest advantage of staying out of the spotlight," he explained, "is that we can go directly for the big payoff without worrying about irrelevant regulations and bureaucratic barriers."

It was not lost on either Atchison Dougherty or Llewellyn Cass that the vote had split along age lines. At nineteen and twenty-seven respectively, Janella and Emile were still, in their own minds, immortal and invulnerable; Dougherty and Cass were not. The big payoff for Emile and Janella would have been fame, fortune, and a secure future. For Dougherty and Cass, the big payoff they were looking at would be far bigger and much more personal.

With Emile's polite abstention, the matter was settled. Dougherty insisted on the return of all copies of the draft paper, telling the few colleagues who had seen the work that there had been a major error in analysis and a break in protocol and promising an early look at the revised work once the problems were fixed. But Janella would not retreat. She argued. She pleaded. She shouted. And she threatened to take the whole matter to the papers. Dougherty, seeing the battle escalating out of control, backed off and proposed a delay while the group replicated a key part of the research.

= =

The Wursthaus in Harvard Square, a local source of hearty German fare and a popular watering hole at the time, was crowded but just noisy enough to make private conversation possible. "Andras," Dougherty said, leaning across the table, "we have to do something about Janella."

"Something. Yes, I suppose. What do you propose, Douglas? You are the one who got us into this with taking her onto the team and into your bed. If she had remained a simple lab assistant, we would not be at this impasse."

Dougherty savored another bite of sauerbraten, then a thumb-sized potato dumpling, before speaking. "You are right. I got us into this, so I suppose it is my problem. I cannot, unfortunately, merely wave my hand and wish her away. Let me think. Let me think."

Andras sipped his dunkelbier and narrowed his eyes in concentration. "If we had the money, we could buy her off, I suppose. She's hungry. It's unclear to me whether her appetite is more for fortune or for fame."

"Well, we're working on the money part, aren't we? Next week I fly to California to meet these wealthy fruitcakes and try to talk them into switching their research funding from mind expansion to expansion of a different sort. I wish you'd take care of it, Andras. I really do not like dealing with pseudo-intellectual flakes, regardless of how many zeroes might be in their bank balance."

"You know I can't, Douglas. Not yet. I still have duties at Dana-Farber. But I am sure some solution will present itself, and when it does, we will act." He sliced off another section of his bauernwurst and wondered what his conservative parents would have said to see him eating pork sausage and savoring every bite. They had never been religious, but they had always taken seriously their responsebility to properly represent the Jewish people and the Jewish way of life to their Welsh neighbors. It was not until he had returned to Boston after his mother's funeral that Andras had tasted bacon and eggs for the first time. He was an instant convert to what in his mind he still thought of as Christian food.

= =

When Janella took up with the young computer scientist from the Netherlands, Dougherty had, in truth, been terribly jealous, but he also wondered if happenstance might have delivered a gift in disguise. Several nights a week, Janella would visit the young man's apartment, invariably returning late and oversleeping in the morning. Dougherty began to hope that this would become her new obsession, that genetic oncology and cell longevity would be forgotten in the flush of new love.

He was wrong.

= =

Janella was still examining tissue cultures under the microscope when the rest of the crew decided it was time to leave for the day. She promised to lock up, then embarrassed Dougherty by telling him not to wait up for her. Feeling powerless and resentful, he had left the lab in silence. He stopped off at the Wursthaus for a beer and a bratwurst before walking the few blocks to his empty house and an early bedtime.

He awoke with a start at the first sound of a key in the front door. Janella was back, at last. He glanced at the alarm clock on the nightstand: nearly two. He slipped into his bathrobe and tiptoed down the stairs. From the landing, he could just see the bottom edge of the front door as it closed. Janella was not in the entry hall. Her purse was on the stand by the door but her keys were not. She must have gone out again, he thought. He returned to the bedroom and quickly dressed. Outside, a layer of fresh snow was marked by the tracks of her boots leading down the street and onto the porch, then back down again and up toward North Cambridge. Dougherty finished buttoning his coat and started out in the same direction, hurrying, following.

= =

He didn't even know the name of her boyfriend, so he was not much help to the police when they questioned him about her disappearance. She had not shown up at the lab in the morning, and it was another two days before he reported her missing. He explained that he simply assumed she was with her boyfriend. "You know how these young kids are these days," he said, with a wink in his voice. Through acquaintances from college, the police eventually identified Bram Dekker as the mysterious boyfriend. Dekker admitted seeing her that night and said that she had headed back to

Cambridge about one in the morning. When asked why he hadn't gone with her or called a taxi, he said, "You don't know Janella. She insists on taking care of herself. She does capoeira—Brazilian judo—and told me she could take down any guy, even a guy like me, easy."

The police found nothing suspicious at Dekker's apartment, and with no body or evidence of foul play and no family to press the matter, the case eventually became just another unsolved disappearance. Dekker returned to Europe when his studies in the States were complete, and Dougherty returned to his quiet research with Andras and Emile.

18

Dougherty set his empty whiskey glass down on the conference table at Selian Atlantic and stared into it for several seconds before raising his eyes to meet Ferguson's. "Do you want to know what happened that night?" he said. He folded his hands in his lap and leaned back in the conference-room chair.

"No," Ferguson said, flatly, "I don't want to know. If you tell me, then I become an accessory after the fact—long after, but still an accessory."

"There is nothing to become accessory to. I did not kill her. I know that's what you have always thought."

"And that is what you have always said. And there we leave it, until the next uncommon occasion when her name enters conversation."

"You don't believe me, do you. You think I would be capable of that."

"I know you are capable of that, even if you yourself do not pull the trigger or push the victim in the back. We both know what we have had to do to keep this enterprise going and its business quiet."

"At least I have never slipped the needle to a patient."

Ferguson's jaw worked as he bit back words. "On whose direction? And who is it who made the phone calls?" He shook his head sadly. "This is getting us nowhere, Douglas. We have real problems to solve. The business with Janella is old business, so old that I am not sure I remember it."

"I do. I remember it as vividly as if it were yesterday. I remember the fight after I caught up with her. I remember her dancing out of reach when I tried to grab her. I remember the fury in me growing as she ran on young legs, and I struggled to keep up with her. And I remember her sudden stop, her spin like a ballerina, and her foot sweeping toward my face like a club. It was a move straight out of a Jackie Chan movie, except it was capoeira, and it was not done with wires. One second she is running away, and the next her foot is meeting the side of my head.

"And that's it. I came to, shivering in that alley, my jaw and my head aching, feeling lucky to have woken up rather than ending up the subject of headlines: 'Harvard researcher found dead from exposure.' There was no sign of her, no longer even tracks in the snow. I knew as much as the police knew, which was nothing. She vanished that night, presumed dead, as they say, but there was no body, no proof, no charges."

Ferguson let out a deep sigh. "I believe you. I guess I have to believe you."

"That spells a very weak belief, Andras. I loved her. Maybe she was the last person I loved. I would have wanted her at my side, even now."

"You would have had to wait many years. Even now it's not reliable for younger patients. Poor Emile. But we learned a lot in the process, didn't we."

It had been ironic. Emile had volunteered to be the guinea pig for the first clinical application of their findings, which made sense to all three of them, since he was the youngest and heartiest, and they knew better than to consider bringing in anyone new at that time. How could they have known that the whole procedure worked better with older subjects, that the very vigor of youth was a barrier, that the gradual and inevitable weakening of the immune system as people aged made it easier to start the process of chimerization, which was the biological key. Emile had died of a self-administered drug overdose when the pain had become too much to bear and when they all worried that the evidence of medical malpractice would soon become too glaringly apparent.

Ferguson pushed his glass away and stood up from the conference table. "Enough reminiscing. Duty calls. I need to get some sleep if I am going to fly out to California tomorrow."

== =

Ferguson's approach to flying was to carry little or nothing and buy what he needed on arrival. It was a lifestyle option open to him but not for everyone. Still, although he had no checked luggage, he went down to baggage claim because he figured that would be where Xander Quarry would automatically expect to meet him. He was standing around, acting the part of the impatient traveler, when someone tapped him on the shoulder. He turned to find Xander, dressed in black pants, a white shirt with bars on the shoulders, and a black necktie reaching only halfway to his waist and held in place by an incongruously large, gold tie bar.

"You, Xander Quarry, look like some goddamned limousine chauffer. Or are we on our way to some costume party?"

"That's me, just looking the part. Let's go."

He led Ferguson outside to the taxi stand.

"I thought you were driving me. Surely we can't be taking a taxi all the way to the ranch. Or have you now obtained your hackney license?"

"No, no, no. But it's too far to walk." He turned to the dispatcher and said that they wanted to go to the Executive Terminal. The dispatcher looked down at the long line of waiting taxis and shook his head. "Here. First cab. This is one cabbie who is going to be thrilled by such a fare."

The driver did not look happy when he heard where they were headed. "You know where that is, right?" Xander asked.

"Yeah, I know. Out to the 101 north, exit at North Access Road, follow the signs." He flipped the meter and pulled out.

"Are you going to tell me what's going on, Xander, or should I just sit back and enjoy the magical mystery tour?"

"I flew up. Had to pull strings with San Francisco Helicopter to be able to land on their helipad here at SFO. It was either that or the Coast Guard, and I figured it would be damned hard to pull enough strings with the Coast Guard."

When the taxi dropped them off at the non-descript Executive Terminal, Xander slipped the driver a fifty and led the way into the building. He greeted the woman working the desk for San Francisco Helicopter with a wink and announced that his client was ready for the Extended Tour. She winked back and waved him through a door marked "Flight Crew Only." Xander held the door for Ferguson, then marched straight through the room to another door that took them out onto the tarmac. There Ferguson spotted Xander's bright red Robinson Raven being readied by the ground crew.

"I had forgotten what fun it was to fly. Ever since that chase to University Hospital, I have been flying every chance I can get. I figured you might enjoy a flight where you can see what you're flying over for a change. Besides, this is a hell of a lot faster and a lot more fun than two hours of fighting traffic at this time of day.

"Come on get in. This trip I've got time to give you a lesson. We'll start with this, which is called the cyclic and controls the tilt of the helicopter, sort of like a joystick. Except on these Robinsons it is this tilting bar, which, if you just tip it up like this," he demonstrated, "makes it a lot easier to slide in and out." He grinned broadly as he walked around to the other side, tilted the cyclic back again, and slid into the pilot's seat.

= =

They were at the Ranch and already sitting at poolside in just over half an hour. Ferguson and Xander watched as Nadia tried for the fifth time to execute a clean back flip off the high board. "Arch your back more, honey. Spot the water," Xander coached her, as she sputtered to the surface.

"How long has she been back?" Ferguson asked. "Where did you find her?"

"She was back the day after you left, towing by his earlobe the poor slob who took off with her. She chewed me out for letting it happen—it was all my fault, according to her—and told me to stay sober or stay out of her life. She acts like she owns this place. Someday she could, since she's my only heir." He poured some more San Pellegrino into his glass, swirled it to reduce the bubbles, and took a sip. "See what I am being reduced to?" he said, holding the glass up to the light and swirling it again. "Mineral water." He set the glass down. "You were pretty quiet on the way down from SFO and, as expected, said nothing over the phone about the purpose of this visit. What's up?"

"The same matter we were discussing on my last visit. Except it seems that you went ahead and hired a contractor without getting the go ahead."

"I did no such thing. I queried an old contact in Vegas, told him that there might be 100K for the right person who could do the job right, and he told me he would get back to me. I never heard anything more."

"Then it sounds like we have a freelancer on the loose. Some 'mechanic' thinks he has a deal and is trying to complete the contract. But whoever it is, he is far too clumsy. Now we have to make this mechanic disappear before he succeeds and brings everything down on top of him—and us."

"I can talk with my man in Vegas again."

"And have this story get around? It's not like your man in Vegas is either a good judge of employees or knows the meaning of discreet inquiries. No, I have a better idea. Do call your man in Vegas, but tell him the job is done and you are ready to make good on the deal. The mechanic just has to come and collect."

"Here? Are you nuts? We want a mafia hit man showing up at the Ranch?"

"Maybe not. Pick a place to meet, some spot he has to drive to.

Make him come to us, where we can manage the stage, someplace where there won't be an audience."

"You know, you are beginning to talk like some of the union goodfellas I bumped into when Bernie and I were riding the building boom in Las Vegas."

"Well, I am a man of many talents and many sides. We need to end this episode and bury the evidence."

Xander smiled and nodded. "That gives me an idea."

= =

From the air it could have been a children's sandbox filled with bright yellow Tonka Toy construction equipment left scattered after the preschoolers had returned home from their play. As the helicopter descended, details betrayed how long the site had sat idle. Rust marred the finish of a front loader, and the larger of the two bulldozers at the site had one track spread out in mid-repair, with weeds growing between the treads. Xander circled once to check for fresh tire tracks or footprints, but there were no signs that anyone had been there for years.

"Now we wait," he said over the intercom, as he spun the helicopter around and retreated over the next ridge. "Are you sure you want to do this?"

"It's a two-man job, you said that yourself. And I need to verify that we have the right man. I have never liked loose ends."

"I could have gotten Frank to fly, you know. Frank asks no questions and has no ambitions."

"Xander, you must know by now that I am really an old-fashioned kind of hands-on doctor who still makes house calls. And look, there comes our man, ready to meet the doctor." He pointed toward a dust plume marking a path through the trees and snaking its way toward the clearing. Xander gently pressed down on the collective to drop the helicopter and then deftly held them hovering barely above the treetops, just out of the sightlines from the construction area. Just as the pickup truck pulled into the open at the site,

Xander lifted the helicopter well above the trees and smartly brought it in toward the clear ground between the pickup and the smaller bulldozer. He set the helicopter down parallel to the truck amidst a whirlwind of dust, then left the engine idling and ducked quickly out of the far side. Ferguson hopped out on his side and advanced toward the pickup with his arms spread, his left hand holding a thick envelope.

The man coming around the front of the pickup truck from the driver side was a walking cliché in his denim jacket, dusty jeans, and cowboy boots. His hair was slicked back and tied tightly at the back of his head. He held his jacket pushed open just enough to expose the edge of a handgun tucked into his waistband.

Images of *High Noon* flashed in Ferguson's head, and he smiled broadly as he lowered his hands slowly, keeping them in plain sight.

"Are you Quarry?" the man asked.

"No, an associate."

"You fly that thing?" He pointed past Ferguson towards the now empty helicopter, which was partially obscured by the still settling dust.

"I have many talents. And what did you say your name was?"

"I go by Adam Cain, a sort of biblical reference, you know. Mr. Quarry knows who can always get in touch with me, should you ever need my services again. Just ask for Adam Cain. Now, you do have the money, don't you?" he said, reaching for the envelope.

Ferguson lifted it away from the man's outstretched hand but kept smiling. "I need to know what you did to earn it first."

"Yeah, sure. I hit the mark. Made it look like natural causes, an accident. It was a surgical strike, so to speak. Ha, ha, inside joke. Don't let appearances mislead you. I'm a college grad and have been in this business a long time. I know a lot of ways to take care of trouble. First I got him scraped up really bad, then a nurse I hired slipped in and spread him with an unstoppable stew of nasty bugs, stuff that modern medicine has nothing to fight. She just mixed specimens from several really sick patients from the research hospital where she works. It was what the doctors call resistant strains, multiple-drug-resistant bacteria. You know what I mean?"

"I do. But you didn't tell all the story, did you."

"Okay, there were some hiccups, yeah. At one point, I thought I saw him out of the hospital, so I took action. I was wrong. He was still in isolation, so I ended up taking out some dumb duck who looked too much like the target. So? Anyway, I headed home before the local police even knew the accident had happened. They're still looking for a stock Ford pickup, white, with front-end damage. I drive a blue job, with custom detailing, clean as a whistle, as you can see. I'm a pro, and the main thing is: I did the job."

"A pro? Are you sure you did the job? How do you know?"

"What do you take me for? It was confirmed. I got a call that said the guy had succumbed to sepsis a few days after he entered the hospital."

"You don't read newspapers, do you?"

Cain looked puzzled. "Hey, do I get my fee or what? I still have to settle with the nurse."

Ferguson handed the envelope over with his left hand and rested his right on Adam Cain's shoulder. "You get your money, Mr. Cain. How much do you owe the nurse?"

Cain pulled a thick stack of used hundreds from the envelope and riffled through it, smiling. "Ten grand," he said, "that's all I promised the bitch, almost nothing."

The spring-loaded syringe plunged into his neck at the same moment as Ferguson grabbed the gun from Cain's waist and stepped back. Cain reached to his neck and struggled to stay standing, then slumped down against the front tire of his pickup. He looked up at Ferguson briefly before rolling his eyes and falling completely to the ground. Ferguson retrieved the packet of bills and the envelope and walked back toward the helicopter.

As Ferguson slipped into the passenger seat, Xander finally succeeded in starting the reluctant engine of the bulldozer. He steered it around the helicopter and straight toward the pickup truck, which he shoved over into the hollow at the edge of the clearing. It rolled once and rested upside down at the bottom of the depression. Xander backed up and sent Cain's body in after it. Then he started methodically reworking the contours of the area, beginning with a huge mound of fill waiting to the side of the hollow. A half hour later, the site looked freshly worked but with no sign whatsoever that there had ever been a pickup or a Mr. Adam Cain there.

Xander returned the bulldozer to where it had started and climbed back into the still idling helicopter. He slipped on the intercom headset and signaled Ferguson to put on the other one.

"Pretty professional work," Ferguson told him. "Where'd you learn how to operate construction equipment?"

"Oh, when we were dealing real estate in Las Vegas, I would sometimes sub in when a development wasn't moving along fast enough. Bernie worked the numbers and the deals, but I've always been good with vehicles—all kinds. Watch this." He advanced the throttle slowly, then edged up on the collective to lift them off the ground. He then worked the controls like a choral conductor, constantly adjusting the cyclic, the anti-torque pedals, and the collective, orchestrating the helicopter in a complicated dance that used the downdraft to sweep the area clean of footprints, tire tracks, and other traces of recent activity.

"That was fun!" he shouted over the intercom. "And you have no idea how hard that is to do when your own dust is blinding you and you're only feet off the ground. Here, take this and dump it out the window." He handed Ferguson a small sack.

"What's in it?" Ferguson said, as he emptied it.

"Weed seeds. We're due for a rain this weekend. In another week, no one will even be able to tell that anyone has been here. Now, let's head home." He pulled up on the collective, sending the helicopter into a sharp climb.

"We have one more loose end. This guy—called himself Adam Cain—mentioned a nurse who he hired to infect Dr. David. We will have to track her down, but I think all we will need to do is settle the account with the agreed fee. I do still worry about somebody stumbling on this site and digging, though."

"Nobody's going to stumble on it, and nobody's going to dig. I bought it through one of Bernie's many shell companies when the owners ran out of cash years ago. The perimeter of the property is posted. I've overflown it now and then just to see if anyone has been poking around. No one is going to uncover our business, and with the business our Mr. Cain was in, no one is going to be inquiring after him. Frankly, one less hit man on the planet seems to me like the makings of a good day's work." He pushed on the cyclic and angled them back toward Quarry Ranch. "I've got a bottle of sparkling Malvasia Bianca from this Hecker Pass winery that will knock your socks off. Lilacs and lime on the nose and mangoes and lemons on the tongue. The perfect way to celebrate. A couple of glasses won't hurt me."

19

Millie moved out on a Saturday amidst tears and hugs, leaving Rosen more confused than ever. She said she would call every week, but refused to tell him where she was going. She argued that if they were still after him, it was better that he not know too much about her plans. He rejected her anxiety as irrational and felt abandoned by her but kept his own unacknowledged anxiety at bay by making plans of his own.

He still did not know who might be after him, other than that they had some connection with Biontolics. Whoever they were, they seemed to be everywhere. They had even been in the house at some point. With no sign of breaking and entry or anything else missing, his laptop had disappeared from the closet where he kept it. He bought himself a slim new netbook at Best Buy for cash and set about meticulously reconstructing his online life from memory—with significant changes. He created new web email and PayPal accounts, new log-in credentials for sites that he needed to access, and a completely fabricated online persona. He knew that he was an amateur but began to teach himself about encryption software that hid files and email from prying eyes, anonymizers that disguised the location of a computer, and safe ways to use public wi-fi. He never worked from the house but began alternating in a random pattern between a Starbucks down in Peabody, one up in Newburyport, and Zumi's Café, his favorite local spot with great coffee and free Wi-Fi.

He delayed returning to Biontolics for an extra week under the pretext of recovering from his accident and the bout with MRSA, but eventually he had to reestablish his office routine, playing the part of the dedicated researcher working on nothing of consequence. He said nothing about Millie at work, but somehow word seemed to get around that she had left him. Jeannine let a decent interval of several more weeks pass before inviting him to dinner. "I hope that's all right. I mean, I heard that you guys had split, but if you don't want to talk, you don't have to. And we don't have to do dinner."

"No, that's all right. It's not what you think. But I suppose we could have dinner, if you like." He could feel his heart pounding but, as usual, was unable to decipher the precise message his guts were sending him. "Do you want to leave from work, or should we meet someplace?"

"I notice you have been leaving kind of early from here since you got back. You used to put in some impressively long hours, but these days..." she trailed off. "Maybe we should meet later. I'm not sure I want to have dinner at half-past five."

"Well, yeah. I didn't think my office hours were quite that obvious, but, face it, there's not a lot of real work to do here anymore, in case you hadn't noticed. So, where do you want to meet?"

"Maybe Michael's in Newburyport, say eight-ish?"

= =

The parking lot at Michael's Harborside was packed, and Rosen ended up having to find a space in a municipal lot. By the time he walked back to the restaurant, Jeannine was waiting. She had changed since leaving work, and the sleeveless black dress she wore showed off her graceful neck. Rosen found himself noticing things: how the color of her eyes matched her light brown hair and how her smile filled her face when she spotted him coming across the parking lot.

Michael's was a noisy mess, with the usual Friday-night crowd multiplied by no less than three special parties. "We should have made reservations," he said, coming back from checking inside. "They're saying it will be 45 minutes before we can get a table, and then who knows how long before we are served."

"Then let's not," she said, taking his arm and turning him around. "We can go to my place. I live five minutes from here. If you don't mind me whipping up something while you have a glass of wine or two."

Rosen was aware that if she had asked him over for dinner, it would have seemed too forward, and he would have declined. But this—this was different, unintended, almost innocent. Almost. He nodded and followed her out of the restaurant.

= =

Rosen speared the last sliver of chicken on his plate, drew it through the remnants of a mirror of raspberry-cilantro sauce, and savored it with his eyes closed. He washed it down with the rest of the Riesling in his glass. Before he could say anything, Jeannine had refilled it.

"That was amazing. You are quite the chef, you know. There is more to you than meets the eye," he said.

"You, too," she countered.

Emboldened by the wine, Rosen decided to go for broke. "If I asked you whether you have been spying on me, would you answer honestly?"

"If I had been spying on you, I would hardly answer honestly, now would I?" She stared across the table as if waiting for some cue from him, unsure whether or not to say more. "Spying is the wrong word, anyway," she said. "Truth? Okay, if you are ready for it." She took a deep breath before continuing. "Part of my job is to keep an eye on people. I get paid extra to let London know what you have been up to. There's nothing sinister. You are valuable property, Rosen, and I think Biontolics likes to keep an eye on valuable property."

"Nothing sinister? You call stealing computers nothing sinister?

How about attempted murder. Is that nothing sinister? Actually, leave off the attempted. A colleague of my wife was killed. Now that's sinister."

"You don't think Biontolics had anything to do with any of that, do you? I mean, that's crazy. You had a traffic accident. Your wife had a traffic accident." She paused, letting her own words sink in.

"Patterns," he said. "Patterns and probabilities: that's what we deal in, Jeannine. First they block my research, then it disappears; then I post a paper anonymously and that disappears; then all the related research disappears, and then my personal laptop at home goes missing." He almost added, "and then my wife," but censored it. "Plus, after I try to get the word out, I land in the hospital and my wife's friend, who looks a little like me, lands in the cemetery. And you are saying this is nothing, nothing sinister."

She turned her head to one side but kept her gaze locked on him. She opened her mouth as if to speak, then closed it again.

"What do you know, Jeannine? Tell me."

"I know I could be fired."

"Maybe. Me, too. Except I've been involved in a lot of independent activity lately, and one thing they have not done is fire me."

"They wouldn't do that because they want to keep you on a short leash. And you just keep chewing it off."

Rosen got up from the table and walked around to squat beside her chair. He rested his hand on her thigh and looked her in the eye. "Please, Jeannine, tell me the truth. Tell me what is going on."

"I don't know. That's the truth. But I do know that all your computers have had loggers installed, that your phone is tapped and your cellphone has been jiggered in some way, and that they know about your latest gambit of trying to contact somebody at *The Boston Globe*. But you said something about other research disappearing."

"Yeah, all the supporting internal studies have also vanished from the project files and archives at work."

"But how would you know that, since I know for a fact that you have not been doing any problematic poking around at the Lab recently. Like I said, everything you do is monitored."

Rosen felt a flash of triumph as he realized that not everything he had been was being tracked. "Alright, then, whose side are you on, Jeannine? Last time I asked, you dodged the question. This time I want to know. When it comes down to hard choices, what would you choose, them or me?"

She leaned slowly toward him and gave him a long, deep kiss, then pulled back. Neither spoke. Rosen looked down at his hand still resting on her thigh then up into her eyes again. "I don't think," he said, but she put a finger to his lips before he could finish and then rose to lead him into the bedroom.

= =

Rosen, who had been with no one except Millie since their college days, felt like an uncertain student again—awkward and eager at the same time. He was shy about the scars that painted his leg and embarrassed at how he kept mentally comparing Jeannine to Millie. Jeannine felt wrong and wonderful in his arms. He marveled at her solid body and the way she wrapped her long legs around him, at how their bodies matched so perfectly in proportions. He savored the taste of her tongue and the exotic smell of her breath, ripe with the Riesling they had been drinking but with another note that was just Jeannine and not Millie. And with each unbidden comparison, he was shot through with excitement and with guilt.

They lay in bed afterward, both staring in silence at the stippled ceiling as if it displayed some secret script to be decoded. Jeannine finally spoke, one word, a word of absolute ambiguity: "Well."

Rosen—who would have preferred the word were "Wow!"—propped himself up on an elbow and asked, "What are we going to do?"

"Not this, not again," she answered.

"Why? What's wrong?"

"This. Oh, don't misunderstand me. I loved it. You were sweet and generous, and you gave me something I have wanted from you for a very long time. But we were not alone in the room. You couldn't escape her presence. Even I could feel it. Each time you thought of her it was as if someone standing in the hallway had spoken, and, for a moment, you would leave and go elsewhere."

"I'm sorry."

"No need to be. I should be sorry for having put you in that position. After all, you are still married."

"Neither of us should be sorry. And I am not so sure that this should never happen again. I'm just, well, out of practice."

She ran a finger down his nose and then kissed it. "Well, you did just fine for someone claiming to be out of practice." She grinned at him and shook her head. "Anyway, I hope one thing is settled."

"What's that?"

"Your question about loyalties. I'm on your side, completely. I hope you realize that. And so, we have to decide what is the best way to use the fact that you now have a double agent behind enemy lines."

20

The Boardroom at Selian Atlantic was being used for actual business, meaning the cover business of a high-roller reinsurance group, so Ferguson and Dougherty arranged to meet at a club in London. The Nights of the Round Table had a silly, tourist-slanted name and a limited menu, but it was a place where a private dining room could be organized on short notice. On this particular night, they ended up not with a round table but with a square one flanked by high-backed wooden benches and lit by a four-branched brass candelabra. Over Yorkshire pudding and a bottle of a private label burgundy that Dougherty had brought with him, they went through their punch list of matters needing review or decisions.

"Oh, yes, we've had to do some shuffling of assignments at the clinic in Russia," Dougherty said, after flicking past several pages on his open iPad.

"Why is that?"

"We lost two of our best technicians there. Really more than technicians. They were working on some independent research that now somebody else is going to have to decipher and carry on."

"Who was it? How did we lose them? Certainly there's nobody around who could hire any of our people away, not at what we pay them."

Dougherty looked down at his iPad and read. "Dmitri Boryshkin and Svetlana Petrova. They worked together in the immunology group. Pity. An auto accident. Those Russians, you know how they all drive."

"Hang on, who did you say?"

Dougherty read the names again, pronouncing them slowly and exaggerating the rolled Rs in each: "Dmitri Boryshkin and Svetlana Petrova. You knew them?"

Ferguson blanched. "I know many people at *Nichevo*. That's where I work, in fact. That is, when I am doing my real work instead of chasing around the globe fighting fires."

Dougherty tapped on the table beside the screen. "This Svetlana— isn't that the Sveta you have mentioned a couple of times? Yes, that's right, now I remember, you were seeing her, not so? You know, maybe you need to be more choosy with your liaisons, my friend. From the looks of it, this woman was pretty wild. She wrapped her car around a tree driving to work one morning. And that happened only days after we got a report from one of our informants that she was talking about some sort of exposé if she didn't get what she was after. Whatever that was. You wouldn't have anything to add to the report, would you, Chas?"

Ferguson's faced turned from white to red. "Anything I might add is no doubt already in your reports. Only days, was it? Coincidence or, perhaps, convenient timing one might say. You offed her, didn't you? You arranged a so-called accident for her because she was beginning to look like what you would call a nuisance. 'Shedding resources' in the management-speak you prefer these days. Without even checking with me."

"And you? It would seem that in your pillow talk you may have said too much, perhaps offered her an inside track without first checking with me."

"I did no such thing. She sussed the whole thing out on her own. She was pretty damned smart, but I had her in a holding pattern. There was no need to take precipitous action, certainly not without our going over it together. Douglas, you are acting more and more like this is your show, and the rest of us be damned."

"It is my show. And yours. There are really no others, not any that truly matter—except as experimental subjects or cash cows or both."

Ferguson knew there was no arguing with his partner, who was both right and wrong at the same time. Certainly it was true that the two of them stood atop a vast pyramid that sustained them, but that was not the same as saying no one else mattered. Ferguson wondered if perhaps he was, at an advanced age, developing a conscience and a sense of ethics. Or was he just going soft? As he thought more on the matter, he concluded that, if anything, he was becoming hardened to the demands of being Pharaoh, perched atop a pyramid, a living god with the power of life and death in his staff.

Suddenly, he became aware that Dougherty was still talking.

"So, as you know from the media reports," he was saying, "Mbutsu's forces have quelled yet another uprising, this time hardly more than a small band of poorly armed mercenaries imported from across the border, but once more the retaliation has been brutal."

"I would think that a few more deaths would hardly bother you anymore, Douglas."

"A few. A few may be necessary—is necessary. But this man and his machete-armed minions massacre thousands at a stroke. I do wish we didn't still need his money. Oh, yes, and I hate to say it, but you may have to go down there again. It seems even Colfax wasn't enough to put everything back right. And Edgar now claims he is overdue for the next treatment. I don't know. You are the physician, the one who keeps track of the schedules and monitors everything. I hardly even understand the technology I helped to invent—not any more.

"You know, Chas, with all the time you spend in tropical Africa, perhaps you should line up a little black honey to warm your hut on that end of your travels."

"No need to be crude, Douglas. We all know about the extent of your own sainthood." Ferguson knew he had hit home with that remark, a reference to the numerous times the organization had acted to extricate Dougherty from a dalliance gone sour. There had been little on that front in recent years, but still, the stories were a subliminal irritant that remained beneath the surface, ready for use by a friend who was still stinging from the loss of a lover.

Dougherty, always the one to be in control, ignored the remark and continued going down his list. "And last but not least, we have the matter of our dear Dr. Rosen David. It seems as if he may have settled down or given up. Or maybe he is just playing us on his line. Holzinger says he's been clean for weeks, and the reports from our onsite minder are becoming boringly routine. As the pioneers would say in the old American films, it's quiet out there, maybe too quiet."

"I agree. After Africa, it's off to the New World for this weary pioneer. I have nothing pressing in Russia, it would seem. Our trusted Doctor Nevsky will handle the reassignments to cover our losses in personnel. We can let the clinic run itself for a while—or be run by others, whatever expression best fits. Reader's choice."

Dougherty gave Ferguson one of his undecipherable looks, closed his iPad, and rose from the table. There was a moment when each of them seemed about to speak, but it passed, and the dinner ended with a wordless farewell and a silent exit.

21

At first, Millie's untraceable calls on SkypeOut had been an added bit of Friday night ritual, a way of touching base and reaching out through disembodied voices to sustain some semblance of connection. But then she would miss a Friday and call midweek to leave a brief message at a time when Rosen was out. As the intervals between calls slowly increased, the conversations they did have were filled with less and less. The distance that had always periodically inserted itself in their relationship, even when they were together every day, steadily grew into an ocean that mere conversation could not cross. Rosen could feel the winter ice thickening in the sea between them, could sense his own feelings cooling as the words became mere words and the "I love you" at the end of their calls was like the ritual "amen" after recitation of a prayer long outdated by disbelief.

Rosen's world had tilted, and as one pole was freezing over, the other was warming. Rosen knew full well that he was entering uncharted waters, but he kept seeing Jeannine, both hoping and fearing that they would end up in bed together again. She managed to keep the prospect at bay by controlling the venues, making sure that they were unlikely to be spotted by any Biontolics people and lowering the odds that they might end up in bed. Rosen admired her ingenuity and integrity, while being irritated at the same time. Ironically, the more she insisted they stick to words and keep their distance physically, the more Rosen found that he was falling in love with her. It was a novel experience. He was coming to realize that he had never fallen in love with Millie, that they had fallen into bed and into each other's lives so precipitously that it had been an event, a discontinuity and not a process. There was before Millie, and then they were married and making a life together. Rosen knew that he had loved her, but it was a memory, like the way he still knew the address of their first apartment in Somerville. The love was—had been—real, as real as any feeling was for Rosen, but even now, so soon after her departure, he remembered it rather than felt it.

For Jeannine, it was all process, a process that had been underway since the day she was hired by Biontolics and had started sharing an office with an enigma. The special assignment she had accepted was a bonus that had given her an excuse to insert herself into Rosen's life, to study him under the microscope of corporate espionage. And then, on the very verge of fantasies realized, she had pulled back to hold him at arm's length. So it was that they ate dinner in safely un-romantic settings and walked the boardwalk in Newburyport without even holding hands, all the time both of them feeling the heat of sublimation radiating, like the glow from a bed of banked coals in a fireplace just waiting for fresh wood to be added.

It was a cloudy-bright day in southern Maine. They were walking a near-empty stretch of shoreline, their hands separated by inches but connected by invisible magnetic lines of force, pulsing in an in-substantial aura that engulfed them. They talked of science and fate and philosophy as the lines of force connecting them intensified.

"Do you believe, Rosen?" she asked abruptly, without offering a context.

"Do I believe? Yes, I believe. I believe in many things."

"No, silly, you know what I mean. Do you believe in God?"

"No."

"Just that? A one word theology? Surely there is more to the story. I know that you don't like going out on Friday night. For a time, I thought it was because of what happened that first time we had dinner together, but then I caught on that you light candles and eat challah at home."

"Yeah, but that has nothing to do with God. I'm Jewish. On Friday nights, we light candles, eat challah, and bless our wine—whether we believe in anything or not." He did not say that his observance had also been about waiting for Millie's calls, even though they no longer came.

"But why? What's that about?"

"Habit. I mean, these customs, these habits, well, it's a deeply rutted road we Jews travel."

"Did you ever believe?"

"Oh, sure, don't we all, when we are children? I went to Hebrew school, learned to read Hebrew and chant Torah, even did a bar mitzvah. But by that time, I had already figured out that men made God and not the other way around. All that stuff is still in me, though. I haven't been inside a synagogue since my uncle on my mother's side died fifteen years ago, but I can still rattle off the *Sh'ma* and the *V'ahavta*."

She gave him an inquiring look.

"The *Sh'ma*. It's a theological one-liner, the first Hebrew you learn and the last words on the lips of the dying. *Sh'ma yisrael*. Hear, o Israel, the Lord is God, the Lord is One. That's followed by," he took a breath and started chanting in rapid Hebrew. "*V'ahavta et Adonai elohekha, b'khol-l'vav'kha uvkhol-nafsh'kha uvkhol-m'odekha*. And so forth. You never forget it."

"And what is it?"

"'And you shall love the Lord with all of your heart and all of your soul and all of your strength.' I'm sure you've heard it before in some form. And you?"

"Lapsed Catholic. But I know what you are talking about. I know most of the mass by heart and can still sing 'Adeste Fidelis' in Latin." She started to sing in her husky alto voice, then stopped. "But you get the idea. You are right, the grooves are cut pretty deep in the cortex."

"I said ruts in the road—different metaphor. You have grooves, we have ruts. But the end result is much the same, I suppose. We grow up. We leave the mystical mush behind, but the muscle learning remains. You can take the Jew out of the Temple, but you never get the Temple out of the Jew."

"Or the catechism out of the Catholic. Do you think it comes from being smart, I mean figuring out that religion is just ritual, a game we invented to comfort ourselves on stormy nights—or on our deathbeds?"

"Possibly. But there has to be more to it than just intelligence or education. Some people set it aside and others cling to religion as if their life depended on it, which, of course, is what religions want us to believe. Nick Borofski, Rabbi Nick, was one of the smartest men I ever knew. He had a PhD in physics, yet he believed—with all of his heart and all of his soul and all of his strength. It's complicated. Look, I'm a scientist, and I know too much to believe in a simple God of creation. The God I was taught in Hebrew school makes no sense to me, but dig deep enough in any direction, and the science stops making sense, too."

"What do you mean? Science is one of the few things in life that *does* make sense."

"Only as long as you don't look too closely, particularly when it comes to the biggest questions. Consider: Why are we here? Why is anything here? How did it start? Anyone who believes that modern cosmology explains the origins of the universe is kidding themselves. Physics and astronomy have become elaborate shell games, in which problems are shuffled between hidden dimensions and in which enormously complicated mathematics disguises ultimate ignorance. Even if the theories are right, they are just descriptions that explain absolutely nothing. So, what if our universe was, as some theories maintain, the result of the collision of infinite super-dimensional membranes in a hyperspace bulk? What does that explain? Where did these so-called 'branes' come from? What created them? We have just swept the question under a cosmological rug. It's stage magic on a galactic scale, mathematical misdirection.

"We can describe precisely and in minute detail the first nanoseconds of the history of our universe, but what came before the Big Bang? What caused it? Saying that the question is disallowed because time did not exist before the start of the universe or claiming that the universe caused itself or that ours is only one of an infinite number of alternative universes in a manifold multiverse—this 'science' is little more than learned and intricate word play, an infinite regress, matrochka dolls nested inside other matrochka dolls without end. For the big questions, the ones that one might say really matter, science is insufficient. It comes up short—wordy and complicated but still short.

"The bottom line for me, Jeannine, is that God makes no sense, but a world without God, a purely scientific universe, also makes no sense. And if you want to know the whole truth, I just prefer not to puzzle over such imponderables, which is why I do the work I do, where the numbers know their places and the equations behave themselves and the problems are all solvable."

"Kurt Gödel would have had something to say about that," she said.

"Well, yes, there is that, too. I remember how excited I was when I first worked my way through Gödel's Incompleteness Theorems. To learn that one could prove, rigorously, that logic and mathematics were themselves fundamentally flawed and limited—wow! Heady stuff! And then there's Heisenberg and quantum uncertainty. Incompleteness, undecidability, paradox—these are in the very nature of science, its methods of measurement, and the mathematical tools it depends on. So we can never know. We can even prove it, that we can never know, that it is not just us but reason itself that is limited. Which brings us back to where we started."

"It does?"

"Yes. Spinoza—you know about Spinoza? Spinoza, the supreme Jewish heretic, set out to prove, through logic alone, the existence of God. In a sense he succeeded, at least to his own satisfaction and that of his followers, but Spinoza's God turned out to be, in the end, one with the Universe itself, identical with the whole of Nature—capital N, as my wife always spelled it—and that, as I have just reiterated, is demonstrably unknowable by science and reason. We are back to another paradox."

Rosen knew that he was on a roll, and his eyes danced with excitement. "We might as well turn Spinoza on his ear. Take the set of all functions that cannot be computed, all theorems that can neither be proved nor disproved, all measurement that can never be resolved, all statements that are undecidable—and maybe throw in all unreachable, unknowable reaches of the universe—take these sets, which themselves cannot be enumerated nor limned but that we can rigorously prove exist, and call them God."

"I like it: Gödel's God. Very clever, Rosen."

"But not really original. It's the God constructed of whatever we don't know: the unknown, the unexplained, just the venerable God of the Gaps reformulated in modern metamathematics."

"God of the Gaps: which number is that?"

Rosen started to smile broadly. "Number twelve," he said. "Number twelve of *36 Arguments for the Existence of God.*"

"*A work of Fiction,*" she finished with the subtitle. "You read Rebecca Goldstein, too?"

"Of course. I loved it. The characters are a little talky and cerebral, though."

"Rosen, we're a little talky and cerebral. But are you sure it's really number twelve?"

"I don't know, I made that part up. I just remember the God of the Gaps, an argument from ignorance."

"This is more than ignorance. I think you have gone one step further. Your Gödel's God is not the God of the Unknown but the God of the Unknowable, the Unprovable, not merely the Unknown or Unproven. You've upped the ante and given God a permanent residence instead of a desert tabernacle retreating in the ever-changing sands of scientific progress."

"Yes, well, and this has been fun, but not where we started. You asked me about belief. God aside—whether Spinoza's or Gödel's or Rabbi Nick's—what I believe, what I personally believe, is that we are here for a purpose, whether preordained or of our own inventtion, it doesn't matter. It is purpose itself that matters. And I do mean 'we'—all of us, collectively, are part of something that, by its very definition, is bigger than our selves. Perhaps it ultimately comes down to the conundrum of self-awareness: we are the Universe becoming aware of itself.

"At least that's the answer I came up with for a philosophy term paper I wrote as an undergraduate."

"You are, in your own oddball ways, a deep thinker, Rosen. And you gave me so much more than I asked. I'm still just that Catholic girl turned mathematician and amateur spy who is trying to sort out what Biontolics is really about and what to do about it."

"You haven't figured it out yet? You don't know what they are doing and why this is a life-and-death issue? You really are a pure math person, Jeannine. You have to spend less time looking at the numbers and more at what the numbers represent. If the cosmologists did that, they would be more in touch with the absurdity of replacing the simple deity of biblical storytelling with an unimaginably complex narrative of numbers and equations that hover beyond comprehension."

He spent the next quarter hour going over in detail what he had learned, starting with the first unpublished paper and leading up to the latest conclusions from his off-hours research.

"I'm still intrigued by what happened to the other original researchers," he announced at the end. "I've learned that Aubuchon died in 1982 of a drug overdose, Llewellyn Cass died on an expedition in Patagonia, but Janella Kai just vanished. This leaves Atchison Douglas Dougherty the only witness to history, their history, but I've hit a wall. I thought I knew how to do online research, but I'm getting nowhere."

"Maybe that's your problem, Rosen? Like your comical cosmologists, you are caught inside a box of your own making. To you, research means online research. You've rewritten Mackenzie's First Law. 'If it's not written down, it doesn't exist,' has transmogrified into the mantra of modern methods: 'If it's not on the Web, it doesn't exist.' Fail, Rosen.

"My aunt Cecelia does genealogy. If she took your approach, we would still know nothing about the Italian branch of our family. She had to go into the LDS microfilm archives to get anywhere. You need to get real, leave the virtual world behind and get your hands dirty. Go do some digging in the Boston Public Library."

They had reached a point on the shore where they would either have to start climbing over bus-size boulders or turn around. Jeannine started to turn before Rosen did and ended up stumbling as they came face-to-face, leaving only inches of supercharged air between them. Rosen caught her, looked into her eyes, and kissed her lightly, as if he could control the energy that passed between them. He pulled back, but she took his face in her hands and kissed him with all the stored up passion of weeks of pretending, leaving both of them breathless.

"I am still too Catholic," she said after a long silence. "I hear the voice of my priest telling me that you are married, that we simply cannot be involved. It makes no sense. It's not like I'm an innocent virgin. But you being married makes it different at some deeply visceral level."

"Those grooves in the Catholic cortex, again."

She laughed. "I'm sorry. You know how much I want you, and I know it's the same for you. I can feel you against me, and I want to make love right here, now, on the beach."

"On these rocks? You can't want to make love that badly."

"Oh, you might be surprised. But. What about Millie?"

As if on cue, a puff of chill wind passed over and between them. "Millie, Millicent, my wife. Yes. I have not heard from her in nearly three weeks. I don't think she is coming back. I still don't understand what happened. She got scared, but that can hardly be the whole story. There are moments when it almost feels like we were never married, that we were roommates for decades, good friends, even lovers, but certainly not husband and wife. Does that seem strange to you? Or uncaring?"

"No. Knowing you, it makes a lot of sense. I don't think you 'do' love, not the way most people do. There is a distance between you and the rest of humanity. It is not that you are never passionate, but your passion is about things, your work, not people and not a person."

"I'm sorry. Do you think it's curable?"

"Don't be sorry. I don't think it's something needing to be cured. You are who you are, and I love you."

They both froze at the speaking of the unspoken, the line that had been crossed so off-handedly. "Yes, I suppose you do," he said. "I am not there yet, which is an odd way to put it—so dispassionately to speak of passion—but I am falling in love with you, which is new and delicious. I am hoping you can wait for me to catch up."

The moment was spoiled by the muffled sound of an electric organ at a hockey game working its way up a chromatic scale. Jeannine cringed with embarrassment and fished her cell phone out of the pocket of her jeans. She looked at the caller ID but didn't answer. "It's my handler, the guy I report to about you. Should I answer?"

"No, just turn off your phone and let him get your voice mail."

She complied, then slipped the phone back into her pocket. "Where were we before ominous interruptions."

"On our way back down the beach and up to the road, where we are going to drive a few miles farther north until we find a nice little bed-and-breakfast. There we will take their best room and make the best possible use of it until morning, whereupon we will have a late breakfast before driving back to Massachusetts."

She ran her tongue over her teeth as she hesitated, but finally spoke, one husky word, "Yes."

22

The invitation, a handwritten note slipped under Rosen's front door, had come unexpectedly. When Rosen arrived at Steven King's office, the furniture had been rearranged and the Chagall poster had been taken down. A palm-sized projector on Steven's desk was painting a blue rectangle of light on the wall where the poster had been.

"Come in, Rosen. You're just in time for the next show." Steven gestured toward the chair that was now backed up against the wall opposite the blue rectangle.

"What's all this?" Rosen spread his hands as he took his seat.

"I'm a modern-day lecturer, which means I am incapable of speaking without my PowerPoint. I wanted to show you what I've been doing and did not want to send you the slide deck as an email attachment, for reasons that I am sure you can guess yourself. Please, close the door. This is a private showing that I do not want the robotics people to see."

Rosen closed the door and sat down again.

"You are a scientist, Rosen, which is a handicap in situations like this. I am a medical doctor, which carries the right advantages. Despite the oft bandied term 'medical science,' medicine is not science, it is applied technology—or, in many cases, still, applied witchcraft. The standards of evidence and the solidity of the underlying theory are less important than whether the patient gets better or worse.

We do not expect or need all patients to respond as predicted, and we certainly do not need to know why something works to make use of it. You scientists, on the other hand, demand that results be reproducible and are dissatisfied with anything less than a complete and consistent explanation. And that is why, Rosen, that you continue to hover around the evidence, accumulating research, still searching for patterns and puzzling over missing pieces, when the complete story has been staring you in the face forever."

Rosen opened his mouth as if to speak, but Steven continued without pause. "Llewellyn Cass was a doctor, a brilliant and aggressively creative one, not a scientist. That is what you needed to focus on. The research you were exploring was suggestive but inconclusive. Even if you had the access and had been able to pull together all the relevant papers, you would still have been talking about patterns and possibilities, because scientifically, that is all that would be there. Medically, it is a different story."

He tapped his keyboard and the first slide appeared with a text cloud full of technical jargon at its center, the size of each term scaled to represent some measure of its importance or frequency. "If we start with the patterns you identified and outlined in your meta-analysis and follow where each lead takes us, we do not get a scientific picture. We get a treatment picture." Spokes appeared extending from the text cloud and terminating in thumbnail pictures of patients or cross sections of human organs or photomicrographs of cell cultures. "We ask ourselves not what does this mean or how does it fit with everything else, but what does it imply as the basis for a possible medical intervention. What would a doctor do with it? Not, what would a scientist make of it?"

He stood and pointed at the wall, now covered with his diagram. "This is what they are doing. It is complicated and messy, but every bit of it is quite doable on the basis of modern medicine. In fact, nearly all of it has been practicable for decades, although the means have improved over the years."

"But," Rosen began.

Steven held up his hand to stop him. "I knew that would be your first word. I can even fill in the rest of the sentence. And the next, and the next. You were going to say that this is speculative, that it jumps to conclusions, that it leaves out chains of scientific inference, that the research does not fully support it. Were you not?"

"Well, that's all true, isn't it?"

"Yes, and all irrelevant, because the picture I am building here is not scientific. I am painting a picture of medical practice. And let me do just that. Let me show you, for each of these nine treatment implications, what I am confident represents more or less what your colleagues are doing and have been doing for a long time."

He took his time working through the presentation, explaining for each slide what his best guess was about the treatment technique and what some of the alternatives might be, how evolving practice and technology in medicine since the original paper was published would impact how the treatments might be carried out currently.

"And that's it," he said, turning off the projector. "That is what they are doing, even though from a purely scientific perspective, they still don't know what they are doing. My guess is they are still busy trying to figure out why it all works and how it all fits together in order to make it work better or make the patient management simpler."

Rosen put his hand to his forehead. "So, the implication is that they are using costly and complicated medicine to keep themselves—or some people—from aging and dying. This is not a line of scientific inquiry but the basis for actual medical practice. And you put this together on your own?"

"Well, I am brilliant. And I do have access to some of the best facilities and smartest colleagues. But, you really did the work. It is all in your paper. Well, most of it is in your paper. You just didn't take it far enough, but it's all there for anyone with the right mindset and the motivation to figure it out. The old paper is merely a clue, yours is a map of the whole mystery. That is why it is so dangerous to them and why they cannot let you publish. But they must also be impressed with your brilliance, because no one else seems to have put it all together so clearly."

Rosen stood and started pacing in the small space. "Knowing the what makes me all the more curious about who. Who are these people and what happened to the other authors of the original paper. I need to know who I am dealing with."

"Is there nothing in the world that you think you might be better off not knowing?"

"Not much. The hour of my death, perhaps, but I believe in knowing. Knowledge is my religion, I suppose, having lost my faith in faith and then my faith in science."

"Will you tell me what you find?"

"Why?'

"Because, Rosen, I also believe in knowing."

= =

Rosen decided to play hooky from work again, having discovered that it was too hard to do his research on weekends, when it seemed that everyone else in the Greater Boston Area was also using the public library. It was slow, frustrating work, requesting microfilm archives, threading the film through the reader, scanning through the images, and finally, finding nothing, exchanging the microfilm for the next in a series. Oddly, the pace of the search made the occasional discoveries all the sweeter. Rosen's eyes were tired, but it had been a sweet morning.

He had started with a date, a reference point from which he could move forward and back in time, the date in mid-February of 1974 when Janella Kai had apparently disappeared. The disappearance was hardly a headline story—there being nothing to report—but one short piece mentioned the police questioning a visiting professor at Harvard who was identified as one Douglas Dougherty. Another, smaller piece in *The Boston Globe* referred to the police bringing a suspect in for questioning. Rosen spun the knob to zoom in on the name of the suspect: Bram Decker. It was more than mere confirmation; it was a new direction. Rosen scanned through later issues and other Boston papers but found no other references to Decker or to suspects in the case.

He switched tactics and used his netbook to go online through the public wi-fi. He turned up nothing useful initially until he accepted Google's offer to search instead for "Bram Dekker" with a double K. Dekker, it seemed, was a common Dutch surname, and, paired with Bram and surrounded with quotes, it still yielded over 8,000 hits. Sorting through the dozens of Bram Dekkers on Facebook and LinkedIn, Rosen narrowed the field down to a handful that were old enough to be the man mentioned in the newspaper article. One, a retired computer scientist whose LinkedIn profile listed a PhD from Tufts in 1976, had a distinguished career. He had spent most of his years at the Technical University of Eindhoven, where he had teamed up with a group of cryptologists to develop new techniques for secure communications and protecting financial transactions. His LinkedIn profile noted that he was retired from the University but still worked as a consultant.

Rosen clicked through to the personal website listed and was greeted by the image of a tall, dignified man with a bushy white mustache, standing, arms folded defiantly, in front of a building that even Rosen recognized as one of Europe's biggest investment banks. Closer examination revealed that the image was a clever PhotoShop composite in which the shadows almost matched.

The contact page of the website gave a telephone number in the Netherlands and an address in The Hague but no email address. Rosen checked his watch, guessed that the time difference was probably six hours, and decided to take a chance on a telephone call.

A female voice answered, *"Hallo. Dekker Consulting is op dit moment gesloten. Laat een berichtje achter na de toon."* Rosen was about to give up when the same voice switched to English, "Hello. Dekker Consulting is closed for the day. Please leave a message after the beep."

Rosen figured he had already paid for an overseas call on his cellphone, so had nothing to lose. "This is a message for Bram Dekker. If the name Janella Kai means anything to you, please contact me by email at rosenkavelier29@gmail.com." He started to spell out the email address when a voice on the line interrupted him.

"This is Dekker. Who is this? What do you want? What do you know about Janella Kai?" The man spoke in a soft baritone, with a pronounced Dutch accent.

"Dr. Dekker, this is Dr. Rosen David here. I am sorry to bother you at this hour, but I am calling from Boston where I am doing some research, trying to find out something about a Janella Kai who lived in the area in the 1970s and did some research that I am interested in." There was a long silence on the line. "Are you still there? I am looking for the Bram Dekker who also lived here in the 1970s and who might know something about her."

"You must forgive me. It has been a very long time since I heard that name, a very long time. I doubt seriously that I can be of any help to you. I really don't know anything about her. What is it exactly that you are interested in?"

Rosen was thinking that two could play this game. "I thought that you might be able to tell me what you know. This newspaper article I was reading said that she had disappeared in 1974 and that you were possibly the last person to see her."

"Why are you interested in such a very old story, Dr. Rosen?"

"It's Dr. David, but you can call me Rosen. I am really interested in a research paper that Kai co-authored: 'Cancer expression, cell longevity, and mosaicism in Rattus Norvegicus.'"

"I think you have reached the wrong person, Dr. David. I am not that kind of a doctor. I am a computer consultant."

"Yes, I know. I'm also in computers. Well, mathematics—same difference these days. Look, I just want to talk with you."

There was another silence of several seconds, then, "I am sorry, but you are wasting your time. As I said, you have reached the wrong person. Good luck and goodbye." The call was disconnected.

Rosen stared at his cell phone before closing it. "I don't think so,

Dr. Dekker," he said to the silent phone. "I think I have reached the right person. But what next? That's the big question now. What next?"

Rosen continued to dig through newspaper archives looking for more stories, but finally gave up after another hour. Before leaving the library, he logged into his web-mail account. There was a message from info@bramdekker.com.

> I dislike email even more than I dislike telephones,
> but I feel that I owe you an apology for hanging up
> on you today. You deserve at least common
> courtesy. It is true that you reached the wrong
> person, because I really do know nothing about
> Janella Kai. But what I do not know is not a matter
> for discussion in email or by telephone. The
> question is whether your travels ever bring you to
> the Netherlands. Perhaps we can sometime share a
> beer and speak of distant days.

"The question is," Rosen said to the screen of his netbook, "What is the cheapest airfare to The Hague." He started to research the question.

= =

It turned out there were no cheap flights directly to Rotterdam-Den Haag airport, so Rosen decided to fly into Amsterdam's Schiphol and take a train. His departure from Boston's Logan was delayed because of inbound equipment, and after landing in Amsterdam, he managed to become completely confused by the train schedule to Den Haag. The address for Dekker Consulting turned out to be in the beach district of Scheveningen, and by the time Rosen figured out the tram system and then walked to the right neighborhood, it was already late in the afternoon. He had deliberately said nothing about his trip to anyone, least of all to Dr. Dekker, so it was with some trepidation that he pressed the button next to the name plate at the entrance. He recognized the deep voice that sprang from the intercom saying something in Dutch.

"Dr. Dekker, it's Rosen David. I'm here to have that glass of beer with you."

A pulse of laughter pierced the afternoon quiet. "Ha! I should have known that this is the sort of serious fellow you were, having tracked me down in the first place. Well, then, you might as well come on up." The door latch released with a loud clunk and buzz.

The office turned out to be a second-floor walkup studio that seemed to double as computer center and apartment. The main room held a desk, a side table straddling a computer and topped by an all-in-one printer-copier-fax, and several swivel chairs. A foldout sofa bed under the windows on the far wall left little exposed floor space. What might have once been a bedroom off to one side now hosted a round conference table ringed by four executive chairs. A credenza against one wall was arrayed with dozens of assorted glasses, a coffee machine, and a dorm-style cube of a refrigerator. On the opposite side of the main room, a kitchen nook was curtained off by a sheet of ecru lace that might have been intended that way or merely discolored by age.

"Not much of a headquarters for one of Europe's top security consultants, wouldn't you say, but then I am really only an amateur, at least nowadays. Please have a seat." He gestured toward the windows and the sofa bed. The windows looked out over a small inner courtyard crisscrossed by colorful plantings of tulips and greenery. "Let me get you that beer. You have come a long way for a drink; it should be something special." He slipped into the bedroom-conference room and returned a minute later carrying two graceful, gold-rimmed glasses of dark amber beer. "This is a favorite of mine, Hertog Jan, from a little brewery in a small town about 100 kilometers from here. I used to have to drive there to get it, but now they have a webshop, and they ship. And, of course, as is the custom among serious beer drinkers here, it must be sipped from the correct glasses, the official ones from the brewery. So," he handed one tall glass to Rosen, raised his own, smiling. *"Gezondheid!"* His soft but resonant voice filled the small room.

Rosen raised his glass and lightly tapped it against the other. "Cheers!"

"Said like a good Bostonian, Rosen," he declared, as he pulled one of the chairs over nearer the sofa and sat in it. "I did love it there. Such an alive city. And for a student in those days, at least in Somerville where I was, cheap living. I was there on full scholarship and had a small stipend and wanted for nothing. Never since.

"But your presence should not be an excuse to indulge in nostalgia. You have come too far merely to humor an old man."

"I came here to meet you." He took a second sip of the beer and savored it. "You live here?" He gestured. Bram nodded. "Not married, I take it."

"Not now. But twice. Once to an Indonesian girl here and once, very briefly, to a girl in Barcelona. Neither lasted, but both had lasting consequences. Those are my two daughters," he said, pointing to a pair of small framed photos on the wall. "Catrijn, on the left, married a Japanese-American and now teaches English in Tokyo. Jacinta, on the right, is a pharmacist in Barcelona, not married, not interested."

"You have beautiful children."

"Past tense. I have their pictures, now, but nothing else. I have a long history of short-term success and long-term failure with the females of the species, starting with my beautiful Janella. I knew her for only a few weeks, but they were intense and wonderful weeks, filled with deep discussions that went on through the night. But I am being too personal, and you must have specific questions, hopefully not about forgotten conversations or long-lost love."

"I want to know what happened to Janella Kai. And I want to know about this paper." He pulled the copy of Dougherty, Cass, Aubuchon, and Kai from his backpack.

"Ah yes, looks familiar." Bram crossed the room to the desk, opened a center drawer, and pulled out a duplicate of the paper. "I knew that someday, sooner or later, someone would find it and make sense of it and do something with it or about it. So, I saved it."

"What about Janella Kai? What happened to her?"

"She's dead."

"You know that for certain?"

"Yes, for certain."

"How is that?"

"Simple. If she were alive, we would have known, the world would know. You have to understand about Janella. She was an unstoppable force, a tiny package of pure, unbounded energy. She would never have walked away from this," he waved the paper, "and she could not have been made to keep quiet, either.

"No, she is dead. I killed her. I killed Janella Kai, my first real love and the most beautiful woman I have ever known and possibly the smartest, as well. I killed her."

Rosen said nothing as he stared into his half-empty beer glass.

"I remember that night, Dr. David. It is as real to me now as this paper is. I can still see her as she left me."

23

Janella stood in the small kitchen of Bram's apartment, her future held in her teeth.

She sucked air to keep from getting the stapled photocopy soggy as she used both hands to engage the slide of her fur-trimmed leather jacket. She zipped it with a sharp flip of her hand, then grabbed her gaudy plaid scarf. With a single helicopter gesture above her head, she wrapped its six-foot length twice around her neck, knocking the paper out of her mouth. She retrieved it, brushed a dirty smudge from the paper, then slipped it into a much-used manila envelope.

Nearly a year of her life was in that paper—perhaps more. She had typed the final copy, and much of the wording was hers. It was also her attentive work with the lab rats that had first drawn attention to the anomalous drug interactions. She understood that the findings were significant but had always had a tendency to lose herself in technical detail and the day-to-day operation of experiments, often missing the grander scientific implications of research, even when it was her own work. Now she understood what was really at stake and how much she was risking in bringing the paper.

She pressed closed the metal tabs on the envelope flap and sighed. "I have to go, Bram. Really."

Bram smiled down at her from the height of his slim Dutch frame. "It's not that late. Stay for a little longer," he pleaded, as he slowly unzipped her jacket again and slipped a hand under her sweater. "You are so beautiful, Janella. And you have the most beautiful little tits."

"They're too little," she said. "It's my mother's fault. She told me that Brazilian girls had small breasts and big butts, as if that made it a good thing." Bram laughed as he shook his head, took another sip of beer, and tweaked her nipple.

"Bram, stop it," Janella snapped. "I really do have to go. Douglas wants me in the lab early tomorrow."

"Oh, so now your Professor has become Douglas? I don't understand what you see in that old man."

"He's not old. And what I see in him is the same thing I see in you, my young Dutch stallion. I told you, I find that the sexiest thing about a man is his brains."

Bram brushed a splotch of beer foam from his blond mustache and flashed a slightly inebriated grin at her. "So, I am your *smart* Dutch stallion, then, a 'Clever Hans' maybe. I can compute powers of two with my foot." He started tapping on the floor. "Does he know, this Professor of yours? I mean about us?"

"Sure, I told him after the party." She had met Bram three weeks earlier at a beer blast in a mutual friend's apartment two floors up. She had arrived with girlfriends from Tufts but very shortly left with Bram to come down to his place. They had been like rabbits ever since.

"You told him? And it's okay with him?"

"I told him; I didn't ask for his permission. I don't think he's completely happy with it, but that's his problem. I think he'd be more upset about our discussing the research than about our making love. He is very possessive about this work."

"I don't understand you Americans. Are you saying that you and the Professor are still screwing? I don't think I approve."

"Do you think I need your approval, Bram? You don't own me. Besides, love is good. More is better. I would expect that you would agree, my adorable Dutchman."

"Where did you get that speech from? Some peacenik flower children you met when you were at that conference in California?" he said, curling his lip in disdain.

"I went to California to deliver a paper, Bram, not to visit communes."

"You? You delivered a paper? Yourself?"

"Yes, myself. And I told you. And stop that." She pushed him away. "It was based on my thesis."

"Your thesis? But I thought you said you never graduated. What are you talking about?"

"I started an honors thesis before I quit. I told you that the night we met. I finished the work on my own time, wrote it up, and got it accepted at this conference."

"More work with Norwegian rats? Tell me, do Norwegian rats squeal with an accent?"

"No, my Dutch dimwit. Why is it so hard for men to take us seriously. Small women have it doubly hard. Do you know what they did? They actually brought out a telephone book for me to stand on so I could reach the microphone and see over the podium. Oh, that was a big laugh—great start to my fifteen minutes of fame."

"What did you do?"

"I walked around to the front of the podium, twisted the microphone down on its gooseneck, held up the San Francisco Yellow Pages, and said, 'My thesis.' That got another big laugh, but at least this time they were on my side."

"Remind me what that paper was about," he said.

"Drug resistance, drug resistance in S. Aureus."

"I'm against it, you know. We shouldn't resist drugs," he teased, pausing for another chug from the near-empty bottle.

"You are incorrigible, Bram Dekker. That's exactly what I mean. You men take us seriously as long as you are trying to get us into bed. Afterwards, it's back to the little jokes. And, seriously, I need to get home."

"You know, I do not think I approve of your hippy philosophy. It should not be that way. One man, one girl: that's the way of things. Or at least one at a time."

"That's not me. Life's too short," she said, squirming as he circled her nipple with his thumb. "And stop that. You have a one-track mind, Bram Dekker."

"It is not true that I have a one-track mind," Bram said, shifting his hand to her other breast. "See? I have a two-track mind."

"I am serious, I keep telling you. I have to get back to Cambridge."

"I'll drive you. It's too far and too cold."

Janella extracted Bram's hand from under her sweater, rezipped her jacket, and pointedly stared down at the Grolsch in his other hand. "No thanks," she said.

"Ah, but the Nederlanders can hold their alcohol better than Americans. See?" he said, taking two steps backward and stumbling into the refrigerator.

"Yes, I see," she said, grabbing her purse off the table. "I'll call you tomorrow after I finish at the lab." She stood on tiptoes to kiss his chin, then let herself out of the basement apartment.

= =

Bram finished his narration with head bowed, then looked up at Rosen.

"What I have never told anyone," he said, "is that she came back to the apartment that night, but I was too drunk. By the time I struggled awake and staggered to the door, she was gone. There was a note slipped between the door and the frame. It said to please return the paper, that her professor, her lover, would kill her if he found out that she had showed it to me and left it.

"That's what he did. He killed her, which means that I killed her, because I was too slow and too drunk to let her in and give her the paper. I never told the police about the note or the paper because I was afraid of getting into trouble. I was still more than a year short of finishing my doctorate, and, selfishly, I didn't want to jeopardize that for a lost cause.

"But I have paid for my cowardice. I have felt guilty ever since, and every year, when the Ides of February approach, I go into a depression that I am unable to fight. We Dutch are given to depression, you know. Perhaps it is because so many of us live below sea level and beneath clouded skies. We are low creatures, creatures of the lowlands, the Netherlands. And in the middle of every February, I sink lower still and drink until I pass out on that very couch where you sit, and no one or no thing can arouse me from that drunken stupor, yet I dream. I dream of a young women with golden eyes and lightning behind them, and I know that I have killed her."

"And the paper?" Rosen asked. "The paper that you preserved and ultimately posted on the Web, do you know what it is?"

"Yes, it is a sort of crude treasure map, a way pointer to the Fountain of Youth. And Janella's professor, Dr. Atchison Dougherty, tried to follow it for the rest of his life. Now his son carries on the search with his Biontolics Research and its far-flung appendages that reach like tentacles into companies around the globe. Oh, yes, I know about his pursuit. I read about his father in the financial press and now I follow the son on the same quixotic quest, but they are both stupid. They did not have Janella nor Janella's brilliance to shine a light in the right direction. Instead, they chase shadows. I read what they publish, at least the abstracts, and they are still missing the mark and getting no closer with time."

"What's this about Dougherty's son? I didn't know he had a son."

"Yes, Junior, the man who now heads Biontolics. I have seen his picture."

"You've seen a ghost. That is Atchison Dougherty. That is Janella's professor."

"No, I think you are mistaken. Dougherty would be in his nineties, and the head of Biontolics is half that."

"You misread the literature coming out of Biontolics. It is a diversion to look like great effort and little progress. The real results never get outside. The real research, based on that work that Janella helped produce, really works. Atchison Dougherty, the one whose picture you have seen, is well over ninety. They found the Fountain, and they are keeping the location secret and saving the waters for themselves."

Bram stood and started pacing, his head nearly brushing the ceiling of the apartment. "For the last few years I have said, knowing what little still lies before me, that were Atchison Dougherty still alive, I would kill him myself, that it would be a good use of my last years, to right the wrong and bring Janella's killer to the end he deserves. And now you are saying that Professor Dougherty, Janella's Professor Dougherty, is still alive and running a company that will keep him alive as long as he wants."

"I am saying that."

"Then you have brought me a great gift—a reason to live—and an end to depression. I will kill this Atchison Dougherty, I will. I am a computer scientist, but I am a cyber-security specialist who has long consorted with people whose work weaves in and out between the light and the dark. I will find a way.

"But, my new friend, there is so much for us to talk about. You must stay. You must have dinner with me. Do you know *rijsttaffel?*" Rosen shook his head. "Then you must learn. Rijsttaffel is Indonesia's contribution to Dutch cooking. Literally, it just means rice table, but in fact it is a near endless parade of spicy delectables. I know a place not fifteen minutes from here, an easy walk, and an eating experience. Come, first another beer, then hours of good food."

24

Atchison Douglas Doherty was approaching one hundred and was not only, arguably, the best looking man his age, but, although never having ever been singled out by *Forbes*, he was the wealthiest. He reveled in both secret ironies, that he was all but invisible, except for his indulgence as CEO of Biontolics, and that he was still around—and young. His time in Aruba under an assumed name and using one of his many passports, had rejuvenated him. The scuba, the sailing, and the lovely and compliant barmaid, had been precisely what his doctor would have ordered, if Andras had ever bothered to be more than a technician. Ten days of diving and dalliance had proven to be just what he had needed to pull himself out of the pool of frustration into which he had plunged.

He was looking forward to a good glass of champagne in his suite. He never drank on airplanes. The wine, even in first class, was never up to his standards, which seemed to rise higher and higher as the years progressed. A thousand-dollar bottle of vintage champagne was routine—and a pittance in the scheme of things. He owned a *négociant* and a winery and large holdings of vines in several of his favorite areas of France and Italy, and the success of those investments only guaranteed a steady expansion of his holdings and an endless supply of the best of the very best. His partner, Andras, on the other hand, was an excellent scientist and skilled physician who lacked all imagination and was limited in initiative. Dougherty knew he would have to replace the man eventually, but eventually was a term that on the scale of Dougherty's calendar could be many decades off. The right replacement would come along, of that he was certain. One only needed patience—and the longevity to exercise it fully—to find that, truly, all things come to him who waits. Dougherty was one who waited and one who enjoyed the wait most thoroughly.

He nodded to his men as he reentered his London townhouse. On the stoop, in the entry foyer, and in the lane at the back, there were the men, his men. Security was easy, even if not cheap. But it was merely part of the cost of doing business for Dougherty, part of the business of living indefinitely.

There was a new man at the entry to his suite, a tall, wiry man with jet-black hair who filled his post with dignity and professionalism, almost imperceptibly speaking into his radio link as he opened the door for Dougherty. When he pushed ahead and led the way into the room, Dougherty began to wonder about his professional zeal.

"Let me check the room for you, sir. It's been unattended in your absence," the man offered in explanation. He switched on the lights, did a quick circuit of the room, opening each door to adjoining rooms, and turning on all the lights. "I think we can safely conclude we are alone," he said.

"Yes, well, I assume we can," Dougherty said, with growing irritation. "Thank you, and good night, Mister, er..."

"Dekker, Bram Dekker, at your service, Professor."

Dougherty turned and studied the man. In bright light, his lined face betrayed the coloring in his hair. Dougherty, calmly reached into his pocket and fingered his personal alarm as he considered his options for the short moments that remained before his real protectors arrived. "I don't believe we've met, Mister Dekker."

"No, we've never met, but that doesn't mean we have nothing in common. Indeed, we have something rather special in common, both having bedded Janella Kai." He waited for the message to sink in.

Dougherty glanced anxiously toward the door.

"Oh, you can relax, Professor. Your security people are not coming. I took the liberty of disabling the receiver for your wireless panic button. I have had nearly a week to decipher all the details and attend to all the minutiae while you cavorted in Aruba. What was that wench's name? Maria? Yes, that was it. Seemed to take a very quick fancy to you, a man nearly four times her age. One would almost think she had some extra incentive. But then, you were also so generous with your bonuses, too. I am certain she appreciated every pound sterling."

Dougherty, his military demeanor restored, stepped back and reached toward the bar. "I trust you will not be offended, Mr. Dekker, if I pour myself a drink. I would offer one to you if I thought you would accept."

"Oh, I most definitely would accept. A glass of the finest is just the thing for a dying man."

Dougherty frowned slightly in uncertainty.

"Oh, I have no illusion that I am going to make it out of here alive after I am finished with you. It's a small price for divine vengeance."

"And you partake of the divine?"

"No, only the vengeance part. As one of the immortals, you would probably be closer to the divine, except that tonight I will conclusively demonstrate that you are not immortal. As to the divine part, that will be between you and your deity. I forget where Dante Alighieri placed the simple murderers. That would be you, were it a simple matter of murder." He noticed Dougherty eyeing the sidearm at his waist. "Ah, yes. The instrument of said divine vengeance. A Glock 29, 9mm, a good choice for your security personnel. With its 'Safe Action' trigger-release safety, even a martial virgin, an inept user such as your humble nemesis here, can be effective without special attention to preparatory steps."

He withdrew the Glock from its polymer holster and aimed it toward Dougherty's chest. "Double tap. That's what it's called in the trade. One to the chest and then one to the head for insurance. Your guards get this drilled into them. There must never be any survivors to offer their own, potentially contradictory version of any 'encounter,' am I right?"

"What do you want, Dekker? I can offer you considerable incentives to walk away from this."

"No, we both know that I would not get to walk very far, and you would still be walking long after I was only a footnote to your history. What do I want? I want you dead. Before that, I want to know what happened to Janella."

"Are you still hung up on some grad-school affair with a teenager? You're a grown man, Dekker, an old man. Get over it." Dougherty started to walk away, reaching the door to the bedroom before turning. There was a Beretta in his hand. "You missed your moment, Dekker, because you wanted to hear me say it more than you wanted to see me dead. The thing to do was to shoot me in the back while you had the chance. Now the chance is gone, the one chance you have been saving up for, waiting and hanging onto for decades—the chance to shoot me and end your own torture.

"You think I don't know about you, Bram Dekker? You, the morose, pathetic alcoholic whose ritual of remembrance is to drink yourself into oblivion, just as you did in 1974. See, I know all about it, the whole story. I have sources—eyes and ears everywhere. I have to, or I would not still be here. Your bright but ignorant new friend thinks it is all about genetics and immunology. No, it is about vigilance. The biology is far simpler than the social engineering of survival. And you still stand there, finger on the trigger, paralyzed by your own ineptitude."

Dougherty fired his Beretta without even taking aim, hitting Dekker in the forearm and sending the Glock tumbling to the floor. "Survival skills, my Dutch dodo. You are extinct. What do you think I do with my weekends? I learn. I practice. At living, I am the professsional. You are the amateur. Maybe I am the first, because who before me has had the time and health to get really good at living?"

Dekker held his arm. The pain and the blood running through his fingers were draining the life from him, sucking away the energy that had brought him to London and sustained him through the logistics of his assault. His vision began to blur.

"So, goodbye, Dr. Dekker. You failed. But you will die knowing not only that, but also the bitter truth that makes it such a pathetic failure. You were right all along. I killed Janella. I caught up with her for a second time just after she finished pounding on your door and was leaving. I strangled her from behind with her own pink-and-purple garrote before she could bring any of her graceful Brazilian martial arts into play. There was no one around on that snowy night, no witnesses. I had a lab at Harvard at my disposal. Disposal of a body was no great challenge. I figured you were a setup as an obvious perpetrator, but you were just a little too clever, so you got off and went home. I have followed you—back to Holland, over to Madeira, home again to Eindhoven, jiggety-jig." Dougherty smiled, pleased with himself and this version of that night's events.

"Why? Why would you do it? Why did you have to kill her?"

"Because she stood in the way, because it had become clear to me that she could never be controlled. She was blocking the way to immortality."

"You sold your soul."

"I don't believe in souls, Mr. Dekker."

"You do not have to believe in a soul to sell it. Hell, you don't even have to have one to sell it, and you sold yours."

"Well, then, I guess that is that. I have nothing to sell and you have nothing I am interested in buying. So, goodbye." He fired once, catching Dekker at the bottom of the ribcage. "Oh, I am out of practice. Too low. Ah, well. Double tap, as you said." He expertly put the coup de grace into Dekker's forehead, then reached around the corner to the wired panic button concealed on the door jamb of the bedroom. "There's been an intruder," he announced to the now-active hidden microphone. "Get your men in here. Now!"

25

A h, Edgar, I am glad you are here," Ferguson said, when Mbutsu arrived at the clinic. "We should talk. You have been busy, from what I hear. Now you are sending troops over the border and claiming a wedge of land on the other side of the river, not so? Here, come sit and we will talk while I ready the first injections." Ferguson gestured toward the examining table.

Mbutsu did not look good. Recovery from his wounds and the two rounds of surgery, even with all the medical miracles at his disposal, had taken a toll. The tall and tempered warrior stood stooped in the doorway, one hand on the doorjamb. The young bodyguards who accompanied him seemed to tower over him. Behind him, almost out of sight, waited an old man who looked vaguely familiar to Ferguson.

Mbutsu gestured for the man to come ahead. "You remember Fallu, Doctor. He was to be my tester, but you talked me out of it. I have changed my mind and will not be talked out of it this time. I want you to give him the injections first—all of them. He is, remember, an old man and of another tribe, so we do not need to worry what will become of him."

Ferguson, sensing that there would be no winning the argument a second time, nodded to the man and patted the padded table. "Here. Sit here," he said in the dialect that fitted the man's style of dress.

Fallu's face lit up, and he answered in kind. "I am not afraid."

"Of course not, a brave old warrior such as you, who protects his president. But, you have nothing to fear from this," Ferguson said, holding up a syringe. "This will do nothing to you, and you can return home tonight to your village and tell tales of how you met the Doctor's doctor yourself."

"I am told that I will not return to my village, but still, I am not afraid."

Ferguson looked over to Mbutsu, who was clearly relishing his moment of small triumph over his doctor. "There is one in this room, it would seem, who is not afraid," Ferguson said pointedly. "And there is nothing to fear in any of these, as I am sure you know, Mr. President. So, let us begin."

Feguson, though he thought the entire exercise to be silly and pointless, played along and put Fallu through every procedure and administered every injection before moving on to Mbutsu. The man's brave front wavered only once, when he was being slid into the big magnet of the MRI. When the rapid fire banging began half-way through the imaging, the man jumped involuntarily and struck his head against the top of the enclosure. It ruined the series, but since it was only an empty exercise, Ferguson pretended that there was no problem and continued as soon as the man was calmed.

At the end of the day, having done everything twice, there was still more to do, and Ferguson realized that his fantasy of a quick visit would not be fulfilled. He pulled Mbutsu aside and spoke to him in English, which he suspected neither the guards nor the test subject would understand.

"Let the man go, Edgar. Let him return home. This business is slowing us down, and you need to complete the treatments."

Mbutsu scowled in contempt. "He is a soldier. He fought in the revolution—on the wrong side, yes, but he fought well and was spared. He cannot return to his village. He has seen and heard too much."

Ferguson, sensing an impasse, said nothing.

"You have grown soft, Doctor. Your life has been too easy. You do not seem to realize that living exacts a price, and the price of living is lives. Some must be taken. It is the way of things."

Ferguson, seeing a parade of faces pass through his mind, glowered at Mbutsu. "Trust me, Edgar, I know about the price of living. I understand sacrifice."

"Good. I hope so. Then I will see you at dinner tonight, and we will talk of other matters."

"Thank you, Your Excellency, but I shall not be at dinner tonight. I am tired and will simply dine in my suite, if that is acceptable. We will have extra days because," he paused, picking his words with care, "because of the new procedure. I will join you for dinner on another night."

Mbutsu snorted his disapproval but nodded in agreement. "Tomorrow, then, good Doctor. More tests and a new tester."

As soon as Mbutsu was out of the building, Ferguson hurried through his chores and slipped into his private office. There was no place on the grounds, probably no place in Mbutsu City, that was truly safe and private, but on this trip, Ferguson had brought with him more than just medical equipment. He pulled the scanner from his medical bag and carefully swept the room before going to the window to open the blinds, count three, and close them again. He poured himself a glass of bourbon from the bottle in his desk, and waited for his meeting.

26

That was fantastic, Jeannine. How do you keep doing it?" Her invitation to Sunday morning brunch in her condo had turned out to mean a spread of a potato-leek frittata topped with goat cheese, a fruit compote with rum-soaked melon balls, and fresh-baked sweet rolls with pistachio topping.

"You've got a caramel-pistachio bit clinging to your chin, dear." She mirror-mimed wiping her own chin as he dabbed with his napkin. "You got it. And this, this was nothing. When my dad was alive, he used to put together a buffet of twice as many dishes every Sunday. My mother and sisters and I would return from mass to a house filled with the scent of fresh breads and sausages and honey-lime ham. Even the drinks were special. He used to make this bergamot-infused blood-orange nectar that he would serve slightly warmed with a stemmed cherry hooked over the rim of the glass. My mother was a good but unimaginative cook. My father, on the other hand, was an artist with a sauté pan and a wire whisk. Neither of my sisters go near the kitchen. They were smart; they married men who could cook. I never found the man, so I learned to cook instead."

"Your father would be proud."

"No, he wouldn't. He was proud of my sisters for marrying well, which he maintained was every woman's first obligation. After that, babies were next on the list. He always said I was too smart, too cerebral. I scared the boys. It didn't help that I was taller than every boy in my class and wore glasses that made me look like a librarian. The final blow between us came when I stopped going to mass. He never went himself, but he expected me to go with Mom, Elise, and Angela. He asked me why I didn't go, and I told him. That was the last conversation we ever had. He was dying in the hospital after his heart attack, and he wouldn't talk with me. He was a stubborn, unforgiving hypocrite to his last breath."

"What did you say to him that triggered that?"

"I told him the truth, that I didn't believe in God. He covered his ears and turned away from me. Mom said he was crushed; she never asked me whether I was crushed to find myself instantly demoted from his favorite, his little girl, to the daughter from whom he turned when I entered the room. When he spoke of me at all, it was as if I were not there, as if I had died when I was fourteen.

"Do you know, that single, two-line dialogue was the only mention of God or religion between us. 'Why won't you go to mass anymore?' 'Because I don't believe in God anymore.' That was it. We had never talked about it before, and we never talked again, or at least he didn't. I tried on many occasions to talk about many things, but he would walk away as if I wasn't there.

"Angela and Elise were always so much smarter than I was when it came to Dad, when it came to men. They never spoke with him about things that mattered, which proved to be good practice for their marriages. I ought to know, because I am the one they have always confided in, still do.

"I was always the one who wouldn't settle. Now, here I am, thirty-seven and single and in love with a married man who talks with me and listens and never turns away. How lucky and how horrible."

Rosen wiped his fingers before reaching across the table and taking her hand. As he did so, he realized that it was a simple gesture that Millie had done many times but was a first for him, such a small thing and yet so foreign. Jeannine started to cry.

"I don't envy my sisters. They have the house and the three children each and busy lives, but I know how empty their lives are. I decided long ago that I would rather come home to an empty house than to an empty life."

She pulled away from him and stood, wiping her eyes of tears that wouldn't stop. Rosen stood with her and wiped his own eyes of tears that he didn't understand but that kept coming nonetheless. "I love you," she said between sniffles.

"I love you," he said, his own voice and rhythm echoing hers, as his tears and his futile fingers wiping at his cheeks mirrored hers. There was the width of the breakfast bar between them, but Rosen had never felt closer to any human being before. He wanted to pull her to him, and at the same time he wanted to stand where he was, where he could see her and marvel in her, feeling her strength and her vulnerability, the very image of his own. It was vertiginous, to see her seeing him seeing her, to understand and be understood and to know that she also understood and was understood. He broke the magic with a word: "Wow!"

She threw her arms around him. "I love you I love you I love you I love you, Rosen David."

"And I love you, Jeannine Carsten, and I don't know what else to say. I love you I love you I love you. That's it."

She sniffled and wiped her nose on his shoulder and pulled back sheepishly. "I've gotten tears and mucous all over you, and you just keep smiling at me and crying with me."

"Hey, what are friends for? Here,"—he reached for a clean napkin—"give this a try while I clear the dishes."

She sniffled again and started to cough. "That doesn't sound good?" he said. "Are you coming down with a summer cold? Or is this allergies? There's so much I don't know about you. I'm in love with you, and I don't even know what you're allergic to."

"Cats."

"Really?"

"Really, I saw the musical and have never been the same since. Anything by Andrew Lloyd Weber gives me hives."

Rosen stuck his tongue out at her. "Really, I want to know everything about you that I don't already know. Everything."

"That sounds like Gödel's God again. 'Just tell me what you don't know and I'll tell you all about it.'" She laughed and started into a coughing fit again, but she was clearly enjoying teasing him as much as he was enjoying being teased.

Rosen grinned over his shoulder as he scraped the dishes and sorted them into the dishwasher. "It is so easy with you, so easy to understand you." He was thinking of Millie and feeling guilty about the comparison.

"That's because I'm you. We have the same goofy, sarcastic sense of humor; we both prefer probabilities to people; we prefer red wine to white, websites to newspapers, and making love to doing dishes." She tugged at his arm. "And, you are, I know, already making an inventory list of counter-evidence, thinking of all the ways that we are not alike, exactly as I was doing the very moment I opened my mouth. Right?"

"Uncannily true, my insightful darling. So, are you saying that it is the very fact that there are so many ways that we are different that makes us so alike?"

"No, dearest logician, I am saying we are alike in needing the differences, illusory or not. We are alike in our need to catalog and contradict each other back into safe corners where we are not quite so exposed and vulnerable. Now, put down the fuckin' frying pan and come make love to me before we both start coming up with a list of reasons why not to."

= =

The afternoon passed in a mist of more tears and teasing and quiet lovemaking. Over a simple dinner of noodles and pan-roasted vegetables topped with toasted black sesame seeds that Jeannine insisted was the simplest thing she knew how to cook, they talked. Rosen filled her in about his research and his surprise trip to Holland.

"I wish you had told me then, had trusted me," she said. "I could have helped with a cover story at work. As it was, I think nobody believed me when I said I didn't know where you were, which probably cast suspicion on both of us."

He scraped at his plate with his fork, rescuing the last bits of sesame seeds. "I would imagine by now that half of Ipswich knows that we are having an affair. It's such a small town and Biontolics is such a small-town company, even if it is part of a multinational hydra."

"That's not what I mean about suspicions. I'm talking about Biontolics, my handler, the German who seems of late to be spending as much time over here as in Europe. He asks a lot of questions about you and why I have nothing useful to report. I imagine he is catching on by now. That's his job, Rosen, catching on to things. I never liked him, but I did like the intrigue. Now I like him even less and the intrigue not at all."

"Remember," Rosen said, "it was your idea for me to dig into real-world records in the first place. I thought I was being smart tracking down this Bram Dekker and getting his story. But the man was obsessed with Janella Kai and convinced that Dougherty had killed her. Last he told me, he was working on a plan to get to Dougherty and take him out. Then nothing. There's been nothing in the news about him or about Dougherty, I get no replies to my emails to Dekker, and all I get is the answering service when I call his office in Den Haag. We have another disappearance to add to the ledger."

"Maybe we need to get out, Rosen, do what Millie did and get lost."

"I don't think that option is open for us, Jeannine. You are entangled with the enterprise, and I am an established threat. All the best evidence is that these people play for keeps, and I am no good at this game. I don't know the rules and am clueless when it comes to tactics and strategy. I don't even know what our assets are."

"Not to put a corny spin on it, but we have each other. And our brains. And we have something that they don't want us to have."

"I would put that in the liability column," he said. "And it's my brains that got us into trouble in the first place. And when it comes to you, I am a definite liability. So, our spreadsheet is speckled with red cells, and we are so deep underwater that we should be wearing scuba gear right now. Our big problem is that we are swimming with sharks, and they see that we are a threat to them."

"Then we need to stop being a threat to them. Either we have to disappear so deep in the woods that even their millions and minions can't track us, or we have to trick them into thinking we are dead. Or maybe we convince them that we are not a threat."

Rosen nodded slowly, then noticed that she was nodding in the same way.

== ==

At first, Rosen had no idea how to do it, but Jeannine showed him the way, the simple algorithm that would home in on a solution. All he needed to do was the opposite of what he thought would take him forward, the inverse of what he thought made sense. He started systematically committing professional suicide, championing lost causes, dropping balls and missing deadlines, citing the wrong people and misspelling the names of the right ones. He got himself barred from posting on websites and managed to get posted papers taken down for rules violations.

In the meanwhile, Jeannine started eagerly passing on information that turned out to be true but of no consequence. She let it become obvious to even the deliberately impervious that she and Rosen were involved, and she accidentally left her desk with a confidential page open on her monitor. Both of them were rapidly gaining reputations as well-meaning but inept people who had compounded their incompetence and bad judgment by falling in love with each other.

The ruse began to work with everyone except those who really counted.

27

Rosen missed the first two notices from DHL, but managed to get off work early enough on the third try to be home when the yellow truck with its red markings pulled up outside, almost completely blocking the narrow street. He signed for the envelope, thanked the driver, and pulled the opener strip. The packet was empty. He was about to dismiss it as a joke, but first inverted it while shaking vigorously. A single, small slip of paper fluttered to the floor and landed blank-side up. He turned it over. There was one word written in neat capitals diagonally across the middle: PATAGONIA. A red X chopped through the word, and in tiny, disciplined script at the bottom of the paper, was the signature: Dekker.

The tracking on the packet indicated that it contained documents, had no value, and had originated with the concierge at a London hotel more than a week earlier. Rosen was about to throw it away when, on impulse, he pried it open once more. Clinging to the inside at the bottom was a sticky note. In the same neat hand was written a name: Charles Ferguson.

Rosen did not recognize the name, but it did not take long to start uncovering the footprints of Dr. Charles Henry Ferguson on the Web, although it was some hours before the link to Patagonia became clear. There was a discontinuity in the searchable records. Dr. Ferguson had been born in 1952, but it was not until early 1993 that there were any traces of him, an unpublished conference paper on medical crisis management of hyper-immune response, a subject that was too far afield to have made it into Rosen's previous searches. Then nothing, as if Ferguson, too, had disappeared from the professional scene. Rosen switched screens to his notes and found that Llewellyn Cass had disappeared on expedition in Patagonia in late 1992. He flipped back to the conference reference and clicked through to an abstract for the paper itself. It was co-authored by Abraham Colfax and Charles Ferguson. A note at the bottom acknowledged the debt owed to the late Llewellyn Cass for the use of his case studies.

"Thank you Bram Dekker," Rosen said aloud. "Now it's I who owe you a beer."

There it was, the missing link from Llewellyn Cass to someone else, a Charles Ferguson. What exactly was Bram trying to tell him? He returned to the first note, with the big red X through the word Patagonia. Not Patagonia. No Patagonia? What? Then it hit him. Cass had not died in Patagonia. There were two survivors from the original research team. Cass was still alive; Llewellyn Cass was Charles Ferguson. Now he just needed to track down Ferguson.

He used SkypeOut to call Jeannine's cellphone, then thought better of it. He looked at his watch and figured she would still be up. Better not to use the phone, he thought. He could drive up to Newburyport and be there in 25 minutes. He closed his laptop but not without realizing that, in his enthusiasm, he had been accessing the Web through his home wi-fi router.

= =

Jeannine was home and awake as expected, but the enthusiasm drained from Rosen when he saw her. She had bags under her eyes and could barely croak out a greeting. "I think I'm really sick, Sweetie. You shouldn't come near me. I've picked up some kind of bronchial infection, and it hurts to breath."

"Then we should get you to a doctor, check this out."

"No, I'll be all right. I just need maybe a day or two off to recuperate."

"Recuperate? What are you recuperating from? No, we need to get you looked at." She wheezed again and grabbed at her chest, wincing in pain.

= =

Rosen spent the night with his arms around her. In the morning, she kept insisting that it was nothing, although her painful wheezing had kept both of them awake through much of the night. He had to almost drag her bodily to the doctors' office.

Dr. Jervis was intrigued and puzzled until he got back the chest x-rays. "There's something there, a shadow. We don't know what it is, yet, but I want to admit you overnight for some tests and a biopsy in the morning. It could be nothing, but we need to take a serious look. Okay?

"And you, Rosen, you go home and get some rest, then come into the hospital around noon or so. By that time we should have a better idea what we are dealing with."

Rosen did his best to stay away, spending the last fifteen minutes the next morning sitting in his car outside the hospital, running anxious scenarios in his head. He finally poked into the room at 11:56. Jeannine was sitting up in bed, propped up with pillows, and staring out the window at the parking lot.

"There's good news and bad news, darling," she began. "They've figured out what I have. That's the good news. The bad news is that they've figured out what I have. I have a tumor in my bronchial tubes. Oat cell carcinoma. No, seriously, that's what it's called. Who knew people even had oat cells? But the doc told me that was just what it was called because of the appearance of the cancer under a microscope. Anyway, it's operable—more good news. The bad news is that it has metastasized and can already be found in nearly every organ of my body. It's extremely aggressive and fast growing. That's bad and good. Fast growing cancers are more responsive to chemotherapy, but..." Her brave verbal front suddenly collapsed, and Jeannine began to sob, her shoulders heaving, sending her into another round of coughing fits.

Rosen held her and stroked her hair. "It's going to be all right. We'll beat this."

She clenched her teeth and choked back the pain and tears. "No, Rosen, you don't understand. The chemo is just an exercise so the doctors can feel they did everything they could. It's months, Rosen, that's it, maybe only a matter of weeks, that's what we get: a few weeks or months, and the last days will be a mix of fog and agony, mind-wrenching pain mixed with mind-numbing morphine. This is what we have left, all we get."

"Then let's go."

"What did you say?"

"Let's go. We'll get them to dope you up and pump you full of whatever they need to pump, then let's get out of here. If you only get a few weeks, do you want to spend them here in this dingy motel they call a hospital?"

"They're moving me over to Dana-Farber tomorrow."

"Just as bad. Classier, more expensive, but still a goddamn hospital. If that's what you want, okay. I'm with you all the way, but that's not where or how I would want to spend my last days, and I was given to understand that you and I were a lot alike. That's what you claimed. So what will it be?"

Jeannine could not suppress a smile. "My sisters' summer place in Maine, on Keoka Lake. Can you deal with the doctors and the paper work, Rosen? They are going to go apoplectic. I just don't feel up to arguing right now."

"I'll do what I can, but you'll still have to sign by all the Xs. Which makes me think of something. We're going to stop off at my attorney's office before we leave the state and get a Durable Power of Attorney and all that crap. And let's clean out your wine cellar. We can stay just this side of drunk for the whole time on some of the better vintages. How about DVDs? Anything you always wanted to see? And some new clothes. Let's do our honeymoon in style!"

"Romantic comedies."

"What? Oh, right, movies."

"Yes. 'Love, Actually.' And 'Spanglish.' O yeah, 'Lost in Translation.' You get the picture. Ha, ha."

"I do. Now, let me go see if there's anything I can do with the bureaucrats that are the real power in these places."

= =

He returned in twenty minutes to find the room was crowded.

"Rosen, darling, come meet the distinguished staff of this hotel. This is Dr. Anschluss, from Dana-Farber. He heads the small-cell cancer program there—which I am assured is no small deal—and he is not sure he believes me when I tell him I have never smoked because the cancer I have is never heard of in non-smokers. And this is the local head honcho, Dr. McKennon, who thinks we are both crazy and that you are uncaring and irresponsible and selfish to want to take me out of here."

McKennon protested, "That's not exactly what I said."

"No, but that's exactly what you meant, which is what really counts."

Anschluss shook hands with Rosen, but McKennon only nodded. "She did say it was your idea," McKennon added, petulantly.

"Now you are being inexact, Doctor," Jeannine interjected. "I said that he had the idea first, but it's our idea."

"We can't force treatment on anyone," Anschluss said. "But her chances multiply if we start aggressive chemotherapy immediately."

"He impresses me as a doctor, Rosen, but his math skills suck. Multiply zero by anything and you still get zip. The six-month survival rate for this particular variant is so small that it might as well be zero."

"But, Miss Carsten, you could be in that non-zero percentage if we get started and get it right."

"At what price? Rosen, you should hear the laundry list of so-called side effects for the cocktail they want to start me on. It's worse than any disease. And, the good doctors here admit that it might only buy us an extra month or two."

Anschluss sighed audibly. "As I said, we can't force treatment on you. The best I can do is give you the information you need to make an informed decision. If you reject treatment and opt only for palliative care, the end will definitely come faster, that is almost certain, and it will not be easy. Breathing will become more and more difficult as the tumor in your chest grows and the cancer spreads through your lungs. The cancer is metastatic, and as the spots on your liver and pancreas grow, the pain will grow, too. A hospice facility will help you manage the pain, of course, but that does not mean it will be an easy departure."

Rosen interrupted. "I don't think we are talking about hospice care anyway. We want to go off on our own, spend the time together."

"That sounds like you, Rosen," Dr. Jervis said, as he bounced into the room and launched into introductions all around. "I couldn't help overhearing; forgive me. So, what about you, young lady?" he said, leaning over the bed and smiling warmly.

"I'm with him." She nodded toward Rosen as she returned the doctor's smile.

"All right, then. Let's strategize and organize to do the best for our patient, eh, doctors?" He gave a quick look around at his colleagues but gave them no time to respond. "To begin with, I recommend we take care of that lump in your throat, Jeannine, otherwise you soon won't be able to breathe, and you will be coughing and cacking around the clock. What would you recommend, Dr. Anschluss?"

"Surgery. It's operable, particularly as we don't have to get it perfect." He looked uncomfortable. "Under the circumstances, that is."

"No, major surgery is itself a big risk and could rob them of what little they have. Plus, recovery from chest surgery is no small matter. We need to kill this thing with as little impact as possible. Get creative, gentlemen."

"It's a short list, Doctor," McKennon said. "Surgery, chemo: both of those are out, apparently. X-rays, radiation: those will require a whole series of treatments and can have pretty substantial side effects, and they typically are combined with chemo. I don't see..."

"Brachytherapy," Anschluss announced. "One course of HDR, followed by permanent implanted LDR. Not the usual approach, but under the circumstances, it makes the most sense. No invasive surgery, an outpatient procedure, minimal side effects—simple anti-nausea medication should take care of most of that. She can be out and on her way in a couple of days with the tumor in retreat."

"Do you want to spell that out for the normal people in the room?" Jeannine said.

"Sure. We put some radioactive seeds directly into the tumor using these long, hollow needles. The first treatment is High Dose Radiation, HDR. The seeds go in, stay there for a little time, and are removed. For the second treatment, we implant Low Dose Radiation seeds and leave them there to continue the work. If the aim were a complete guaranteed cure, we might just do several rounds of HDR and combine it with other therapies, but in this case, we are looking for short-term benefits with the fewest side effects."

Jervis nodded enthusiastically, "That's very creative, Dr. Anschluss, genuinely patient-centered medicine. My respect for the oncologists of the world just went up a notch."

28

It was the end of the week before they were ready to take off. The most prominent evidence of her time at Dana-Farber was a dressing over the patchwork of tiny marks on her chest where the array of needles had been inserted. Dr. Jervis, insisting on seeing them off, showed up at Jeannine's condo at eight in the morning carrying a brown paper bag. "A going away present," he said. "Don't get caught with it, or they will think you are a drug dealer. And the stuff is ultimately traceable to me, so I could lose my license. And here, fill these prescriptions before you leave town, then see this guy up in Bridgeton to write you another script. Gil and I went to medical school together, and he already knows what this is about. Don't be afraid of it; use as much as she needs to keep the pain under control. You don't have to worry about her becoming addicted at this point. I see that you like wine," he said, nodding toward to the rack against the wall. "Do be careful about alcohol. The combination can depress breathing. She can drink, but don't overdo it, especially as you start upping the dosage. There are side effects, so pick up some laxative while you're at the drug store.

"Enjoy each other," he said, gravely but smiling. "It's a gift you've been given." He turned to leave.

"Thanks for the gift," Rosen said, shaking the bag.

"Not what I meant. I was referring to the other gift. I've known you for a long time, Rosen, since before you graduated. You've been handed a lesson; learn it well."

Rosen was about to ask a question, but then, concluding that he already knew the answer, simply nodded with the same serious smile he saw on Jervis's lips. Jervis excused himself and left.

"What was that?" Jeannine asked as she entered the living room wrapped in a bright orange towel.

"The good doctor bearing meds." He shook the bag. "We had better finish loading the car and be on our way. You said we would probably have a few hours' work ahead of us to open up the place."

Her smile broadened. "Who said we have to open it today. We can leave here later and grab a motel room for the night. I think we have business here that also needs attention." She untucked her towel and let it drop to the floor. "We haven't made love since I started treatment."

"That's because I don't want to be nuked by close contact with my radioactive lover."

Jeannine scooped up the towel and snapped it at him. "Rosen David, you come with me now, or I will show you what nuking really is."

Rosen grinned, walked over, and dropped to his knees. "Okay, love, but how about if I focus my attention down here where it's sweet and warm and the gamma rays don't reach."

= =

The rustic cabin was a dark brown box dwarfed by white pines and surrounded by a carpeting of pine needles that also covered the roof and the open porch that looked out over the lake. Jeannine coached Rosen on how to clear the needles from the roof with a long-handled push-broom and how to undo and store the shutters that blocked the windows. While she got the spring-fed water system operating again, he started a blaze in the fireplace to take the chill out of the cabin. They stood holding hands in front of the fire for several minutes before she led him to the open sleeping loft that looked down over the fireplace. They made love under thick down comforters, then spent the afternoon in bed, talking and dozing off until the dying fire demanded their attention.

The hardest time at the lake was the following weekend when both of Jeannine's sisters arrived. It was, Jeannine had explained, part of the deal to use their lakeside summer place. She and Rosen had agreed to maintain a pretense that the treatment had been a complete success, that Jeannine was cured. Still, it was Elise and Angela who needed the comforting and support. By the time they left on that Sunday night, Jeannine was emotionally and physically exhausted, but she and Rosen quickly settled back into a routine without routine. They watched movies on Rosen's netbook or made love or paddled around the lake as the mood of the moment dictated. The days were languorous but rushed, as they shared the stories and the dreams and confessed inner conflicts that shrunk into insignificance even as the words were formed.

Jeannine worked her gastronomic magic in the small kitchen of the cabin for the first several weeks, but as she weakened and upped the dose of morphine, she had less energy and interest in cooking. They took to eating out until they had worked their way through all eleven restaurants within a twenty-mile radius. Then began the take-out food, alternating among pizzas and subs from a place just down the highway and pretty good Thai from the nearest ethnic café two towns over.

It was the fights that most surprised Rosen: fiery volcanoes of searing words, rivers of resentment, and floods of cold anger. Nothing in his experience had prepared him for the intensity of Jeannine's heat or cold—or his own.

"I think," he started to say, as he pushed his breakfast plate away, "that you are only looking at—"

"I don't give a flying fuck what you think, Rosen," she snapped, interrupting him. "What do you feel?"

Something seethed in him. "I feel, I feel, I..." He stood up suddenly, sending his chair flying. "I feel cheated. I feel alone. I feel trapped in a storyline I never wrote. That's what I feel, damn it!" he shouted. "And I feel, no, I resent that you...no, I *hate* that you seem to think that this is only about you, as if you were the only one trapped in this tragedy, as if I weren't dying, too, because when you die, Jeannine, a piece of me as big as Kansas will die with you. And then, damn you, I have to clean up the next day and go back to Massachusetts and somehow plod through days and decades without you.

"And then, like right now," he said, dropping his voice, "I feel guilty, guilty and angry at the same goddamn time. Because, you are the one who is dying, and who am I to complain, and you are just being so goddamn selfish." He threw up his hands. "And self-centered, and..." The words stuck in his throat, and when he opened his mouth a cry of primal agony escaped. "I don't want to do this, Jeannine, and I have no choice." The millrace opened and tears gushed from his eyes. "I hate it and I am scared and I love you."

"Me, too, Rosen. Me, too." She joined him on the floor where he had dropped to his knees, and another storm had passed.

= =

Jeannine had her good days and her not good days, and the fraction shifted inexorably toward the latter despite her increasing medication. Then there was a sudden reversal so dramatic that Rosen secretly wondered whether she might miraculously recover.

Rosen had cooked fresh pasta under Jeannine's direction, a simple penne with fresh local tomatoes and basil, extra virgin olive oil and garlic. They had accompanied it with a Brunello di Montalcino that Rosen declared to be the best Italian wine he had ever experienced.

"It had better be, my dearest of dears, because that was also the single most expensive bottle of wine I ever bought."

"Don't tell me how much it cost. I want to enjoy it for itself." He divided the last of it between their glasses. "You are in fine fettle tonight, darling."

"It's been a good day. My love cooked a wonderful dinner for me, and a peachy, gibbous moon is rising over the lake. Come, bring your glass, and let's sit on the dock."

They sat and sipped without talking, their heads tilted together as they watched the moonrise.

"The trouble with these Italian wines," she said, breaking the silence, "is that the bottles are too small. See." She raised her empty glass until it was silhouetted against the moon, now only a thin crescent short of full.

"You want more? Are you sure? I mean, are you okay?"

"I am okay, and yes, I want more—more wine, more you, more of everything. Start with the wine."

"What wine? I think that was the only Brunello we have."

"There's a bottle of Fragolino chilling in the fridge. Here, how about a fresh glass?"

Rosen returned with two juice tumblers holding a few fingers' worth each. He sat down and they clinked. "L'chaim," he said.

"I like that: to life!" she said. "Thank you for teaching me."

Rosen took a sip. "Strawberries?" he commented.

"That's how the grape got its name, because it tastes like strawberries, but it's grape wine. Pretty nice, huh? And will you look at the moon down there." She pointed toward the reflection in the middle of the lake. "There's no wind and the water is like a mirror. Perfect, absolutely perfect." They both sipped in silence, listening to the syncopated chirp of early crickets.

Jeannine stood suddenly, steadied herself by reaching down to Rosen's shoulder, then straightened. "The perfect night for canoeing. Help me put the small canoe in the water. I think I want to take a little paddle around the lake."

"I don't know, Jeannine. Let's use the other one; I can take the stern."

"No, I just want the solitude. I'll do this alone, Rosen. I won't be long."

"Are you sure?" The air was dead still, and his question hung in it for long seconds.

"Yes, I'm sure. I'll be all right."

They slipped the canoe down the bank and alongside the dock. Rosen helped her into the canoe and handed her the paddle. "Here. Smooth sailing." He knew what was expected, but he almost couldn't say the words. "I love you."

"Me, too," she said, the words hardly more than a whisper. He leaned out over the canoe and kissed her lightly, his eyes open, their lips barely brushing. She pushed off and glided soundlessly away over the glassy lake.

= =

There was still no wind, and in the predawn stillness, a lightening sky revealed the capsized canoe adrift in the middle of the lake. Rosen busied himself cleaning up, restoring shutters on windows, and burying the remnants of their stash. It was late morning before the local sheriff arrived with the news.

"She was ill," Rosen said. "I probably shouldn't have let her go out alone."

"I know, son. Word had gotten around the lake; it's a pretty small community, you know. I am sorry. Just don't blame yourself. When you feel up to it, drop by to answer some questions."

Rosen watched the patrol car disappear down the dirt road before he started screaming and smashing dishes.

29

The unreality of the retreat at the lake and the reality of Jeannine's death left Rosen numb. He returned to work, but quickly realized that he could no longer sustain the pretense of doing make-work that was made all the more meaningless and unbearable by the solicitous manners of his coworkers. On the third day back, he gave his notice and left the office after lunch. He was now completely adrift, like the canoe on Keoka Lake, in a windless doldrums. There was no Millie in his life, no Jeannine, no work. Before the week was out, he had finished off more than half of the dozen bottles that still remained from Jeannine's wine collection.

The funeral arrangements he had left to the family. He was only the boyfriend, after all, and her sisters had met him only that once in Maine. Still worse, Jeannine had confided in them that he was still married, which would put him in the second circle of Hell.

The funeral was being held at Immaculate Conception in Newburyport, and Rosen figured that showing up would be rude and inappropriate. That, at least, was the rationale he used to convince himself that he had no reason to go. Instead, he opened another bottle of Riesling from the last of Jeannine's wine cellar and drank it for breakfast, toasting her memory until he passed out on the kitchen floor. It was eleven in the morning.

He awoke to the sound of bells and banging. The wall clock said it was three in the afternoon, but it felt like three in the morning.

Rosen struggled to orient himself, then looked up to see Dr. Jervis' round face peering in the kitchen window. "Are you all right, Rosen?" he said, rapping on the window. "Are you all right? Let me in."

Rosen staggered to the kitchen door, holding on to chairs as he went. "Not a good time, Dr. Jervis," he said, as he opened the door. "Not a good time."

"I suppose not. I suspected this would be how you might cope. I am sure you were strong as long as she needed you, but none of us can be nonstop grownups; eventually we crash. However, young man, this is not the way. I think there is something you can do about Jeannine."

"Do? Doctor, she's dead. What is there to do?"

"Right now, get some coffee and splash some cold water on your face. That won't solve your problem, but it will help you feel better. Then I have something for you to read."

Rosen blinked, trying to steady his vision. "What do you have for me to read, Doctor? I already read the obit. I wrote it. The least I could do, I figured. Pretty good, too." He continued to babble as he tried to regain his equilibrium. "I don't think her sisters liked it though, and the paper wouldn't let me say 'survived by her lover, Dr. Rosen David of Essex,' so I told them I was her husband, but that she had always called me her lover. Quick thinking. They changed it to 'survived by her loving husband, Dr. Rosen David of Essex.' The sisters must have raised a royal stink, because the next day the paper published a correction. I didn't even know they did that with obituaries."

Dr. Jervis took his shoulders and looked him in the eye. "You get the coffee going, and after the second cup I'll let you read something."

= =

The coffee helped, but not enough to stop Rosen's head from throbbing and not enough to make the letters stay anchored on the page. Rosen handed the printout back. "Just tell me what it's about, Doc."

"Jeannine's cancer was a rare type, as you already know, and extremely rare in non-smokers. The pathologists at Dana-Farber had actually never seen anything quite like it before. I started to do some research. Turns out there were references in the literature to this particular variant. They were published some years ago in one of those third-rate commercial catch-all journals with a few hundred subscribers who pay a thousand bucks a year each. Elliot Longtree, M.D., and Barbara Hecht, Ph.D. Names mean anything to you? No? Me neither. But I did recognize where they worked—a lab down in North Carolina by the name of Biontolics Southland, LLC."

Rosen jerked, suddenly fully alert. "What?"

"They were researching virulent human cancers, implanting them in laboratory animals, and studying their progress. This one proved so potent that they didn't even have to inject it to implant it. They would spray the cells down the throats of their subjects, and the poor doomed mice would obediently develop oat cell carcinoma of the bronchia. The strain they were cultivating would metastasize in every case. The authors were excited because it was such a reliable, reproducible research vehicle, but after the first two papers, there's been nothing more."

"And there won't be," Rosen declared, "because it was important work. That's how Biontolics operates, even when it's off-topic from their main interests. They were saving this one against a future need, in this case a need named Jeannine Carsten."

"You really think this was deliberate? I was thinking that maybe it was some kind of accidental exposure at the lab. You know, in connection with her work."

"She was a statistics wonk, Dr. Jervis. She worked with numbers, like I do. Did."

"So you don't think she was exposed to this in a lab accident at Biontolics."

"Oh, she was exposed all right, but it was no accident. Look, not a word about this to anyone, not anyone. Okay?"

= =

Rosen knew that the best thing for him to do would be to sleep it off, but his heart was pounding and he was already getting too wired to sleep, so he grabbed his netbook, slipped the paper that Dr. Jervis had left with him into his hip pocket, and headed for Zumi's to do more coffee and more online research.

It was not until late that afternoon in Zumi's that the thunderclap jarred him fully awake. They wanted him alive, because if they had wanted him dead, he would be in a grave, just as Jeannine was. Either they had changed their minds, or he had been wrong that they were out to kill him. This meant that he had time and that he still had some chips to play, even if he did not know what color they were or what they were worth.

It took weeks of dogged work before Rosen finally had enough to go on. Ferguson had been canny, but even a light-footed traveler leaves tracks in the snow. Dig deep enough, dig wide enough, and eventually your shovel hits something. Each hit led to more, each name he uncovered offered another line of research, each company connected with Biontolics was another lead.

Patterns, it was about patterns and connections, and this was what Rosen did, and now, with nothing else in his life, this was all he did. He lived on coffee and donuts and adrenaline. Bit by byte, he assembled the dossier until he had telephone numbers and addresses and affiliations. Biontolics and Revic AG were part of Averica SA, which was partially owned by Health Sciences and Services Holdings, Limited, whose board included two members of the Board of Directors of the Gerard and Hannah Berkowitz Charitable Foundation, which funded Biontolics and a research unit of PanAfrica Pharmacometrics. There was a consortium, formed out of something called the Exaction Group along with Slavic Estate Enterprises and a German bank, that actually owned an entire city in Russia.

Eventually, the returns on the Web research dwindled, and Rosen turned to hacking. Even there, the Web was his friend. All the tips and techniques he needed to know in order to hack into private networks and encrypted sites were waiting for him and for anyone else interested. Rosen figured he was leaving his own trail behind him but also figured that if he worked fast enough, it wouldn't matter. Still, he started cultivating his paranoid tendencies: randomizing his schedule, glancing in reflections as he passed store windows, checking his street and his rearview mirror for recurring vehicles.

Every time he became discouraged, he would picture Jeannine, feathering her paddle as she followed the trail of the moon into the middle of the lake. Every time he was too tired to try another password or compare another list of corporate officers, he saw her eyes, open like his, reflecting the moon as their lips brushed for the last time. Knowing. Both of them knowing.

It was all about knowing and being known, and as Rosen began to know his adversaries, their movements and actions began to make sense. He still had no idea what he would do if he ever reached his destination. The pursuit itself had become his purpose—to meet and confront them. And then, suddenly, a door opened in front of him, an appointment on the Exchange Server at Biontolics in Ipswich, where he had kept open the hidden access that Jeannine had set up for him: Ferguson, Berkowitz Foundation, Tuesday, 09:30. Now the only question for Rosen was what to do about it, how to bet the chips left to him.

30

First class on the flight from Boston to London Heathrow was full, but Ferguson didn't care; he had his favorite seat, one in the middle, which meant that an aisle separated his partially enclosed, full-flat, mini-suite from his neighbors on either side. After takeoff, he accepted the salad but declined the entrée. He was finishing his coffee—they had a real espresso machine on board, especially engineered to operate at altitude—when the left window-seat passenger in the row behind stood and started toward the lavatory. The man stopped just past Ferguson's seat, turned, and flashed him a broad smile. He wore tinted glasses and sported a fashionably close beard in the style currently favored by the young intelligentsia.

"Doctor, Doctor Llewellyn Cass. How good to see you. On our way to London, are we?"

Ferguson jerked, startled. "I'm afraid you're mistaken, young man. I've never heard of..."

The man knelt beside the seat and lowered his voice. "What, never heard of the famous oncologist, the Welsh wunderkind, world traveler, and medical entrepreneur?"

Ferguson held the man's gaze without blinking but shook his head. "I really and truly do not know what or whom you are talking about. I—"

The man interrupted again. "You were born in Swansea in 1928 to a prominent Jewish family, taught yourself English at the age of five by listening to the BBC news on the radio, followed your father and grandfather into medicine, finished your studies at 22, then decamped for Boston where you quickly rose to dominate the sarcoma scene. You prefer to be called Andras, drink but never smoked, and you certainly don't look your age."

Ferguson's heart was racing but he kept his voice to his best patient-calming resonance. "This is absolutely preposterous, young man," he said quietly. "My name is Charles Ferguson, as it says on the passenger manifest and on my passport, and the only part you got right is that I am a doctor. Now, please, I would like to get at least some sleep on this all too short hop to Heathrow. I face a day filled with meetings after we land."

"Please forgive me for being so rude, Doctor," the man said, as he reached across to shake hands. "I should have introduced myself. I'm Dr. David, Rosen David. We've never met, but still, we know each other, Andras. May I call you Andras? I do feel I know you as few others might."

Ferguson quickly changed tactics. "You can call me anything you want, Dr. David—after we get to Heathrow where my limousine will meet us. Until then, please, just enjoy the flight." He frowned. "How odd, I wouldn't have thought you could afford first class on Virgin Atlantic on your salary, but..."

"I can't afford it, but one has to ante up to enter any high-stakes game. As you should know, if you have kept up on recent personnel changes in Ipswich, I am currently unemployed. There has been such a high turnover on the North Shore in recent months, hasn't there? First, there was the sad and untimely loss of one Jeannine Carsten, statistician and sometime spy, paid by both Biontolics and the Berkowitz Foundation, it seems, so I am sure the name must have come to your attention at some point. Died of small cell carcinoma, a rare type that seems to have been a specialty of some of your colleagues down in North Carolina."

Ferguson blinked and tried to channel his friend, Douglas

Dougherty, with his unreadable face, but Rosen, noticing the momentary flash of discomfort, pressed closer. "Yes, right, clearly a matter we will have to discuss further, Dr. Cass."

Ferguson started to protest, but then held his tongue.

"Nothing to say? Well, then later. I do look forward to that limo ride and the chat. So, sleep well. Goodnight, Andras," he said, winking and rising to return to his seat.

Ferguson, too agitated to sleep, finally gave up. He punched the buttons to motor his bed back upright into a seat, then turned on his reading lamp. Glancing over his shoulder, he noticed Rosen was also awake, flipping through papers on his tray table, and munching on an outsized chocolate chip cookie.

At Heathrow, the two men deplaned without exchanging a word, Rosen following Dougherty a half step behind. The limo was waiting at curbside when they exited the terminal. Ferguson greeted the chauffer by name as the door was held for them. As soon as the chauffer was back behind the wheel, he discreetly raised the privacy window at his back.

"So," Ferguson began, as they pulled out, "you think you know something about me, do you?"

"I know a lot about you—and your organization. Or should that word be plural?"

Ferguson snorted with skeptical amusement but said nothing. Rosen reached over and tapped him on the chest, hard enough to hurt and to make an audible thump. "You know what you are, Dr. Cass? You are a professional killer, an assassin. You kill for a living, you and your colleagues. You kill to keep your secret." Ferguson pushed Rosen's hand away from his chest, but Rosen returned it and thumped again with his index finger, relishing Ferguson's discomfort. "You killed Jeannine."

"You know less than you think, Rosen David. I had nothing to do with that. It was somebody else, acting on his own, an unauthorized initiative."

"Ah, yes, the German, your man Holzinger. See, I do know. I had even figured that his last meeting with Jeannine was about the right timing to take advantage of your group's special insights in oncology. But, if you must know the truth, I no longer really care so much about the details of who did what and who said what and whose initiative was involved. I'm not even here for revenge.

"As I said, I've been doing some research. Anyone could do it with the right starting point and enough persistence. I am surprised that no one has ever tried to expose any of your small circle of friends."

Ferguson, emboldened by the safety of his own turf, responded directly. "Oh, they have, but there are so many ways to deal with such matters when you have the resources. And as you say, the circle is small, although I would not call most of them friends. Patients is the word I use."

"You have some interesting patients, Andras."

"Please, among friends I am now called Chas. Charles is too formal, and Chuck has that American abruptness. Chas was started by a Boston colleague. It's got an old money, faux continental ring to it that appeals to me in an amusing way."

Rosen, realizing the momentum was now with him, replied, "Among friends, you can be whomever you please, I imagine. But, Andras," he said, stressing the name, "we were talking about your patients, right? Let's start with one of the rich and famous who was not hard to figure out: Edgar Mbutsu. You've been keeping that bastard alive, haven't you?"

"What can I say?"

"You can tell me why."

"Because we still needed him. He's our oldest surviving patient and has been under treatment the longest, so he has become somewhat of a living laboratory, a look into our own future. And he foots the bills—not all of them, but the biggest share. He was our banker, our insurance policy, and a guinea pig all rolled into one big black package."

"He's a monster."

"The world has known worse."

"Try the slaughter of over a hundred thousand people who happened to belong to the wrong tribe in his fiefdom."

"It's a democratic nation, not a fiefdom. Granted it's a one-party democracy with rigged elections and a president-for-life who seems to be enjoying an exceptionally long life. You know, when their constitution was amended to grant the title for life, I do suspect they had no idea quite how long a president might live. But Mbutsu didn't slaughter the Bunto-speaking minority; the Lusanyu-speaking majority did that for him. Didn't you even read his Wikipedia entry? Besides, as monsters go, he's minor league. What's a few hundred thousand when the Hall of Famers do millions. Try six million."

"Ah, the old Nazi comparison ploy. After Hitler, who can compete in the atrocity sweepstakes? Not very imaginative, Andras. Do bigger monsters make the smaller ones less monstrous or their collaborators less accountable? I don't think so.

"But, let's see. Who else is in your circle? It's hard to tell in some cases. Obviously, records can be doctored, but there are still scattered sources that contain clues. I found that newspaper archives can be particularly useful to establish probable dates of birth for people who just seem to hang around past their welcome. Of course, I'm just guessing in some cases. Atchison Dougherty is a no-brainer, though. Actually, if he were not CEO of Biontolics, I don't think there would be much of a trail for him."

"It's an ego thing," Ferguson said. "I tried to dissuade him, but he likes to see himself as still leading the charge, herding his intrepid little squad of researchers, even though it is no longer little and not really his to lead anymore. An off-scale ego is a common trait among my patients; one might say it's almost a prerequisite for participation in our program."

"Ah yes, so let me guess on another. Julian Costa at Boston University."

Ferguson's expression was one of embarrassed chagrin. "It's Gabriel, Gabriel Costa. And yes, I'm sorry to say, he is one of my patients. We funded some of his genetics research, he sussed us out, and he's had us by the nuts ever since. But he won't last forever; his time is coming, maybe sooner than he thinks."

"From what I could learn, he seems healthy as a horse, one of the old guard who knows how to play all the palace games all too well. I don't see him retiring anytime soon. His faculty hate him and would love to see him go, from what I read."

"No, he won't retire, but he still won't be around all that much longer." Rosen opened his mouth as if to speak, then seemed to change his mind. Finally, Ferguson said, "Yes, Dr. David, to answer the unspoken question, we do that. Not as often, as you think, and not if we can find an effective alternative, but we do what we must to keep the ship sailing smoothly and on course. Remember that. Costa continues because he does not ask for much, and he knows better than to threaten. Mbutsu continued as long as he did because we needed him, and he actually plays on a small stage in a faraway country. Plus, he sends cash. Or diamonds, which are, at times, even better."

"Yes, I do get the idea that it's mostly only the super-rich who get to join your club. There are some who have been vocal about life extension that are ambiguous cases, maybe they're in the club, maybe not.

"Put your mind to rest. Venter and Kurzweil have nothing to do with this. We don't deal with high-profile amateurs no matter how rich they are."

"So I take it de Grey didn't make the cut."

"Poor Professor de Grey. He writes with such passion and tries so hard to be persuasive, but, no, he didn't make the cut. There are scores of others, hundreds. They have the unwarranted sense of self-importance, they see the singularity looming, but they can't swing the ante. It's a costly club, Dr. David, and the price of admission has been going up as the enterprise grows. The principles are relatively simple, but what it takes to sustain it over the long haul are unimaginably complicated.

"We do not, strictly speaking, arrest aging. We do not have some kind of shot that freezes you in time once and for all. But then, you already figured that one out, I imagine. It's like standing still on a unicycle, which is impossible. The unicyclist is always peddling, forward and back, twisting and returning. It's actually more like balancing a unicycle atop a small stool, a balancing act between competing pulls, between cell death and cancer, between organ failure and rejection of new tissue. In the process, the human chimera that is our patient becomes ever more complicated, comprising the genetics of a growing number of individual cell lines, and the balancing act grows in complexity with the passing years. Fortunately, our research and development have kept pace, although not by a very wide margin. We do not yet know where it ends. Our oldest patients are over 100 with a biological age in their fifties and with little or no aging from year to year. Our simulations and projections tell us this game can be played for another two hundred years or so. We think—"

Rosen interrupted him. "Do you believe in God, Dr. Cass?"

"You think we're playing God, right?"

"No, I just wondered whether you believe in God."

There was a thoughtful pause, then a quiet response. "No. I do not believe in God."

"I, too, do not believe in God. But I believe in good and evil. Do you believe in good and evil?"

"I think the universe is intrinsically indifferent. Good and evil are human inventions, and we are the perpetrators of both. Is that how you see it, or did you mean something more mystical?"

"No, that's pretty much how I see it. As I see it, what you and your enterprise are doing is among the greatest evils ever perpetrated in human history. It is the end of progress, the death of childhood, the triumph of ultimate selfishness."

"Oh, please."

"A few hundred years of Mbutsu? Tell me that's not evil in every sense of the term. An aging academic blocking progress in his field?

On another scale, but still evil. A cabal accountable to no one but themselves cornering wealth and secretly pulling strings to one purpose: to perpetuate their own stranglehold on everyone else?"

"Melodramatic, wouldn't you say? I would have expected something more calmly rational from you, Dr. David."

Rosen ignored him and continued. "You would end death, Doctor. What could be worse than that? Do you know what the late Steve Jobs told the 2005 graduating class at Stanford? Do you know? He said that death is very likely the single best invention of life. He called it life's change agent, because it clears out the old to make way for the new."

"Do you think I haven't heard this hogwash before? It's a matter of scale. If everybody lived as long as Methuselah, it would be different. But we are not talking about everybody, we are talking about a handful—someday, some distant day, as many as thousands, maybe—but never millions. The world can't afford more. Our enterprise is a creator and concentrator of wealth, but it is also a consumer on an enormous scale. So we will always just be one small piece of the story, and the story we are writing is innovation itself. We are the true agents of change. Do you have any idea how much basic and applied research we have underwritten? You know only the tip of the iceberg, Dr. David, only the tip."

"Perhaps, but I also know you are shaping a worldwide research agenda to fit your own ends. And what about the research that you have decided does not suit those ends, the countless studies and promising lines of investigation that you've killed."

"You have to understand some of the subtleties, Dr. David. Obviously, we have a vested interest in progress in all these many areas, but at the same time we have to limit exposure. It is another balancing act, like maintaining political and economic stability in a country in order to enable real progress, slow but steady."

"That may be how you see it, but what about Mbutsu, whose personal wants and wishes become the agenda for an entire country? Forever."

"Not forever, Dr. David. Nothing lasts forever. In the case of Edgar Mbutsu, forever may be far shorter than you or President Mbutsu think. In any case, sooner or later somebody would get through his vaunted security and do him in. Even his legendary luck must run out. You can be certain of that."

"They've been saying that for many years, and with every year, his survival skills are sharpened and his opposition dwindles."

"Life has always been a form of gambling, Dr. David. Survival is always a roll of the die. We may have loaded the dice, but they are rolled, nevertheless. Every day is another roll, another spin of the roulette wheel. We can inhibit aging, but we cannot stop a bullet or prevent a plane from crashing or an assassin's blade from slipping between the ribs."

"Or a pickup truck from colliding with a small car."

"That was a mistake, a misunderstanding."

"A misunderstanding that almost got my wife killed and did kill one of her coworkers—a middle-age school teacher with four school-age children."

"I said it was a mistake."

"Yes, a stupid mistake, the kind of mistake that comes all too easily from single-minded dedication to one cause, one purpose, one end. All other priorities and perspectives fade before that one, all-important objective. Jeannine Carsten was no accident, though, no mistake. You sent her to an early, watery grave."

"She took her own life. You and I both know that."

"So, it would seem that you have been following the developments in the New World rather closely. Suicide or not, you killed her."

"I already acknowledged that it was our security man acting on his own. Look, Dr. David, we are not stupid people. We are a small cadre, yes, but we are also diverse. We have political scientists working for us, and there is even a politician among our small circle of friends—I am coming to like that term of yours—who not only serves the agenda but also helps shape it."

"My God, I just put it together. Senator Thurstone, right? He's rich and he's been around forever."

"You are rather fond of that word, forever, aren't you? Yes, but he will have to retire from politics before too long and find another career. At some point it becomes unseemly and raises suspicions. We prefer our membership to be out of the public spotlight. Like many an old club, we prefer a low profile."

The limousine slowed and pulled into a circular driveway in front of a large brick-and-stone building.

"Wait a minute," Rosen said, leaning toward the door. "Where are we?"

"A small private clinic outside of London. You are almost overdue for your second treatment, so you might as well get your money's worth out of your airline ticket."

"Second treatment? What the hell are you talking about?"

"In the hospital, in Boston, the experimental course of antibiotics. There were, shall we say, some extra ingredients in the formulation. And who do you think developed the new drugs that fought off your infection? It was all Biontolics or some other unit of our enterprise. Is that your evil? If we are cut, do we not bleed? If we are infected, do we not fall ill? Much of the most innovative medical research in the world today is directly or indirectly funded by us."

"You said second treatment. You mean..."

"Yes, you are one of us, a chimera, one of that small circle of friends. Your application for membership was approved—expedited, I should say. It was my idea, and now we have every intention of keeping you around."

Rosen looked pale and felt sick. Suddenly he was catapulted from thinking he might soon be killed to seeing now the years stretched out before him without any end that he could see. He swayed with the sudden knowledge as he stared into the gulf.

Ferguson noticed Rosen's discomfort. "You'll get used to it. You'll have lots of time," he said, as he stepped from the limousine.

Rosen got out slowly, stood next to the limousine for a moment, looking around as if trying to get his bearings. "I'll have to think about this," he said, then started walking back down the drive.

Ferguson waited until Rosen was nearly out to the road before calling out after him. "If you want time to think about it, I suggest you return and accept our hospitality. Otherwise, you might find that time has run out."

31

The marshes were studded with mounds of salt hay heaped high to dry in the early autumn sun after the harvest, a practice only recently resumed in this part of Ipswich. Rosen turned reluctantly from the view to find a young woman standing in the doorway of his new office.

"I'm sorry to interrupt," she said. "I can come back another time."

He smiled, shrugged, and motioned for her to come in.

"I'm working on productizing your visualization program so that others can use it. I had some questions about some of the parameters."

"Have we met?"

"No, I don't think so. I was hired when I finished up at Stanford. It was after...after you left. I'm Alana Grossman. Software Engineering."

Rosen studied her face, a face that was pretty because she was young but might become ordinary as the years added up. A nervous smile flickered and fled her face before she looked down at the notepad she was carrying.

"I'm rewriting your visualization program as a Web app," she began again. "I've reverse engineered most of it, but there are some parameters that...well, I'm not sure what they mean. I know what they do in the program, but I meant...I, well, what is the significance to the user? What are they about?" She was clearly becoming uncomfortable under his unflinching gaze, but Rosen kept looking at her, as he might ponder a painting at the Peabody Essex Museum. She swallowed. "Look, I'll come back another time. Or maybe I can email you. I was just thinking..."

Rosen was thinking about her dying, this young woman, barely old enough to buy booze in Massachusetts, this young professional just starting out her career, and he was looking at her as if she were already at the edge of death. She was more than twenty years his junior and she would die before he did. Her face would turn pudgy as she put on weight; the breasts that now proudly filled her tee-shirt would wrinkle and sag; her professional skills would grow rusty, and her mind would become less nimble; the vertebrae in her back would compress, and she would gradually go from short to shrunken. And she would die. Rosen would still be much as he was today, and this young woman would be dead.

The thought, strange though it was, did not trouble Rosen. What troubled him was that he could look at her this way, look at her pretty young face and see her dying—and feel nothing. It was like looking at a cell culture under a microscope. She was life, but alien life, a different species. He continued to stare in silence, dispassionately.

Annoyance spread across her face, and she stood suddenly. "Look, this is getting a little too weird. I don't know what your problem is, but I'm just trying to do my job. I'll find some other way to figure this out." She backed away from his desk without turning.

"The parameters link the oblique factor rotation to the distribution of terms in the corpus," he said. "I'm sorry. I was...trying to remember. It seems like a lifetime ago that I wrote that program. Well, it was, in a sense, another life. Please forgive me. I was lost in...lost in thought. Sorry."

"Okay, no problem. That makes sense. That's why they feed into the color map, right?"

"Right. See, you probably would have figured it out without me.

And, again, forgive me for being 'weird.' I've only been back for a few weeks, and I am still not used to my new life, my new job."

"Sure, I understand." She smiled broadly at him, turning on a megawatt smile that Rosen realized would take her far and get her many things. She turned and bounced out of his office.

His new job, a senior position created especially for him and justifying regular trips to London, was part of the deal of his new life. So were the surges of energy and debilitating bouts of nausea that followed his last series of treatments. He was in process, becoming somebody else, something else, a new species, dependent on medications and on medication for the medications. His briefcase carried a new laptop and a half-dozen bottles of pills. His Outlook calendar was stippled with asterisks that kept him to his complicated schedule and would remind him each time he had to book another flight to London, a redundant reminder, since he now had his own secretary who handled all his appointments and travel bookings. She, too, was young; she, too, was dying. Everywhere Rosen looked, he saw people dying, even the children who laughed in the playground adjacent to his new apartment. Everyone was dying, everyone except him. And Ferguson. And Dougherty. And Mbutsu. And Gabriel Costa.

Rosen did not know the whole list. He wondered if he would recognize other immortals when he met them, if there would be a shock of mutual awareness. I am one of you and you are one of us. We are the watchers. We watch the world, the world of the dying, a world that is not ours.

Of course, that was not quite true. Gabriel Costa was not immortal, because Gabriel Costa was becoming an annoyance and was no longer useful. Stay useful, do useful things, that was the mantra of immortality in the world into which Rosen had been admitted. The mantra was a perversion of Steven King's TANSTAAFL economics. Everyone contributes. Contribute, and you get to live.

The briefing at the London clinic and the earlier presentation from Steven King had prepared him for most of the physical effects, but not for these changes in the world around him, a world that was losing its color as it pulled away from him, becoming monochrome through the wide-angle lens of his extended life. Of course, it was he who was retreating, panning back, zooming out from the people he would have to watch die, making them smaller and smaller in his worldview. It was a radical refocusing of his experience, ironically made necessary by the very feelings to which he had become more open. A younger Rosen David, already detached, would not have had to undergo this surgical separation that removed him from himself and from humanity.

He had acquiesced to their trickery in London to buy himself time, thinking that the purchase price had been his soul. Now he was coming to realize that it was not an outright sale but a mortgage with high interest and regular payments.

He looked at the clock on his desk, its second hand frozen. He looked at the calendar beside it, the date unchanged since he had returned. He looked at his face reflected in the glass top of his new desk, the eyes unblinking, the nostrils not even flaring with each breath. In his mind, the world had stopped, and time stretched out before him, a line of lonely isolation, an infinite arrow, a vector rather than a line segment. He laughed at his own metaphor. Only a mathematician would see it that way.

"I am not a mathematician," he said to his reflection, which sprang into life as he spoke. "I am a mathematical biologist. And I have a soul, still."

He started thinking about what it would be like to be celebrating the next turn of the century—or the one after. He was neither elated nor depressed by the staggering number of years that might lay before him, the things and places he might do and see.

He got up and walked past his secretary in the outer office. "I'm going for a walk," he said, without looking at her face, which was unlined and attractive and would remind him that she was dying. He walked out the front door without signing out, which would have been unnecessary now anyway, since the new guard, along with everyone else at the Labs, knew him on sight, the Lazarus who had returned from the lost to win a cushy new position. How little they knew.

He turned left out of the driveway, heading toward the Crane Estate and the beach. Although he had worked for years within an easy stroll of the Estate, and the beach had always been one of Millie's favorite local haunts, the seashore had never meant much to him. Now he would often hike to the end of Argilla Road and walk the sands and stare out across the visual infinity of the Atlantic, sometimes until the autumn sun set and the beach patrol chased him off. Late, on weekdays after Labor Day, the beach was sometimes all but deserted.

Today, he looked out across the whitecaps churned by a fresh wind out of the northeast, hypnotized by the visual music that was regular and chaotic at the same time. He could look at this non-human beauty and be moved by it, the unending beauty of Nature with a capital N.

His reverie was interrupted by the sound of the beach patrol approaching, and he realized that he had walked far from the entry and that the sun was a red-orange blob sunk almost to the horizon. The patrol had begun to recognize him and would joke about his taking up residence on the beach. He knew the names of the two regulars, Fred and Julio, and waved when he saw them approaching. Usually they talked, mostly about the ups and downs of the Red Sox, but sometimes about bits in the news or local gossip. Tonight they brought news of a different sort.

"You used to work down the road, didn't you, Doc? At that lab?" Fred said, talking through his soup-strainer moustache.

Rosen smiled and nodded. "Still do," he said.

"Well, then, you probably already know. It was in the news this afternoon. Bionholics, right?"

"Yeah, Biontolics," he gently corrected.

"Right, that's what I meant. Well, the CEO, this limey from London, was in the headlines today."

"What was it? What did he do?"

"Not what he did but what somebody did to him. A crazy from Europe somewhere broke into his apartment and shot him. He died in the ambulance."

"Who died in the ambulance?"

"The CEO. The security guards got the guy from wherever, but not before he had gotten off a couple of shots at your boss."

"Was the guy, the shooter, from The Netherlands, from Holland?"

"Yeah, that's right. So you already knew the story, huh?"

"Yeah, I already knew the story."

Julio leaned toward his partner. "See, I told you. And you still gotta get off the beach, Doc. Rules. We close at sunset, you know."

"I know. Give me a couple of minutes, and I'll be out of your hair."

"Better start hiking back, Doc, there's a lot of sand between you and the entrance."

Rosen grinned broadly and reassured them that he was on his way. The tide was coming in, anyway, and with the erosion from the heavy winter storms of the past several years, there were places where the water would soon be lapping against the fencing that separated the beach from the protected dunes.

"So, you finally succeeded, Bram," he said, talking to himself as he watched the patrol roll out of sight down the beach. "Good for you. You found a purpose and you filled it." The thought gave him comfort, but only for the brief moment before his mind started searching through scenarios and highlighted one labeled Patagonia. Was The General really dead or had they faked his death as they had with Llewellyn Cass? "It's hard to know what's real," he said to the wind. "Death, now that's real, at least for most of the human race. Beyond that, it is hard to tell anymore."

= =

News of the second death reached him later in the week. It was impossible to miss, what with all the special features and retrospectives, the file footage and the talking heads of the analysts.

"Brutal Dictator Dies." "Butcher of Busanyu Dead." "Future Uncertain in West African Country." "Busanyu Military Assumes Control, Promises Early Elections." "Cause of Death Uncertain for African Leader."

When the follow-on stories began flooding the cable channels and the Internet, Rosen realized that he had gotten his answer about what was real. The President for Life of Busanyu had succumbed to a rare tropical disease that had recently made its reappearance in West Africa. Rosen didn't need to read on; he already knew the name of the invariably fatal disease: Charles Ferguson, once known as Llewellyn Andras Cass.

The commentators made much of the two faces of the late President: the stability he had brought to the whole region and the brutal violence that had been the instrument of his pacification. The old question about whether ends justified the means was displayed on text crawls at the bottom of screens and posed in interviews with political pundits.

Rosen walked the sands at Crane Beach that day, posing his own questions, talking aloud like some displaced denizen of the streets of New York City.

"What is the point? What does it matter that any of us were here. Immortality? For Mbutsu, it turned out to be less than a century. Who will remember him in another hundred years? Who will remember me?"

His secretary had reminded him on his way out of the office that she had booked him on an overnight to London for the following week. He didn't need the reminder. He had already postponed it more than a week and was beginning to feel the effects of the delay, but he still needed time, time to think. He found it easier to think aloud, so he talked with Jeannine, walking barefoot on the beach with her, feeling the electricity between them again even as their hands did not touch. He was aware that his mind was becoming affected, but it didn't worry him. He never worried. That was someone else's job. His job was to figure it out. There were moments when it seemed clearer, moments like now. It helped to say the words aloud, where he could hear them clearly. At least his hearing was still good, he thought.

"Why are we here?" he said, looking first to the clouds and then to the sea that reflected them. "No, the question is why am I here? That is the question every man must answer for himself." He started mumbling, then merely mouthing the words, then there were only the thoughts. And Jeannine. If there is no God, he said to her, then we must choose our own purpose. If there is a God, then perhaps it had been chosen for us, but still, there is the personal choice to be made. Do we meet destiny or run from it? Do we make our point or leave only an ellipsis?

And what is the point? Bram Dekker may or may not have lived with a purpose, but certainly he had died with one. What had been the purpose of Edgar Jabari Mbutsu's life? Of his death? What had been the point of your ever so much shorter life, Jeannine? To teach me, he thought. To teach me how to understand imaginary and complex numbers, to teach me about mystery and miracles. He smiled at the thought of her smiling when he told her what he meant.

"And what of me?" he said, once more speaking to the waves. "What will be my point, and when will I make it?" He looked down at his feet, noticing the packed sand scribbled with the tracks of the darting shore birds. Millie would know what they were, who had made the tracks, but Rosen had forgotten—if he ever knew. Plovers. Or was it rovers? But now he noticed that among the bird footprints there were what looked to him like Hebrew letters. Rosen knelt on the damp sand and started to scan the tracks with his hand as if reading an ancient text: *Im ein ani li, mi li? U'k'sheh ani l'atzmi, ma ani?* Questions, they were questions that he recognized. If I am not for myself, and if I am only for myself, then what? But there was one more, one more of those pointed questions from Hillel the Elder, questions that were themselves answers. "If not now, when?" he shouted above the susurration of the retreating tide.

"Indeed," he answered himself. If we are all headed for the same destination, better to make a point on arrival. Jeannine had made her point, even if the only one to hear it in the still of the night had been Rosen. Now it was up to him to make his point in a way that could not be ignored, that would be heard everywhere. It would be tricky. He would have to buy still more time, and the cost could prove to be too high. But he knew he would have to delay his final move until the very last.

Suddenly, completely rational again, his mind sharpened by his resolute choice, he fished out his cellphone and dialed his own office, knowing that his secretary was working late on her regular weekly report to London.

"Marti, it's me. I need you to book another trip. I really need to get away from the office for a few days, change the scenery, get some really good food and some fine French wine. Get me on a morning flight to Montreal and book me into a good hotel for a long weekend. I want to fly back in time to change and catch my flight to London, that way you won't have to rebook that trip. Okay? And get me a car so I can get around a bit."

"Consider it done," she said. "And say hello to Quebec for me."

"Will do. I'll see you after I get back from London." He thumbed the phone off. He would need to use cash, and even then he would not be able to stay off the radar for long, but he only needed an extra week or so. They would know as soon as he missed his return flight from Canada, but they wouldn't be certain until he was a no-show for London. He knew there were still ways to cross back into the U.S. without passing through Customs: logging roads or fire roads without gates or patrols. Jeannine had told him and pointed out the general area to him on the wall map up at Keoka Lake. Keoka itself was not an option for him, much as it appealed to his sense of symmetry. It would be tricky guessing when to resurface, but there was now no doubt in his mind of where and how to do it.

"I will not retreat in silence," he said, as he turned toward the water, the opening lines of a long forgotten poem rising, unbidden, to his lips:

> I will not retreat in silence.
> Let the shofar sound at last
>   its plangent call, both sweet and shrill,
>   one long and final blast, *tekkiah gadolah.*
> Remind the echoing hills
>   that we were here and passed before,
> And left our footprints in the winding streets and dusty stalls,
>   and scratched our marks, still incomplete,
> Upon the city's sun-hued walls.

32

A salt-laden wind swept the deserted beach. Ferguson's new partner turned toward him with quiet fury, snapping his words off between clenched teeth, twisting the rolled newspaper as if it were a snake to be strangled. "You did what? Do you want to spell that out again, just in case I misheard or misunderstood you?"

"I gave him saline. He started feeling much better immediately and sent me on my way. The placebo effect works. Even for the likes of Edgar Mbutsu, it works. Or maybe especially for the likes of the Butcher of Busanyu, a man who long needed to believe in magic and in medical miracles. Given the delay in treatment and his already deteriorating condition, it didn't take long for the cellular cascade to set in."

"And now what? Where does this leave us?"

"Right here, on holidays in the Cayman Islands, carrying on business as usual."

"Are you out of your mind, Andras? You think they won't figure this one out and go after you, after us? It must be obvious what happened."

"No, it is not. They will not. The President's new personal physician was handpicked. He has diagnosed idiopathic hemorrhagic fever, of which there have been a growing number of unexplained cases in West Africa. He has, as expected, done everything in his power, including obtaining shipments of powerful medicines dispatched from the Institute for Tropical and Uncommon Diseases in Switzerland and from its commercial partner, Revic AG. But, as you know, IHF is unresponsive to even the best antibiotics and is almost invariably fatal. I knew that the fear factor would insure that there would be no autopsy. This is Busanyu we are talking about, not Boston. And, of course, there is no such medical diagnosis as cellular cascade, anyway. We are in the clear."

"And en route to bankruptcy. We cannot operate without the flow of funds from Busanyu. You know that. How could you be so stupid? And how could you be so arrogant, to take action like this without first consulting with me?"

"Is that the procedure, Bertrand?" He pronounced the name in the French style, with a guttural R, an accented long A, and a nasalized N. "We need not consult before, say, shedding resources in Russia, but Africa is different and requires consultation?"

"Is that what this is about, Andras? About your Slavic slut with the soulful eyes and the big mouth?"

Ferguson grimaced. "No, this is about an African dictator who was diverting funds for a new initiative to take over half the territory of his neighbor to the north. It was about our supposedly peaceful and unambitious President for Life deciding that his safety and security required pushing back the borders, plunging Busanyu into open warfare that would have been fatal for our relationship. Mbutsu was already talking about scaling back his support for the organization. What would the outbreak of war in the region do to the economy?"

"But now the money stops anyway, Andras."

"For God's sake, Bertrand. How many years does it take before you remember my name is Charles, Chas to you. It took me all of two days to master Bertrand Francoise Lyon, never called Bert. And what do you take me for? The payments have been made automatic. The Secretary of the Treasurer and the executor of Mbutsu's estate are both on the take. Each thinks they know the story and each knows a different one. They both think the funds being siphoned off will be there for their own enrichment when the need arises. But there are many layers to the onion. And, after many years more, when they finally peel it back, they will learn how little remains in the center waiting for them.

"In the meantime, there are those who were interested in seeing an imminent end to a long-running regime. They have a very large stake in seeing to it that there is a peaceful and orderly transition. A death by simple if uncommon disease, rather than at the hands of rebel forces or infiltrators, has improved their chances. And you and I have been paid bonuses by special-interest groups and individuals who gladly hastened the end to the reign of their dear departed dictator. They think they simply paid to keep me away, to guarantee that I would not come in and rescue him at the last minute after he fell seriously ill."

"And who will they suspect, when the inquiries become heated?"

"Each other, enemy agents, the gods, fate—but not us. We are now out of the picture, and a few extra millions richer for everyone having bribed us to stay out of that picture. I would say that we can count on the spigot to stay open for at least several years more, maybe longer. It will depend on how the Busanyu economy continues to grow, how well the country is run after the elections that they don't yet know they will be having soon, and how well our friends connect their self-interests with ours. In any case, there will be time to adjust our investment strategies and identify new revenue streams. In Busanyu, I have been cultivating talent for some years, so things there should go rather smoothly now that the President for Life is no longer President."

Dougherty's name may have changed, but his expression was, as usual, unreadable. "I suppose it makes sense. Mbutsu was always a bit of an embarrassment, even if nobody knew the connection. It had to end eventually, of course. He was too visible, too prominent. Another ten or twenty years and it would have been evident to anyone with eyes that he had some inside track on staying alive. I think I might have chosen different timing and different methods, but this will work."

"I am so glad you concur, Bertrand." It struck Ferguson as odd that the end of their relationship with the brutal Mbutsu had finally been reached, not because of his brutality but because of his insecurity. Economics trumped ethics and pragmatism triumphed over political values, as always. "I am also relieved," Ferguson continued, "that you finally listened to reason about Atchison Dougherty, who was also well past his use-by date. It did not take an orthodontist to see that he was becoming rather long in the tooth. The CEO of Biontolics had a long and rewarding run, but it was time to pass the torch to those protégés that he had so carefully cultivated over the years. I trust that you, Bertrand, will learn from his mistakes and stay out of the spotlight."

"We were lucky, that's all, lucky that a ghost from the past gave us a story."

"I still don't know the whole story or the complete rationale for the timing of our friend Douglas Dougherty's demise."

"It was Dekker. Do you remember the name, Bram Dekker?"

"It sounds familiar, but I am not sure."

"He was Janella's boyfriend. Turns out he had been following my career, as it were. He blamed me for Janella's death. Or disappearance. In any case, he blamed me and decided as his last act to get his revenge. He was a security consultant of sorts and somehow slipped in under our radar. I have had Holzinger taking our security organization apart and putting it back together right. His review uncovered some surprising holes and lapses, including a trusted asset in Ipswich who seemed to have been less than trustworthy, but it turns out Holzinger had already taken care of that.

"Fortunately, in my case, Dekker was a bad shot and I was not. I tell you, Andras, you should take the hand-gun training, too. You never know."

Ferguson scratched his ear. "I don't know. I've always believed the demographics that people who carry guns are more likely to die by them."

"Don't confuse cause and effect, Andras. Oh, all right, Chas. Why do you think people arm themselves in the first place? I'm surrounded by armed men for a reason, and this deranged lowlander was one of the reasons, proof that fortune favors the prepared. Unfortunately, Dekker acted with less preparation, so we had to put him on ice while we figured out how best to make use of his sacrifice. It took a little time to finish my new papers and fill in the blanks in the revisionist historical record."

Ferguson picked up a flattened stone and sent it skipping out over the blue-green waters. "Does it ever bother you, Bertrand?"

"You mean taking on a new identity? I don't think I've had enough time to notice much about it."

"No, I mean the cost, the lives, so many lives over the years."

"People die, Chas, at least most people. Some die so that others might live. It's always been that way. A soldier is killed on the battlefield in keeping the war from reaching his home. A research subject dies in the course of a study that finds a cure for a disease. That's life."

"But this is different. We are choosing who dies in order that we can live."

"Don't lose sleep over it; I don't. They choose themselves. Every one of them made a choice. They nominated themselves for the roles they played." He looked down at his iPad. "Have we covered everything?"

"Do you carry that gadget everywhere? We are on the beach, for God's sake. You don't see me with a phone or a computer. You need to develop some new habits to go with your new hair and name. Save the damned technology until we are back at work, which will be good for both of us. I have one more trip to the States, and then I can get back to basic research, back to the clinic where I belong."

"The Boston problem? Still?"

"He is a single-minded, chap, our boy. He skipped out on the last treatment, a no-show."

Bertrand shook his head in disbelief. "Keep me informed, Chas."

"I will, Bertrand. I will."

33

The nurse taking Rosen's pulse seemed small and lost amidst the spider-web of cables and tubes enmeshing him. Her uniform was ill-fitting, and she was taking his pulse. Rosen was puzzled. He could hear the slow, steady beep from a monitor. He knew that his every heartbeat, every breath, every change in blood chemistry was tracked, recorded, checked, and analyzed. But she was taking his pulse. No, she was only holding his hand in the light, little-girl grip that he remembered from Millie. He looked into the blue-gray eyes above the nurse's surgical mask, eyes that watched him, studied him, and he saw the lines at the edges deepen as if she were suddenly smiling.

"What are you doing, Rosen?" she said.

"I'm dying."

"But why? Why here, why now?"

"If not now, when?" He squeezed at her hand, a bare twitch of pressure. "Millie?"

"Yes?"

He closed his eyes. Minutes passed before he reopened them. "You came back."

"I'm still here," she corrected. "And I'm still waiting for your answer, Rosen. What are you doing?"

"Dying. Dramatically. On-stage. This is Mass General. That's why I stayed away, then walked in unannounced. The world watches.

People want to know. They ask, 'What is happening here?'"

She answered his rhetorical question after a long pause. "The Markarov Siamese twins were separated yesterday. Both girls are still in intensive care but doing better than expected. Pediatric cardiology did the first in utero fetal heart transplant this morning, and Bulkowski's knee will keep him off the Bruins' line-up for the season. That's what's happening here; that's what people want to know about. And you?"

"I want them to know about me. No, not about me. It's not about me at all. It's about them and about why I am dying. Death. My death, a warning, a call to arms."

She reached out and traced small circles on his forehead. "A friend who works on the ward told me you were here. She lent me her uniform and helped me get in. It was not too hard. There was no swarm of reporters and only one extra guard in the hall."

Rosen inhaled sharply. "They'll come. They have to. The truth needs to get out. This will be too big to ignore." His voice shook and his eyes moistened.

"My Rosen, always the same. So smart and so naïve."

"Are you really here, Millie, or is this some dying vision?"

"I'm here. I'll stay for a bit, while I can. I'm sure you're right," she reassured him, "they will know. Somehow they will know." She stood beside him, holding his hand, looking at him with love. He noticed.

"I did love you, Millie."

"I know."

"I was not good that way, you know, not then anyway," Tears pooled in his eyes. He reached to brush at them but was too weak to raise his arm more than a few inches. She tugged a tissue from the box by the bed and dabbed at his tears, then leaned over and kissed his forehead through her mask.

Then she was gone.

= =

Dr. Goldin turned from the computer cart where he was updating the patient's chart and shook his head. "You know, I've been at Mass General for twenty-one years now, and I have never seen anything like this. A man staggers in here on Thursday and on Saturday he is dying. I still have no idea what we are fighting or how to fight it. The patient's organs are failing. We can't find a pathogen, not a plausible one. The ones we do manage to culture are clearly opportunistic infections. It's as if his body were at civil war, insurgents fighting rebel factions who are battling separatists—it's biological chaos, utter chaos. I asked for a consult and now they tell me a team of experts from the CDC arrives tomorrow, along with a specialist on tropical diseases from down in North Carolina, which makes no sense to me. I'm skeptical. And in any case, it doesn't look like they will be arriving in time."

"The patient, Doctor. He's trying to say something." The nurse's eyes were filmed with fatigue, and her voice was hoarse after a long shift.

"Okay, see if you can suction out his mouth."

Rosen looked up at the lights swimming, weaving a figure eight above his head. There was something he knew he was supposed to do, something he needed to say, but in his thoughts it kept bobbing and weaving, dancing like the lights before his eyes, beyond his reach, just out of his grasp. It was a rut in the road of life. A word. It started with a word. If only he could remember the word, the last word, the word that he was supposed to say to start, the word he needed to say to be able to finish. He could hear it in the distance, faint. Listen, he told himself. Listen. That's it. Listen. *Sh'ma.*

"*Sh'ma,*" he said, a rasping, barely audible whisper squeezed from between his cracked lips, "*...yisrael...*" The word faded into a hiss as his last breath escaped and his lips and tongue continued in silence until the lights stopped dancing before eyes that no longer saw.

There was a long pause while the doctor watched the man's lips flutter stubbornly one last time.

"Amen," he said.

"What did you say, Doctor?"

"I said," he hesitated, thinking, remembering something from his own distant past, a childhood of forgotten faith and reassuring ritual. "I said, 'I attest.'" The nurse gave him an odd look. "I attest," he repeated, thinking quickly. "I attest that the patient died at," he glanced at the wall clock, "11:07am, Saturday, 20 September." He reached for the pen in his pocket and stared at it. "It's Shabbat. I forget."

She gave him another odd look.

"Shabbat, Nurse Wilson, the Sabbath, a day of rest, no work. But it's a mitzvah, a commandment, to save a life—or to tend to the dead. Even on Shabbat." He finished writing the record and returned the pen to his pocket.

Epilogue

Millie had read the story at the library in the online edition of *The Boston Globe*. She didn't have cable, and the local paper hadn't even covered the news. "Hospital sounds all-clear," declared the headline. "Rare jungle fever not a threat, experts announce. Essex man, only victim, dies." For the drama it alluded to, the story was surprisingly succinct.

> A spokesperson for Massachusetts General Hospital told reporters at a news conference today that the hospital, in consultation with experts from the Centers for Disease Control in Atlanta and medical doctors in the African country of Busanyu, had determined that there was no risk to Boston-area residents or anyone else in the Commonwealth from the fever to which an Essex man had succumbed over the weekend. "Idiopathic hemorrhagic fever, type 2, is a serious but rare tropical disease that is not highly contagious," said Linda Furtganger in a statement read to the reporters. "In accordance with established protocol, the patient was at all times kept quarantined in complete isolation in our secure unit."

The patient, earlier identified as Dr. David Rosen, a research biologist employed by the North Shore firm of Biontolics Research, LLC, apparently acquired the infection through improper handling of tissue cultures sent for analysis by the firm from doctors in Mbutsu City, capital of Busanyu in West Africa. Doctors there had enlisted the help of the Ipswich high-tech firm after President for Life, Edgar Jabari Mbutsu, succumbed to the fever last month.

Symptoms of the disease include high fever, violent tremors, and vomiting of blood and tissue as internal organs are destroyed by the virulent pathogen. After the onset of acute symptoms, death usually follows within 48 hours. There is no known treatment. Doctors at Mass General reassured reporters at the briefing that all possible measures had been taken to keep the patient comfortable. He died quietly on Saturday morning. The body was immediately placed in a special biohazard containment coffin before being transferred to a facility in North Carolina for further study.

It was bullshit, all bullshit. Rosen, who would not even scoop carrot peelings from the kitchen drain, would never have handled tissue samples of any kind, least of all in his work in mathematical biology. Surely the reporters would have checked his background and learned that he was just a computer geek, that 'biologist' had been a flag of convenience under which he sailed the seas of science. The North Shore Lab was not even the kind of facility that would have been called on to help diagnose Mbutsu. And, of course, it was not idiopathic hemorrhagic fever that had killed either of them. They had, she knew, died in a biological civil war as secessionist cell strains fought a losing battle against each other.

What infuriated Millie most unreasonably was that the reporters had not even gotten Rosen's name right. Still, she knew better than to contact the paper. She had been careful so far, and there was no point in taking an unnecessary risk just to score a personal point.

The school year had started weeks earlier, but she was not teaching. She was living in Falmouth Foreside under her maiden name, although she had kept the apartment in Cambridge and continued to pay the rent and the cable company. She had done all her research on public computers at the library, where she also made copies on a coin-operated machine. Since moving back to Maine, she had never even used her cellphone.

Millie chewed on her lower lip as she slipped one more speckled copy into the last of the 32 Express Mail envelopes. She knew they had underestimated her. Everyone underestimated Millicent, the scrawny little woman who taught middle school and banded birds on weekends.

She glanced over at the refrigerator where magnets in the shape of shore birds held printouts of the newspaper story, a quotation from Steve Jobs, and the action plan that she had drafted after talking with Steven King. Red tick marks decorated all but the final item on her list.

She had considered using UPS Next Business Day delivery, but in the end worried that a corporation, even a big one like FedEx or UPS, might too easily be breached. If Mass General and the CDC could be compromised and *The Boston Globe* hoodwinked, who could she trust? She had settled on the U.S. Postal Service. She reasoned that it might be an inefficient and uninventive bureaucracy, but, at least, it was not corrupt and might not be corruptible.

Numbers were the enemy of conspiracies and the friend of whistleblowers. Millie figured that the further she spread the word, the less likely it was that the word would be lost or silenced. They can't be everywhere, she told herself. The thick packets she had assembled contained most of the story and much of the documentation, at least what she could still dig up on the Web and could recover from the hard drive she had swapped out from Rosen's laptop before it had been stolen.

She was particularly proud of that maneuver, which meant that no one could find anything incriminating on his computer, regardless of what forensic methods they employed. There was nothing there to be found and never had been; it was a clean, factory-fresh drive with an unaltered OEM copy of Windows. One could not fault the level of technical support she had received from the computer company. Once she convinced them that the hard drive really was dead, the replacement had arrived the next day by overnight courier, and she had slipped away with the original. She liked to believe that Rosen had lived at least a little bit longer because of what she had done. She also hoped that the story in *The Globe* had been accurate, at least on one count, that Rosen had died peacefully, without pain.

In addition to Maine's two senators and the Governors of Maine and Massachusetts, there were packets addressed by name to people at *The New York Times*, *The Times of London*, and a dozen other newspapers, including one to a former classmate who had become a senior editor at *The Sacramento Bee*. Millie was not sure whether the one addressed to WikiLeaks would ever be delivered, but she felt it was worth a try. Each packet also contained the full list of all the recipients. Her reasoning was that this way the disappearance of any one would let the others know that the story was real and needed to be gotten out as fast as possible.

The organization, as Rosen had referred to it, would come after her, she assumed, but it would be too late. By then, too many people would know too much. Even if they killed her, the damage would already be done. The scientist in her hoped to live to see how the story played out, what the world would ultimately do with the knowledge—the knowledge of good and evil as well as of life and death. The realist in her assumed that she would not likely live that long. Rosen's far-flung children might; protected by the anonymity of their own medically-assisted conceptions, they might live to see the dénouement. She hoped they would inherit his brains, then thought better of it and wished only that they would get his hair.

She walked over to the refrigerator to tick off the last item on her checklist. In the process, she knocked loose one of her magnets, and a sheet of paper fluttered to the floor, the note from Rosen that he had mailed to her old address in Cambridge before leaving for Quebec. She picked it up and reread the quotation before fastening it again to the refrigerator.

> No one wants to die. Even people who want to go to
> heaven don't want to die to get there. And, yet,
> death is the destination we all share. No one has
> ever escaped it. And that is as it should be, because
> Death is very likely the single best invention of Life.
> It is Life's change agent. It clears out the old to make
> way for the new.
>
> Steve Jobs, Stanford University Commencement,
> 12 June 2005

Millie grabbed her car keys from the pegboard by the door and left.

= =

At the Post Office, Hazel Shaeffer greeted Millie warmly when she entered. Hazel had been a clerk in the small office for what seemed forever and had even remembered Millie when she had come in the week before to pick up the Express Mail envelopes and the multi-part address forms. Hazel was one of the reasons that Millie liked being in a small town again, a community where people knew each other and looked out for each other.

"Looks like some serious mailing you're into there, Millie. That'll cost a pretty penny. Sure you wouldn't prefer to send them just Priority Mail? Only takes a few days, you know. Usually. Most places."

"No, thanks, Hazel. I want them to go out overnight rate. There's a lot of work in those packets. I want to be sure they get there right away."

Hazel started weighing and stamping each piece. "The Governor? Do you have friends in high places, Millicent Geller?"

Millie laughed but said nothing. When Hazel finally finished with all the packages and had processed Millie's credit card for payment, Millie asked, "Now you're sure those will go out today and be delivered tomorrow?"

"Not the overseas ones. Can't promise when those will make it once they are out of the capable hands of the U.S. Postal Service. But the rest, don't worry about them. I'll take care of them myself."

Millie sighed and smiled. "Thanks," she said, as she gathered her purse. "It's important."

"I'm sure it is," Hazel responded. She watched as Millie left, crossed the street, and got into her car. Hazel was thinking about the man with the German accent who had started talking with her at the coffee shop the day before. She was also thinking about what retirement would be like on a decidedly modest USPS pension. And she was thinking about the little Geller girl, remembering how she used to stand on tiptoes to see over the counter and shyly ask if she could have a lollipop.

Hazel gathered the packets, balanced them in her arms, and pressed her chin on top to keep them from slipping. She headed for the back and walked over to the canvas sorting bags hanging in their frames. She paused for a moment in front of two of them off to one side, one labeled "Express Mail" in neat block print, the other with a hand-lettered sheet that read "Postmaster – Special Handling Only." She hesitated for a moment but knew that if she stood there for more than a few seconds, someone was bound to ask her if anything was wrong.

She had no idea why these particular packets were so important or why they might be worth so much to some foreigner, but she did know that she was an Assistant Postmaster in the United States Postal Service. Some things you do because that's just what is done, she thought. That's how it's done here in Maine.

She lifted her chin, letting the pile cascade noisily into the Express Mail bin, then turned resolutely on her heel and returned to the counter where another customer was waiting.

Also by Lior Samson

**Bashert | The Dome | Web Games
Chipset | Gasline | Flight Track**

The Four-Color Puzzle

Available from Amazon and other booksellers